THE KRAKEN'S CASTAWAY

A DARK MONSTER ROMANCE

FOR THE LOVE OF TITANS, BOOK 1

CASSANDRA MEDCALF

For the monster girlies who've read about the knots and orc cocks and crave something a little...
bigger.

CONTENT WARNING

Whew, boy, do I have a list for you!

Let's start by saying, this book is not for the faint of heart. Okay? We've all read the cozy little monster romances starring a gentle, clock-punching Orc or a Minotaur who likes to snuggle. We love them: they're chicken soup for our weird little souls.

But this is not a chicken soup monster romance.

Oh don't worry, we still have a Himbo with a Heart of Gold, but he's a little... tortured.

So I have some serious content warnings. For those of you who aren't looking for a dark story that deals with grief and references to self-harm, this may not be the right book for you at this time.

But for those of you who *are* ready to take the plunge, here's the list of triggers and tropes:

PCOS/fertility issues
Pregnancy loss (mention)
Suicidal Ideation (mention)
Attempted Suicide (mention)

Nonconsensual sex (mention)
Dubious consent
Enthusiastic consent
Sexomnia
Hypnosis
Magical Manipulation
Possession
Mind-break
Ancient Norwegian angst
Forbidden love
Forced Proximity
Age gap (in the like, thousand-year-old faerie with a 30 year-old sense, not in the middle-aged-man-with-a-teenager sense)
Breeding Kink
Oviposition
Cumflation
Orgasm denial
Greek mythology b-sides
Cephalopod shifters
Tentacles. So many tentacles.
References for Swifties
Bi awakening
Polyamorous Awakening
and... sounding? Maybe? I uh... well, to be honest, I don't exactly know WHAT to call the thing that happens at the end, but let's just say it involves a really, *really*, REALLY big penis.

Godspeed!

CHAPTER 1

LILLIAN

I snap my book shut and press it against my burning face, as if that will somehow cool me down.

Spoiler alert: it won't.

Of all the things I expected when I cracked open a monster romance, blushing like a teenager buying condoms for prom night was not one of them. But here I am, sitting in a cheap plastic lawn chair, thighs pressed together, feeling things I haven't felt in... well, let's just say I'm gonna need to schedule my battery-operated boyfriend some overtime.

I exhale slowly, sneaking a glance at my best friend beside me, hoping she doesn't notice the heat crawling up my neck. Maybe choosing *this* book to read in the middle of a girls' trip wasn't my brightest idea.

But after three years of nothing but solo adventures and cheesy Harlequin romances? I needed a little... inspiration. I just didn't expect it to claw its way under my skin quite like this.

Ha. *Claw.* Monster smut. I stifle a giggle and set the book down on my lap.

Tiffany looks up from her Kindle in the beach chair beside me. She raises an eyebrow at me.

"You're finished already?"

"What can I say? I'm a fast reader." I reach down into the sand next to me for my tiki drink. "I should have brought a couple more paperbacks. That was my last one."

"Or you should just take the plunge and get an e-reader," Tiffany says. "Seriously, Lillian, the way you read? You'll save so much money."

I shake my head. "Nope. Sorry. I like the feel of the paper in my hands. The smell of that mass-market wood pulp." I breathe in deep and stretch, rolling my shoulders back and raising my arms above my head. My tankini bottoms roll down, *again*, and I tug the waistband back above my belly button. "Ugh, I hate these things. What am I going to do for the next two days without any more books, though? That was my last one."

"Dean could drive us into town for karaoke," she pipes up eagerly. I flatten my gaze at her. "Or you know, maybe we just cut this vacation short and go somewhere else for the rest of the week. Dean can drive us around the midwest. Make it a road trip. See some new sights."

I snort, and gesture with a hand out at the gorgeous lakeside view. Off in the distance, a small embankment shrouded in tropical-looking sumac trees sparkles in the setting sun.

Every year, the weekend after Labor Day, Tiff and I rent the same cabin on the same private beach of Lake Superior in the Upper Peninsula of Michigan, miles away from anything that might bother us, for a girls' trip. We load up the car with booze and mixers, snack foods and staples for taco nights, and escape to our perfect little lakeside oasis in the middle of nowhere. It might as well be the beach, for how huge the lake is, only the water is fresh and clean and there are no other tourists to bother us.

But this year, it feels like Tiffany would rather be anywhere but our traditional lakeside retreat. And I'm not sure how to take that.

Because this is the last one we'll ever have.

Tiffany sips her passion fruit seltzer, hand resting lazily on her small baby bump. She's now comfortably in the second trimester of her first pregnancy, and we're taking full advantage of the last bit of freedom she has to enjoy a vacation before having a baby to take care of. Or at least, that was the plan.

When we were preparing for the trip, it felt like there was something she was holding back. She didn't seem nearly as excited for the getaway as I was. I haven't had this much time with my best friend in months, and I've been missing her something crazy. It was important to me that we have the chance to spend some time together before the baby comes.

But her fiancé, Dean, refused to let us go by ourselves. And, despite the fact that the two of us have been coming here every year for a decade and never had any issues, he *insisted* on tagging along. And Tiffany took his side.

Oh sure, he tried to play innocent.

"I won't crash the cabin! I'll bring my own tent. You won't even know I'm there."

Yeah, right. That little fantasy collapsed the second Tiff and I tucked into bed for the first night, and she snuck out to get freaky with him on the beach.

"Tiffany..." I sigh. This has to be the fifth time she brought up leaving the beach *today*. I've lost track of how many times she's mentioned it since we left Chicago. "This is our last girls' trip together before you become a mother.

The lake is *our* place. Why do you keep trying to convince me to leave early? It almost feels like Dean wants you to sabotage it."

"We're not trying to sabotage it!" She sits up, rubbing her arms. "This has nothing to do with Dean. Maybe I'm just a little more sensitive to temperature with all the hormones in my system. It feels colder than usual, and I just don't like sitting out on the beach all exposed."

"Are you sure that's all it is? You've been acting weird ever since we started planning for this last hurrah. Are you okay? Are you sick?"

"I'm totally fine."

Unease swirls in my gut. If she isn't unwell, then what's the problem?

"You know you can tell me if something's wrong."

She closes her eyes and takes a deep breath, before opening them and meeting my eyes. "I know. Trust me, I'm okay. I haven't even gotten queasy in weeks!"

"Then why won't you get in the water?"

Seriously. We've been here three days; I've been swimming six times already. Whereas she hasn't even gotten a toe wet.

"I told you already, I'm cold. A big chilly lake just doesn't seem appealing to me right now." She rubs a hand on her exposed stomach. Even four months pregnant, she looks better in a bikini than I ever have (or will). "Why don't we go into town to grab a bite to eat? I'm craving a big, greasy burger from the Yooper Diner."

I roll my eyes, but I'm hiding a smile. "You and your pregnancy cravings."

"Better than morning sickness!" Tiff laughs. "Those first three months were *awful.*"

"I can't imagine..."

I can, though. She knows I can. It's been harder than I want to admit, watching her soldier through all of the ups and downs of this milestone of womanhood. With Dean.

Given our history, I thought she might want me to be with her to celebrate all of the little landmarks along the way. I've tried to let her know I'm there for her. But she keeps pulling away from me, and I can't help but feel like she doesn't want me to be part of the next chapter of her life.

And look, Dean's a great guy. Truly. A real peach. Caring, affectionate—literally everything she deserves and more. Dean is absolutely head-over heels for Tiffany, and she for him. The way they look at each other is pure magic, like everything I've read in my romance novels.

The thing that my novels don't cover, though, is what happens to the heroine's best friend after she gets her happy ending.

Obviously, I know that once Tiff and Dean start their family, she and I won't get as much time together. I'll still come over, help out, and be the best Auntie Lil I can possibly be. At least, that's my plan.

But lately, I feel like she doesn't even want me to be that. I'm missing out on all the benchmarks of our pre-family friendship. They didn't have an engagement party. She hasn't asked me to be maid of honor, claiming they're just going to do something small for their wedding after the baby comes. Which means we haven't even had any fun wedding or bachelorette parties to plan, either. Despite the fact that I know they love each other, the whole thing feels rushed.

Not that I know that for certain, because since she got pregnant, she's barely spoken to me.

I'm not *mad* at her, exactly. I can't be. I'm thrilled that my best friend has a great man in her life and, deep down, I know she'll be an amazing mom. But the more she pushes me away, the more negative feelings come to the surface.

And then when she's constantly blowing me off for Dean…

It just makes me realize how alone I am without her. She gets a husband, she gets a baby, and I…

I get a big, empty hole in my life where my best friend used to be.

When am I going to get *my* happy ending? When will some amazing, sexually affluent well-endowed heartthrob with beefy arms come into my life and sweep me off my feet? Keep *me* satisfied and knock *me* up with his babies? And then, instead of leaving, be worried enough about me that he'll crash our girls' trip and worry over me like I deserve?

I scan the surrounding beach for Dean, but true to his word, he's "gone" for the day, at the fishing hole a mile down the beach. His truck is nowhere in sight. And aside from the tent behind the cabin and the occasional *ping* of Tiff's cell phone alerting her to a text from him and the *tap-tap-tap* of her replying, there are no signs of his presence.

I clear my throat.

"Well, I could stand to go for a swim. I need to move a bit." And after reading that spicy book? I kinda need to cool off. "Wanna come with? Even just to soak your feet?"

She doesn't look up from her phone. "Why don't you go on ahead? I've gotta call Dean with a check-in."

"You really need to call him? Again?"

This is the third time since breakfast.

She frowns at me, a little wrinkle divoting her brow. "Yeah, Lillian. It's getting late. I'm pregnant and far away from him. Of course I need to check in."

"But you're not far away from him. He went fishing a mile down the beach. He's literally sleeping twenty feet away from us every night."

"He just asked how I was feeling. I should at least let him know."

"Isn't that what you've been doing?" I nod to her phone, where her text conversation with him is lighting up the screen.

"If I don't call, he'll worry." She bites her lip. "You of all people should understand that."

I close my eyes, and take in a deep breath.

Ever since we first became roommates in Chicago, Tiff and I have been each others' person. I was there for her through countless boyfriends and girlfriends before she found Dean. We shared our first apartment, a shitty studio in the southside, because neither of us could afford anything better. We were each others' personal references for our first big-girl jobs.

She was the shoulder I'd cried on when, three years ago, my boyfriend of five years left me because I got pregnant. And then again, a month later, when I found out I wouldn't be having a baby after all.

That year, our annual girls' trip was the only lifeline I'd had. I was battling so many emotions: grieving a relationship, a child, a future I hadn't realized I wanted. And battling the guilt for feeling some nugget of relief that I wouldn't be navigating the world as a single mother. Every positive thing, every silver lining in those months just wound me deeper into a web of self-loathing.

But Tiffany had been my rock, convincing me that all I needed was some fresh air and the healing waters of Lake Superior.

And, weirdly, she was right. The trip got off to a rough

start: I slipped in the mud while we were out hiking and had to trek back to the cabin alone and crying while I found a change of pants. But later that night, we joined back up for a sunset swim and something... changed.

Like the weight of the world was suddenly off my shoulders. Like I could go on, and everything would be okay.

The rest of the trip was amazing. One for the books, for sure, and Tiffany and I were even more inseparable after that...until she met Dean a few months later.

So when she goes and says something like that to justify letting Dean shoehorn his way into our special bestie's vacation, it rubs me in all the wrong ways. Like she's using my history against me, to buy her more time with her boyfriend, when this has always been the time of year where we reset *our* relationship.

Luckily, though, I bite my tongue long enough to realize this is *Tiff.* She's the only reason I was able to bounce back from my own miscarriage. And, if I'm honest, I'm probably the reason she's so scared that something might happen to her and her baby.

Everytime Tiffany makes a noise even slightly resembling a gasp or a groan, I zero in on her faster than a dog with a bone. Because I care about her, and the last thing I'd ever want is for her to go through what I did.

The struggle comes from balancing that concern and understanding with the part of me that's frustrated with Dean's constant interruptions. When I ask if something's wrong, she's quick to assure me she's fine and brush it off. But *he* gets a half-hour phone call three times a day.

Is she actually scared? Or does she just want to get away from me?

After another second of calming breaths, I force a smile.

Maybe it has nothing to do with me. Maybe he's just as much of a mother hen as I am. "Right. Of course, that makes sense. You'll come in in a bit, though?"

She doesn't meet my eyes, packing away her Kindle and unlocking her phone. "Yeah, I'll be back in a few minutes."

I watch as she grabs all of her stuff, slips on her flip-flops, and walks back to the edge of the treeline, where there's better cell reception.

Fine. So she can't be by my side every second of our girls' trip. That's fine. Just...fine.

I can still have fun. I can still relax. Enjoy the beautiful scenery. This is one of my favorite places in the world, after all: the freshwater beach of Lake Superior.

I look over the lake to the little island embankment in the middle. All the years we've been here, I've never actually swum far enough to explore over there, always staying close by the shore. I wonder if there's anything out there.

I'm a strong swimmer. It's one of the few forms of exercise I've always really enjoyed. I don't have to worry about finding a sports bra sturdy enough to support my boobs, or feel self-conscious about how I look in my yoga pants. The sensation of weightlessness and anonymity as I move through the cool, deep waters of the lake is one of the greatest feelings in the world.

Just thinking of the soft lapping of the inland waves rocking me out in the open water makes my skin tingle. Still a little hot from my book earlier, I suddenly wonder how the lake water would feel against *all* my skin, and not just the bits exposed around a swimsuit.

Maybe I can use these few minutes of "me" time to my advantage. Now that I have a little privacy, maybe I can *really* have a little fun...

After all, Tiffany's getting her rocks off every night with Dean. I should let off a little steam myself.

I check back over my shoulder to see if Tiffany's watching. But she's long gone. Maybe she went off for a little "me" time herself while she talks to Dean.

How long do their phone calls usually last? Twenty minutes? Half an hour?

It's a private beach. And even if it weren't, this is the weekend after Labor Day in the UP. Nobody's camping now that summer's over. And hunting season hasn't started yet.

You know what? I'm doing it. YOLO.

My stomach cheers as I strip out of my control-top swimsuit bottoms, and my breasts positively rejoice when I unbuckle the tight tankini top. The feeling of relief is instant.

Thank God, I'm free!

Okay, but seriously, why have I never done this before?

The water laps at my feet as I step carefully along the pebbled beach and into the surf. It's somehow both invigorating and relaxing. And chilly: the lake maintains a remarkably cool temperature even into the peak of summer up here, because it's so deep.

Lake Superior doesn't give up Her dead.

Goosebumps erupt along my arms and shoulders as the old saying pops into my mind. I'm brought back to three years ago, when I first heard that phrase.

The elderly cashier at the campsite welcome center made friendly conversation with Tiffany. I hid behind a rack of local books and brochures, not up for socializing.

One pamphlet caught my eye though, and despite my sour mood, I couldn't help asking about it.

"Hauntings of Lake Superior?" I read off the front cover. "There are hauntings up here?"

"Oh yes," the old man said, his gaze suddenly a million miles away. "You've heard the old saying, of course?"

Tiffany and I looked at each other. "Old saying?"

"Lake Superior doesn't give up Her dead." He pointed at the rack of books, one in particular with an old ship on it. "For hundreds of years, ships have wrecked in surprise storms, or ice floes in the winter. Unequipped to handle the waves of the lake waters. They get lost, you know, sink way down to the bottom of the lake, never seen again. The deep waters... it'd be suicide to try to retrieve 'em."

"Does it still happen?"

"Haven't had one since the Edmund Fitzgerald back in '75. But there are still the rumors."

"Rumors?" Tiffany asked. Even she was getting pulled into the story.

"Oh, there are all sorts of monsters out in the lake, eh? The Ojibwe tell stories of Mishipeshu, the Great Lynx, then of course there's Pressie, who's more like our own Lochness Monster."

"Uh-huh..." I met Tiff's eyes, holding back an eye roll.

"Haven't been any reliable sightings in years, o' course. But that doesn't mean they aren't out there..."

Despite all of the history, I've never felt anything but awe whenever I take in the lake in all its glory. Its waters always welcome me, drawing me in, accepting me as I am.

Still, there's something forbidden about stepping in naked, without any protection between me and the icy waters.

I ease deeper and deeper into the surf: first up to my knees, then my thighs...

I gasp as I feel the water lap against my mound. This far out and this deep, the tide exerts a little more pressure around my body, making it harder to stand completely still. I let the push and pull of the tide knead into my muscles.

This is a vacation, after all. And dealing with Dean butting into Tiffany's and my trip has forced a lot more tension into my neck and shoulders than usual.

Up to my waist now, I take a deep breath before reaching my hands forward and submerging completely. My whole body goes tense at first with the shock in temperature, but then relaxes as I feel Superior's gentle waves embrace me. I take a few strokes, then surface again, feeling the surface of the water lap against my ribs.

A slight breeze chills my exposed skin, and my nipples harden.

I've never gone skinny dipping in my life. *How bizarre is that?* Tiff and I have been coming to the same private beach for almost a decade now, and we've never gone skinny dipping?

I spread my hands out to my sides above the water. How would it feel to float out here, completely naked, half submerged with only the tips of my toes and the peaks of my nipples sticking out of the water?

I glance again to the shore, but Tiff must still be on the phone, because I don't see her anywhere.

Fuck it.

I arch my back, allowing my legs and lower stomach to rise to the surface as I sink my head and shoulders back into the water. Lazily reaching my arms out and above my head, I slowly stroke out and back, no real aim in mind. Just allow the tide to carry me wherever it wants. I'm a strong swimmer, after all. It's not like I'm going to get lost in the middle of the largest lake in the world if I just float here for a few minutes.

I spread my legs, starfishing in the surf. Cool water rushes to caress the hot skin between my thighs. *God, that feels good.* Surprised, I moan.

It's so nice out here. Nothing above me but the open blue sky and the tops of evergreen trees that flock the north shore framing my vision. Nothing below but the crystal clear water and pebble beaches of the lake. *I wish I didn't have to go back.*

Back to my regular life, and my regular job. Back to a world where Tiff and I grow further and further apart as she prepares to become a mother. Where she and Dean build their future family together, eventually forgetting that funny, chubby ol' Lillian even exists.

I close my eyes, letting my head fall back and my ears and hairline fully submerge, blonde locks fanning out around me in a halo.

With the gentle movement of the water, it almost feels like a caress. Like someone brushing out the strands with a gentle, loving hand...

CHAPTER 2
ERIK

S ix months. Six full moon cycles since I last shifted. The longest I have ever gone.

The first few weeks were the hardest. Spring is a long, slow thaw on this desolate island. At times, it felt like there was no escape from the cold and wet. I longed to just give in to the monster within and hibernate in the lake depths.

But in good faith, I could not. The longer I stay in that cursed form, the more I feel myself changing permanently. As if there might be someday I shift and never change back.

My previous record of four months in my human body was broken in a frenzied haze, brought on by the rush of tourists in the early summer. I had been unprepared, already hungry after a long winter surviving on small fish alone, and my monster had gotten desperate. Too desperate. I had lost control.

But not this time. Last winter, I prepared. Allowed myself to shift to hunt large game while the humans were not around in the cold season. Found purpose for some abandoned equipment left by campers, using their grills and charcoal to prepare feasts of meat and fish and keep the monster satisfied.

There was a time, long ago, when I had kept count of how many days I had been trapped here in this place. An inland loch seemingly as vast as the ocean I once crossed to arrive in this new land, this new world: so green and full of promise.

Until it was only full of regrets.

I am the last remaining member of my once great crew: explorers of the Northern sea, settlers of lands unknown. The greatest shame of our people was this failed journey, and I am its sole bearer.

I have since lost track of the years I have been trapped here by the curse. I know it must be in the hundreds. But now, I have reason to count again.

I can control the monster.

And if I can control it, then maybe I can at last escape it.

The small, horseshoe-shaped island in this giant loch I have been cursed to call home is limited. Each summer, I find myself trapped here, self-contained in my small wilderness, where I hide in the secluded lagoon that has remained isolated from the many humans that vacation here in the warm months. Families with young children stay close to the loch's broad southern shores, and the fish-ermen in their boats steer clear of the rocky entrance to my oasis's waters. Those who have ventured too close over the years have not returned.

They became tribute to the monster within.

I am grateful for the end of summer this year. When the humans leave, I find comfort and safety in my solitude. I feel the approach of autumn on the breeze, and my body yearns for it. Perhaps the season's chill can contain the heat that boils beneath my skin. Perhaps, without the temptation of easy human prey, I can maintain my human form—maintain control of the monster.

I try to ignore the tension building inside me like the falling sands of the hourglass. It is a pull: a horrible, deep urge like nothing I have known as a man, but that I instinctively recognize as something powerful and monstrous.

Time to breed.

In all the years I have been trapped here, it has only happened once before. The fever overtook me on a full moon, brought on by an all-consuming wave of heat—one that still haunts my nightmares to this day.

She was the daughter of a fisherman. A sweet thing, waife-like and ruddy-faced. The nymph of my dreams. I watched her from my rocky shore at nights by the light of the stars and waxing moon. In the cool summer evenings, she would shed her clothing, submerge herself in the cool lake waters, and bathe by the celestial lights.

I was foolish then. I did not know that my desires would stoke the monster's, too, until it was too late.

The pull within me increased with the moon. The night it hung pregnant in the sky, illuminating her precious body like a beacon, I could no longer suppress it. Every night I watched her, thinking it was only my loneliness that stirred the heat within my belly. Rising with the heat of summer, hotter and hotter as the days grew long and heavy with unrequited longing.

I did not realize that *I* was not the only one who longed for her.

I can still feel the way the desire coursed through my body, first tickling, then burning its way through my lungs, to my bloodstream, through my muscles and into the furthest reaches of my limbs. I dove into the lake, my limbs outside of my control. My body shifted in a delicious shudder until I was more monster than man.

Its movements were mine, but I was helpless to stop them. I could only watch as my tentacles wrapped around her legs, yanked her under the water. Horrified, I took in the havoc my grotesque body unleashed upon her. My beak, nipping along her achingly soft breasts. My tongue, lapping at her nipples hungrily.

Her arms submitted to my unbreakable grip. And when she was bent, back arched like a bow primed to launch a deadly arrow, it was my cock that pierced her perfect flesh. It was my seed that filled her. And it was my uncontrollable lust that kept her submerged far too long. My carelessness that killed her.

It did not matter that the monster had overtaken my will and forced me to action. *I* was the one who was responsible. The monster had killed before, of course, but always in self-preservation.

A child here, a lone sailor there. Women, men... I lost count of how many humans died to the insatiable hunger of the lake beast. His hunting sustained us both, and while I mourned the death of my fellow humans, I could not fault the monster for eating to survive.

Hunger, I understand. For a beast is still a being of nature. It still deserves to eat, does it not? Just as men eat the fish of the lake, or the fowl of the sky. But before that night, the monster always feasted for hunger.

Never for lust.

That, I could not justify. Nor would I lend it my body to achieve its perverted ends.

I have stayed secluded on my island ever since.

To my knowledge, the monster has no children. Other than that one tragedy, I have resisted the pull of the monster to breed. The maiden perished in the attack, and the heat quickly abated in its grief over the failed mating. But many years have passed, and now that heat has begun to build again.

I cannot give into it. I will not.

Yet as I submerge myself for a celebratory swim—*six moons without succumbing to the beast!*—I reach for it. Express gratitude for its compliance. A summer with no kills is an admirable feat indeed, and I am grateful. Now that the warm season is coming to an end, we can once again hunt our waters without fear of the temptation to seek out human prey.

As I float peacefully, knowing I am alone, I allow the beast to uncurl its many legs. A warm wave envelops my body as my own muscled limbs transform and multiply. The giant tentacles unfurl and lengthen, undulating in the cool and soothing lake water.

And then a paralyzing scent wafts through the waves.

No.

The monster growls within me, its beak clicking hungrily.

Mate...

I try to clamp down on the monster, but it is too late. As one, my legs coil and forcefully push themselves straight, rocketing us toward the delectable scent. One I have not allowed myself or the monster to breathe in for so long: *woman.*

Weaving through the sharp rocks of the lagoon's entrance, the monster takes control, speeding toward the coast. And then I see her.

She is nothing like the fisherman's daughter. Where she had been small and slender, this maiden is strong, rounded. Her legs and arms drift gracefully through the loch's undulating waters, her sweet breasts' splendid points peek out above the waves. Her hair spreads in a shining, golden halo around her head.

The man in me, the one who has fought for and claimed dominance over the monster for months as its hunger built, rages.

No, I scream at it, *you will not destroy this maiden like you did the other!*

Using every ounce of internal strength I have built for the past six months, I bring the beast to heel.

It screeches inside my mind, and once again I feel that devastating heat. The pulsing low in my belly, the *desire.* In the middle of the swirl of tentacles, I feel my cock begin to rise and harden.

No!

My mind is a hazy fog of lust and primal desire. It is untenable, nigh all-consuming, but my will is strong. I force it down, opening my eyes...

Only to realize that my human body has gained control somehow. I have human eyes to open, and a human head for them to reside in. My arms and legs are back to their tanned and muscled shape, my fingers and toes separated and grasping as I paddle through the water.

One thing, however, stays the same. My cock is still pulsing with desire, unlike anything I have felt for over a hundred years. That heat still scorches in my loins, coiled and tense.

I look up towards the surface of the water. Instinctively, I swim closer to the curvaceous shadow of the beautiful woman above me. Her golden hair is so close, I could almost touch it. Weave my fingers through it. Feel her softness across my skin...

We do not have to kill her.

The voice of the monster is low and deep as it slithers in from the furthest reaches of my mind.

I blink. No. This voice is not mine. So why is it saying such things?

It does not make sense. He wants only to kill. All he has ever brought is destruction and danger. It is why I cannot allow myself near humans, why I should not be here now. Why I have resisted shifting for so long...

No, human. Neither of us want to kill.

I freeze. Water passes in and out of the slits along my neck, an evolution I acquired from the curse of the monster those centuries ago. That, and my immortality. Condemning me to a long and hungry life in this lonely loch.

I breathe in slowly, the warm pulse of desire still a current in my veins.

What do you want? I ask the monster.

This is dangerous, I know. Entertaining the beast within me. Letting him spin falsehoods in my brain.

The same thing as you. To break the curse.

What? I pause.

So many years. Uncountable, the number of days I have lived this cursed life, and all this time... there has been a way to free myself?

How... it can be broken?

It whispers simply, its voice a teasing tendril stroking my brain into a fuzz. So gentle, I could almost forget the horrors it has wrought around me.

I must breed. To break the curse, I must bear young.

Above me, the beautiful woman kicks her legs. I watch eddies form around her toes, swirling a current up her delectable thighs. Delicious thighs...

No, I respond, fighting back against the way I can feel

the voice altering my senses. My vision blurs slightly around the edges, and I know this is the monster's doing. Before, the heat in my veins had brought about an eerily sharp focus, but the shapes around me are soft and pulsing now. *Stop it. Stop your lies.*

I will not die with you, it whispers. ***I know you've been waiting to take me with you from the world. A noble pursuit indeed. But as long as I am with you, you will never die.***

My stomach roils.

So that is why. And he has known. The weeks I subjected myself to hunger in an effort to starve myself. The recklessness with which I first navigated the rocky shores, throwing myself against them, years and years ago.

It never worked. I would always survive. He would always take over, and I would heal. I would eat. I would live.

It is not I that am immortal. The monster inside me is. And I am cursed to live for as long as I carry him.

So if I am to die...

Then I must breed. Around me, the colors of the pebbles below and the sky above intensify. My vision pulses once more, and then... returns to normal.

The sun has set now. The moon is a warbly globe above the current, and the beautiful woman above me is backlit by the white light of its full face.

The heat surges anew in my loins. My cock pulses hungrily. It is not only the monster. I, too, want this woman. Want to bury myself within her. Want her to take my seed. It has been so long since I have felt the softness of a woman in my bed, and I am so lonely...

No! No, Beast. You will kill her.

I will not, it argues sweetly, assuringly. ***For if I kill her,***

she will not bear my young, and we will not be free. We will love her. We will take care of her. And together we will break our curse.

I swallow, the tingling desire almost too much to bear. My hands twitch, desperate to relieve the ache in my cock, but I know it will not be enough. This is not merely my human desire. This is the desire of the monster, the drive of the curse.

I cannot fight this forever. If not this woman, it will be another. I will only be delaying the inevitable, like I have been for years.

She must choose it, I insist at last. The realization sits bitter in my throat: the beast will not die until it breeds. I cannot kill it. And it will not let me kill myself. *I will not subject her to carry this curse unwillingly. I will not let you rape this woman. Please. Allow her the choice.*

The monster coils within me, considering, and with each passing second the heat of its lust and frustration build. My cock feels as though it may burst. Could I withhold the beast if it decided not to heed my direction? It has taken me over before.

Am I actually strong enough to contain it?

I gasp out a breath as the pressure becomes unbearable. Bubbles escape my open mouth, and I choke a bit on the water entering my lungs through the wrong hole.

Acceptable. The monster gives in at last. **Persuade her.**

No, I insist, emboldened by the hope rising in my chest. *Not persuade. She must choose it—of her own free will and desire. And she must survive after.*

For a moment, I feel the monster's tension writhe inside my stomach, and the heat flares again. I grunt, fighting the overwhelming drive, its anger shooting a twisted dart of pleasure through my loins, as if it might finally consume me once and for all. I concentrate with all my might, keeping myself from giving into the urges. I will *not* let this creature's lust betray my honor ever again.

Stop it! I plead. *You shall not take control this time! I am stronger now. You need me!*

She will survive! It snaps back, as if it is insulted. As if this agony inside me is a punishment for me doubting its sincerity. **She will thrive! And at the end of her term, so shall my children.**

At his words, an unbearable climax pulses through me. And then, just as quickly as it spikes, the wave subsides. I feel myself soften, the desperate ache in my cock receding to a dull throb. I breathe out in relief, a column of bubbles spiraling out of my lips.

You have three days. Or I will eat her and her friend.

Another body appears at the shore of the lake. A more slender frame, but with a slight swell to her belly. She is with child.

But I—

You will lose strength eventually. Just as you always have. You humans are all the same. You think you are invincible. But you are not.

The threat weighs heavy in my gut. If I cannot stop him, he will devour these two women. Just as he did the fisherman's daughter.

I pray it will not come to that.

CHAPTER 3

LILLIAN

Tiffany barrels up the shore, shouting loudly enough to break me out of my reverie. I've lost track of how long I have been floating out here, and there is a slight chill in the air that tickles the back of my neck when I right myself in the water.

Thankfully, Tiff hasn't seen me yet. She's seen me naked before, of course, but I don't like to make a habit of flashing my friends without warning.

"Lil?? *Lil!!*"

"Relax, I'm out here!"

I kick a little harder with my legs, and I'm able to wave an arm above my head to get her attention. She squints at the shoreline, just barely visible in the evening dusk.

"Are you... *naked?*" She shouts, sounding out of breath. I can just make out the yellow swimsuit bundled in her hands—*my* swimsuit, that I left on the shore.

I shrug my bare shoulders as I tread water, not that she can see the gesture all the way out here. "I wanted to try skinny dipping. And you were occupied."

"About that." Tiffany stops along the edge of the surf, and her voice drops. "I think we should go home early."

"What?" I groan. This again? "Tiff, this could be our last vacation together for years. You want to cut it short?"

"Dean says he saw something in the water when he was fishing just now. Something big. I think it's Pressie. The Lake Monster. You shouldn't be out there."

"*Seriously??*" I swim closer to her, too angry to have this conversation without my feet on the ground. I need my arms for gesturing right now, not doggy paddling. "The *mythical* lake monster. Dean thinks he saw Pressie?"

"I know it sounds silly, Lil, but I've had this weird feeling all day–"

"You know what I think?" My shins hit the pebbly ground beneath me and I gather myself, rising out of the water until my torso is exposed to the night air. I cross my arms and raise an eyebrow. "I think that feeling is called *horny,* and you're using local mythology as an excuse to get your boyfriend in a cozy hotel for the night."

"What?" Her face flushes enough that I can see the hot pink even in the dim light of the moon. "Just because—Lil, no, that's not it. I care about this vacation as much as you do!"

"Really? It doesn't seem like that. You haven't even gotten in the water this week, Tiff!" An angry puff of breath shoots out of me as I try to calm down, try to make her see my side of things. But my hands clench inside my elbows as I fight to keep my temper under wraps. "This has always been *our* time. This little girls' trip, just for us. For the past three years, these vacations have been the only time I've known I could actually count on you to really be present with me. Ever since you and Dean moved in together, we hardly hang out just the two of us. And now that you're engaged, I feel like I never get to see you anymore!"

She shuffles her shoulders uncomfortably. "Lillian, come on. You're being unfair."

"*I'm* being unfair?" I raise my hands and walk closer, the water now down to my waist. Great. I guess I'll have to have my boobs out for this conversation anyway. "Tiffany, you are leaving the only time we've carved out for each other in the past year to call your fiancé three times a day. You're texting him constantly, like you've done every time I've tried to take you to a movie or out for drinks since you've gotten engaged! And if you aren't texting him, it's because he's tagging along. You never hang out with me anymore!"

Tiffany's face glows red. She *knows* she's wrong. But she refuses to admit it. "We still hang out!"

"Yeah, with Dean!" I yell. "It's never just the two of us. I miss talking to you without having Dean coming between us. I miss my best friend!"

She's silent for a second, and my racing heart drops. I walk closer, searching her face to try to see what she's thinking.

Just say you miss me, too.

"I don't know what to tell you, Lillian." I freeze when she finally speaks, only a few yards away from her now. She fidgets with the swimsuit in her hands. "I want to go home."

"*Why*, though? What did I do?"

"Nothing, I just *do*, okay? There's the lake mon–"

"Oh please, it's *not the fucking lake monster!*" I stomp my foot, sending water splashing all around. A few drops spray Tiff's face, and she wipes at them. My face is wet, too, but it isn't from the lake. "Tell me the truth! What is it? Why don't you want to spend time with me anymore?"

Tears stream down my cheeks, and my throat clenches around all the frustration I've been holding back. I need her to acknowledge it. That she's been drifting apart, trying to leave me behind. I just want her to *admit* it.

Tiffany stares down at my swimsuit still clutched in her hands. "I just... look, can you put some clothes on? This is awkward."

She tosses my suit to me. Surprised, I just barely manage to catch it.

"Not until you answer my question."

"I don't... I don't feel safe here. Not now. Not with..." She puts her hand on her stomach, and I feel that flash of unfairness again.

Okay. Now she's just trying to deflect. She has to be, because *something* isn't adding up here. I'm a decent swimmer, but Tiffany swam competitively in high school. Half the reason we even started coming here all those years ago was because she wanted to swim in Lake Superior. I get that she's pregnant, but exercise is good for pregnancy. Swimming, especially. Why would she feel unsafe here?

"Nothing dangerous has happened here in the ten years we've been visiting. What is really going on?"

She throws up her hands, and there are tears welling in her eyes now, too.

"Look, maybe I'm just done with this phase of my life, okay? Going out to bars, partying with the girls. Maybe I'm about to get married and have a kid and I think it's time for me to move on from all of that."

"That *phase?*" Okay. Now I'm angry.

I may be many things, but I am not a *phase.*

"What the hell are you talking about, Tiff? I'm not

asking for you to party *with the girls*. I'm not asking you to drink, I'm not asking you to be reckless and put yourself in danger. I'm asking you to spend *one* week—one *measly* week—with *me*. Your *best friend*."

She stares at me, rubbing her stomach. I clutch my swimsuit in front of me.

"If you can't understand, then maybe we're not as close as we used to be." She looks away, and I hold back a sob. "I *did* make time for you, Lillian. We've had three days out here together. And it's been fun. But now I want to go back home. Yes, with Dean. He helps me feel safe. Is that too much to ask?"

He helps her feel safe.

Because, supposedly, she doesn't feel safe around me. Or part of what she considers "home".

"Fine." I toss the swimsuit into the surf. "But I'm staying here. If you're not going to enjoy our girls' trip, then I will. For both of us. Enjoy your ten-hour car ride with Dean."

The last words crack on my lips as I turn away from her, submerging myself back into the water.

I can't believe it. Three days. Three days, in a whole year. That's her "making time" for me.

I've been trying to be a supportive friend through the biggest changes in her life, through the engagement and the baby and all of it, and she can't bear to spend more than a couple of days on the beach with me before running back to her fiancé.

What happened to us? What happened to the best friend who'd brought me back to life after I fell apart, after I lost everything? The one who promised we'd always be there for each other?

I knew things would change when she and Dean got

engaged, but I didn't think...

You know what? Fine. She can leave. I'll find new friends. Maybe I'll even find a boyfriend or partner of my own, finally. Someone way better than Dean. Someone who will actually let me spend time with my friends, who actually cares about what I want and who I am. Instead of just changing me into someone else entirely.

Without even thinking, I dive under the water and take long, powerful strokes across the lake. I don't even think about how far I'm going, or how long it will take to get back.

I just know that I don't want to be around to see it when Tiffany finally leaves me for good.

CHAPTER 4
ERIK

I retreat back to the lagoon, pondering the deal I struck with the monster.

He needs to mate. And soon. But once he does, I will be free.

Will I die instantly? Or will my body simply revert to aging naturally after I am no longer cursed by the sea monster? Do I even have a preference? Any outcome will be welcome after my thousand years of imprisonment.

Since my body was possessed by the curse, I have maintained my youth and vigor. To any outsider, I likely appear no older than the thirty summers I was when my peoples' ship capsized in the lake. Tall, strong, with my crew tattoos coiling down my arms and around my thighs, my body is that of a Viking warrior in his prime. My hair has grown wild in my many years alone, my beard is full and unbraided, and I gave up tying back my long, blonde mane centuries ago. The clothes I wore in the crash have long since deteriorated, and large furs are hard to come by along the loch's shores. So in the summer, I leave my skin bare to the elements. Just one more reason I cannot venture onto the mainland with the humans about.

I lose myself in my thoughts, roasting fish on the open fire of the lagoon's sandy shore, when I feel the monster stir in the base of my stomach.

You will eat soon, I tell it.

We have company.

I start, sensing the presence of a human approaching. But who?

Silently, I creep through the island foliage towards the shore. As I peek through the trees, my heart constricts in my chest.

It is the woman from before, lying against a boulder on the sand, chest heaving with labored breaths. I feel my own breath catch as my eyes follow the movement, watching her ample breasts rise and fall with each intake of air.

The stirring in my stomach is back, but this time it is not the monster. Loyal to our agreement, he is mercifully silent, though I can sense him still coiled deep within me.

He is giving me space. To feel her presence and approach her as a man.

And the sensations I am feeling? Entirely my own human desires.

She is beautiful. Water drips from her flaxen hair, which fans out behind her head against the rock. I was already admiring her breasts as she breathed, watching the round, full swells bounce—not unlike the well-fed tavern maidens who populated my fantasies as an adolescent back home.

Pink nipples—delightful, pert buds—poke from the center of each one, and I find myself inexplicably yearning to suck one into my mouth, to taste her puckered skin. I shake my head.

I have been living in the water too long. Have watched

too many fish with their pouting lips swarming in their mating schools.

Her lips, however, are full and dark, parted with her exertion. I watch as she lifts a strong arm to her round cheek, and swipes at a few damp hairs that curl around her face.

Her light hair, her strong arms... she reminds me of the women I knew from long before I ever sailed to this cursed land.

The rest of her body is lush and full. The tightening in my stomach, that old and familiar feeling that I know to be human need, almost overwhelms me.

I swallow as my eyes drift down to the sweet tuft of curly hair at the apex of her thighs. The water on her skin glints in the moonlight, and a sudden thought makes me shudder.

Is she as wet within?

I shake my head, casting my lust aside for now. There are more important questions to be answered now. How did she get here? I cannot believe that she would swim across the lake to the island. That is no simple feat; few humans attempt it, except for the occasional display of competitive athleticism they hold every midsummer. But this maiden is alone. There is no one to compete against. And she seems... tired.

Her eyes drift closed, and the water droplets that cling to her long lashes clump and fall in rivulets down her cheeks.

But then I realize that it is not only lake water causing the tiny rivers to fall. She is crying.

"What hurts you?"

She and I both jump at the words as they crackle from my mouth. My voice is rough, more growl than speech, from many decades of silence. I could not remember the last time I opened my mouth to speak aloud.

She turns toward me, squinting at the tree line. Realizing I have made a terrible mistake, but not seeing any way to rectify it without frightening her further, I creep out into the light from the cover of the low-hanging evergreen branches.

Her eyes widen. Like I did with her, she appraises my body, scanning her eyes up and down. She hesitates when her gaze travels below my waistline before darting back up to my face. Pink tinges her pale cheeks.

It is mesmerizing.

"Who are you? Why are you naked?"

Her voice, piercing and melodic, rings out like a bell in a storm. I cannot remember the last time I heard music like it.

"I could ask the same of you," I respond, voice still rough from lack of use. She blinks, then looks down in shock before scrambling to cover herself with her arms. I shake my head and reach out a hand.

"No! Please do not cover yourself. You are too beautiful to hide." Slowly, I approach her, taking small but steady steps across the sand. "What brings you here?"

Her tone is wary when she answers. "I come here every year. Well, not *here*. The cabin. On the main shore."

I nod. I know I have not seen her on my shore before. I would have remembered a beauty like her sunbathing on my island.

"What about you? You look... like you've been here a while. Are you lost?" Her brow wrinkles, and silence stretches between us.

My chest shakes. Like bubbles rising deep from my stomach, peals of air propel themselves up my torso and out from my mouth in short barks. The sound cuts through the crisp night air, bouncing off the trees and echoing around us.

Am I... *laughing?*

When did I last laugh?

My whole body fills with warmth. My lips split into a wide grin, and my entire body feels... *lighter* from the action. This maiden... this woman, she made me *laugh*.

"In a way..." I begin, as the last of the laughter dies on my lips. Her face creases more, and I realize that the wrinkles between her brows are conveying concern. Concern for me. "No. I am not lost. This is my home."

"You live here." Her expression flattens.

She seems not to believe me.

"Yes. I have for many years. Alone."

"And you... don't wear clothes?"

Her eyes dart down below my waist yet again. My cock has been hardening as we parlay. I do not attempt to hide it. I have been alone for too long to be troubled by shame or embarrassment at my nakedness.

"No. I have no need."

"It gets cold here in the winter, though, doesn't it?"

"I stay out of the air in the winter."

When the autumn winds shake all the brown leaves from the trees, I retreat to the depths of the lake. My monster and I both are more comfortable there.

Not that she needs to know that just yet.

"Huh." Slowly, her hands drop to her sides. I feel myself harden further as I take in her full beauty once more.

Stunning. Simply stunning.

I hope I can convince her to stay. To mate. I do not understand the full consequences of the ritual He needs to perform to break the curse, but my monster did assure me she would be safe. Live. Thrive, He even said.

Perhaps after, she might even choose to stay. Perhaps, she could be mine.

My cock pulses at the thought, and the maiden's eyes flicker to the movement. I smile.

"What is your name, lass?"

She raises her eyes to mine. The white light of the moon and stars glitter in their dark blue depths, and I find myself drawn to them like the lake waters in winter.

"Lillian."

"Lillian," I repeat, and for the first time, the sounds coming from my mouth do not sound like they are being pulled through the jagged rocks of the lagoon. Her name floats on my tongue and resonates in my chest, like the music that it is.

"My name is Erik."

CHAPTER 5

LILLIAN

Erik.

Erik is the completely, totally, way-too-normal name for the fucking mountain of a Viking lumberjack that stands before me. Easily 6'5", with shoulders like The Rock, and buck-naked as the day he was born.

But unlike Dwayne Johnson, this man has a full head of long, curly dark blonde locks and a beard to match. His massive, sculpted chest is smudged with dirt, as if he's been living naked and alone on this island for months.

But none of that even matters, not really, because the most remarkable thing about this crazy homeless Viking man is the massive erection jutting out from his pelvis. Jesus Christ, I've read enough romance novels that praise the penises of their leading men, and like many other readers I usually roll my eyes at the fawning of the heroines over the size of their dicks. If I have to read one more girl wondering "if he'd fit," I'll gag.

Scratch that. Bad choice of words. Now all I can think about is how I would actually gag on this man's cock if it were ever in my mouth. He's *huge*.

Suddenly, I understand what it would take for a woman to question whether or not a man would fit inside her.

I feel my cheeks heat. Again. I remember that I, too, am naked. And my jiggly belly, fat ass, and floppy titties are on full display in front of this Adonis of a mountain man.

Whyyyy did I think skinny dipping was a good idea?

"Okay, Erik. Nice to meet you. I uh, I should be getting back–"

"No! Please, maiden, do not leave."

Maiden?

Okay, what's with this guy? He sounds like he hasn't talked in a hundred years, and it seems like he has the vocabulary to match. Or he's one of those nerdy neckbeard types that likes to LARP as a paladin on weekends or something, and I'm the first female he's seen in months.

I need to get out of here.

"Sorry, I should really get some clothes, you know? It's a little chilly out here." I turn to swim back to the shore, despite being pretty tired after I just ran away from Tiffany.

Yeeeaaaah, maybe that wasn't the brightest idea I ever had.

A pain shoots through my chest at the thought of my former best friend. How long has she felt like she's outgrown me, and just been too polite to say anything about it? Has this just been since she became pregnant? Or has it been building ever since she met Dean?

You know what? On second thought, nothing about her leading me on the way she has is "polite." She's a bitch, is what she is. Cutting our vacation short so she can go dick her boyfriend. They're probably already on the highway home to Chicago.

I take a few more steps back towards the water, tears springing to my eyes once more, when a hand grabs my wrist.

Instantly, a shock zings up my arm. Not like a static electricity shock—this is like a warm tingle that zips from my wrist to my neck and down my spine, sparking a fire in my stomach.

Oh.

I whip my head over my shoulder, and see that Erik's big, calloused hand is gripping my arm. His hold is strong, and up close, his body is even more enticing. I can feel the heat radiating off of him, and I can smell him. My nostrils widen as I take in a deep breath, and realize with a start that even though he looks dirty, he doesn't smell bad.

No, he smells... *musky*. Loamy. Manly.

Fuck. It's hot. He smells *hot*.

The heat that started pooling in my belly at the sight of his rock-hard cock spreads lower, until it pulses in my pussy like a heartbeat. I look down in embarrassment, and remember that, of course, I didn't shave before going on this trip.

So not only am I fat, naked, vulnerable, and gross with lake funk, but I also have a full bush situation going on.

Great. Just great. I finally get a man's attention, and it's at the worst possible moment.

I tear my arm from his grasp. Surprisingly, he lets me go. But I don't walk away from him just yet. Instead, I just rub the spot where he grabbed me with my other hand, and give him a hard look.

He looks back, completely nonplussed.

"What? What do you want?"

He stares deeply into my eyes before answering, and the warm tingling returns in earnest. His eyes are so dark, almost black, and they glitter with a swirling intensity. I'm unable to look away, utterly hypnotized, until he speaks.

"I need you, Lillian."

Say what now?

"You... need me?"

I couldn't have heard him right. Sexy naked Viking man needs *me?*

Uh, yeah, no. Not unless he needs someone to help him patch his canoe or something. Or maybe he hit his head on one of those big boulders along the north shore?

That would explain it. Why else would anyone this unjustifiably hot claim to need a lonely wreck like me?

"Yes. I need your help."

"I mean, I can call the coastguard for you—"

"No! Only you." He reaches for me again but hesitates, his giant hand hovering just above my shoulder. I can feel the heat of his palm, agonizingly close, warming my skin without actually making contact.

He's waiting for my permission to touch me, I realize. But I stay perfectly still, eyes wide as I wait to see what he does next.

He pulls back his hand. Conflict swirls in his dark eyes for a moment, and by the light of the moon, I see a shadow cross his face. It almost looks as if he's fighting some kind of war with himself.

No, that's silly. What does that even mean? A war with himself?

I must be seriously dehydrated from the long swim. I need to get back to the cabin.

But just as I make the decision to swim back, Erik sighs. A full-chest exhalation, like the weight of a thousand years is crashing down on his lungs. His whole body seems to deflate, with the exception of his cock, of course, which still bobs temptingly below his waist.

This poor man. What happened to him?

"No. I cannot ask you to stay. I'm sorry. Please, leave here. Hurry. Do not come back to this lake. It isn't safe here."

"What?"

I'm not sure what I was expecting him to say after a sigh like that, but it wasn't *that*. It isn't safe here? What on earth was he talking about?

First Tiffany, now him. What is wrong with everyone today?

"If you need help, I'm sure–"

"Now! Leave!" He shouts, the gravel of his voice cutting deep into my heart.

With that, something snaps between us, and I crash back to reality.

I'm naked on a strange beach, and a crazy unhoused man, albeit a smoking hot one, is yelling at me, literally telling me I am unsafe.

Granted, *he's* likely the one putting my safety at risk, but regardless, I should take my chance while I have it.

I need to get out of here.

With one last look at the stranger, I wade out into the lake and start swimming back to the mainland. The moon shines high in the sky above me; night having fallen in earnest now.

Tiffany's likely long gone.

My arms ache as I arch them up and stroke into the water again and again, breathing heavily with the effort. I kick with all my strength, the fear of what I just encountered sinking in.

Who *is* that man? What is he doing out on that weird tiny island in the middle of the lake? And why was I so drawn to him?

Those broad shoulders, his sculpted body. He looked like he could fucking bench me if he wanted to without a problem. I suppose if anyone is able to survive alone on an island in the middle of a Great Lake, it'd be a frickin' Viking lumberjack.

Fuck. I'm exhausted.

About halfway between the island and the mainland, the adrenaline starts to wear off. I slow my strokes a bit, switching to a treading doggy paddle as I catch my breath. This is not an easy swim, and I've already done it once today. I've been in the water for the better part of three hours today. I need to take it slow, otherwise–

Gah! A cramp seizes my calf.

"Fuck!" My leg lights up with pain, and my mouth sinks below the surface as my kicks falter. Water fills my mouth, and I cough. *Charlie horse! Shit!*

Desperately, I flail in the water, my nose and mouth bobbing in and out of the lake as I kick and pump my arms as best as I can, trying to stay upright while I bite through the pain.

It's not letting up!

God, when was the last time I drank water? I was drinking cocktails all day while I was reading on the beach. Of course, now I'm dehydrated, and still a mile away from shore...

The cramp grips my calf like a vise, and this time my whole head dips below the water. My mouth opens in panic, and I take in a huge lungful of Lake Superior. I wave my arms helplessly, coughing and sputtering as I briefly surface, only to plunge back down under the surf as a particularly bad pain bolts through my leg.

"Gah!" I cry, but it's too late. I'm sinking. My eyes flare

open, stinging in the lake, as I wildly search for something, anything, to help propel me back above the surface.

But there's nothing. Just a black blur, getting ever larger in my vision, and a pressing pain squeezing my lungs, until finally, it all goes dark.

What was it that the old man said? All those years ago?

Lake Superior never gives up her dead...

CHAPTER 6
LILLIAN

Weightless. For the first time in my life, I feel truly... weightless.

It's like swimming, but instead of the pressure of the water around me, everything feels warm and floaty. Fuzzy. Is this real? Am I alive?

Trying to get any concrete thoughts to form is a battle. I know I'm Lillian, and I'm an adult... what does that mean, adult? Don't adults have responsibilities?

But what kind of responsibilities?

Cooking food... raising children...

I have to be forgetting something, don't I?

No... no, there's no need for me to get up just yet. I don't have any children. I'm not hungry. Just a few more minutes. This bed is so comfortable...

"That's right, Lil, we're on vacation. Sleep in as long as you like."

"Tiffany?"

My voice feels odd as it forms the name of my best friend, almost like I'm talking around a mouthful of cotton balls. But I'd know that voice anywhere.

"That's right, hun. Just relax."

Strong, soft hands start to rub my shoulders, and I have to admit, it feels amazing. The fingers knead into the sore muscles at my neck and collarbone, reaching down to stretch and soothe my tight chest.

"So... sore..."

"You swam a lot *yesterday, Lil. It's a wonder you didn't drown!"*

Drown?

Drown...

Bubbles spilling from my mouth, legs kicking, arms reaching—waving—struggling. Why is everything so hard? Why is everything so heavy??

"You're safe, Lil. You're here with me."

"Tiffany, what's–"

"Shhh, don't speak. It's okay. I know everything you need. We have *everything you need."*

We?

A second pair of hands comes around to massage my feet, my ankles, my calves. Together, the two of them rub every limb, sending me deeper and deeper into total relaxation.

"It could be this everyday, you know. The three of us. Together."

Tiffany's voice is low and sweet as her hands explore lower down my body, almost meeting the other set as it climbs my legs and begins to tease at the apex of my thighs.

"Tiff–"

"I've always liked you, Lillian. But you haven't let me in. I never wanted to steal Tiffany away from you. Not when you two feel so strongly about each other."

Is that... Dean's voice?

Dean... that's right. Tiff's boyfriend. They're getting married. Without me...

"Let us in, Lil. Let us in, and we can all be together. Make this vacation last forever."

"Va...ca...tion...?"

Each syllable is a Herculean effort, the air just not coming. My lips word soundlessly as I whisper-shout, until I feel a soft mouth nip at my own.

I let out what little air I have on a moan, and it rumbles through me, a million times louder than anything I've been able to say.

"We're at the cabin, remember?" Tiffany coos. "The lake house? This is our last trip together."

Lake! Lake water. Cold, so cold, so heavy, everywhere—my lungs, I can't breathe, I can't—

"Help her, please. I can't help her, I can't..."

A low chuckle echoes through the vast emptiness around me. And then a voice, sultry and seductive, feels like it fills everything around and within me as she speaks. The hands on my body grow stronger, writhing and twisting as they wrap me in their embrace, squeezing and sucking and...

"I knew you'd come back. Back to my healing waters. Perhaps it's time you stay..."

Darkness! Immeasurable darkness, pressing on my eyes–

"Accept my gift, Sweet Lillian. I can see your deepest desires, your desperation to be wanted. I want you, now. Stay with me. Let me in..."

More arms than I can count now, so many more than four, long and thick and languid, pull apart my legs, reaching into my most sensitive places.

I let out the last of my air on a sigh...

.   .   .

I open my eyes to find that my surroundings are quite dark. So dark, in fact, that I wonder if I actually *did* open my eyes, or if–

Ow!

Ooookay, nope. Seeing as I just poked myself in the iris, they're definitely open. Magenta spots bloom in my vision, blocking out my view even more. Slowly, I rub my face and allow myself to adjust to the low light.

I can barely make out anything.

Except... I'm naked. My pale skin is one of the few things shining through the inky depths. But there's something dark wrapped around my arms and legs. Cords? Ropes?

Slowly, my eyes adjust.

Seaweed?

Where am I? And what was that crazy dream–

You're safe, Lillian.

The voice sounds low, sensual. It resonates around me, vibrating through my body, and feels strangely... familiar?

"Who's there? Who are you?"

No sound comes out of my mouth. It's like the dream again, only instead of cotton, bubbles float from my lips. My eyes widen, and I panic.

I can't speak.

And I can feel pain.

Which means I'm awake. Awake and–

Underwater!

Your friend. The one you were dreaming about. You've been here with her before, have you not?

My mind races as I try to place the voice. Where have I heard it before?

One of the tendrils of seaweed floats from my leg, tickling the inside of my knee. And that's when I remember.

She's the voice from the dream.

Mmm, yes, I suppose you never saw me before. But I know you, Lillian. I know you so much better than you think.

I try to speak again, to ask who she is, but my mouth fills with water when I go to take a breath. I start to cough, only for more bubbles to launch themselves forward. My eyes sting with invisible tears, and I–

Easy, Lillian. You can breathe. Through your gills. Just like you've been doing.

Gills?!

I close my mouth, and attempt to breathe through my nose. Miraculously, instead of passing through my nostrils, I feel the water current through filters in my neck.

I'm breathing underwater.

What has she done to me?

She chuckles again, the sound filling my brain just like it has been, as if she has a direct line of communication into my very soul.

Oh, Lillian. I saved you. For I'm not the only one who's interested in you and your friend. It appears you've collected an admirer.

Wha–

All will become clear in time, my dear. For now, sleep. You over-exerted yourself, and now, it's time to rest.

The commanding presence filling the underwater cave dissipates. And suddenly, my eyelids are too heavy to hold open any longer.

Tendrils of seaweed wrap around my legs, coiling and uncoiling around my body, stroking up and down, higher and lower, closer and closer to my center. They brush against my rib cage and breasts, and I shiver as one skirts over my nipple, before delving ever nearer to the space between my legs.

Despite the fact that I'm clearly underwater, I feel wetness pool between my thighs. Is this a dream? Is any of this... real?

One of the tendrils suctions itself to my upper thigh, and in that moment I realize: this isn't seaweed.

These are tentacles.

I gasp, and once again, my mouth makes no sound. Only bubbles rise from my mouth and nose as I struggle against the tentacles' firm hold, feeling them rise to stroke against my lower lips.

"No!"

But my cries are useless. Even if I could speak, my body only betrays my words. Memories of Dean's and Tiffany's hands exploring me earlier rush to the surface of my mind, and I become a slave to the sensation. Heat spreads inside me, more wetness gushes from my pussy, and one long, thick tentacle slowly works itself between my folds and teases at my entrance.

I squeeze my eyes shut. This can't be happening. This has to be a dream.

But what about the voice from before? Was She a dream? Was Dean? Was Tiff?

A suction cup latches onto my clit, and at last, I hear a sound echo from my throat. But it isn't a cry of resistance or pain.

It's a lusty, desperate moan.

Don't stop, I breathe, the words something between a thought and a flutter of bubbles. The monster obeys, and I feel my pussy stretch around a deliciously textured tentacle. It thrusts inside me, while another latches on and shudders against my clit. More appear, wrapping themselves around my torso, curling up the sensitive skin along the insides of my arms and up to my breasts, squeezing around the squishy globes, and teasing my nipples with their flexible tips.

Oh, God!

My whole body shudders as a second tentacle enters me, thrusting in and out in an opposite rhythm to the first, undulating inside me, alternating so I'm never empty. Water gushes in and around my gills as my breathing quickens, my heart beating in triple time. Where before, I couldn't hear myself making any sound at all, now I'm too loud. My desperate moans and gasping breaths echo within the dark, wet cave, and the lewd sounds only make me even hornier.

I'm going to come. I'm going to explode around these tentacles. Hard.

Another gush of wetness trickles down my legs, soaking the strong arms that hold me in place. Then I feel one of them retreat, chilling my slick thigh with its absence.

Where–?

And then it answers.

Slippery with my own wetness, the tip of a tentacle slips between my ass cheeks, pressing at my tight hole.

Another moan reverberates around us as a wave of pleasure cascades through me, as suckers thrust inside me and ripple past my g-spot again and again. My pussy is a swollen mess, clenching around each thrusts, and I find myself pushing my walls open for them. I'm trying to take them deeper; I want this. I want to come harder than I could have ever dreamed.

Because this has to be a dream, right? I'm breathing underwater. I'm surrounded by lusty tentacles. Some merwitch gave me gills. I can't possibly be awake right now...

And if I am, don't wake me.

I feel my pussy twitch, and all the muscles around my entrance begin to flutter uncontrollably. The tentacle at my asshole pushes gently inside.

And then it starts to wriggle. It burrows against the tight bud, opening me up as it delves deep inside, deeper than I've ever let anyone try with my ass before.

But this is different. It's not pinching, or hurting. It feels... amazing!

I'm a slick mess, already loose and dripping with arousal from the monster's onslaught of my pussy and clit. This added pressure against my tight hole is alarmingly good. It's almost tempting. Like if I could just open a little more for it, then maybe...

An orgasm overtakes me, and the sucker at my clit suctions off of me with a loud pop that echoes around the chamber. I cry out, not even caring that it's nothing but a column of bubbles, too busy shaking with my release.

And the tentacle that had been spelunking my back hole redoubles its efforts, plunging into me so hard my legs spread wide to make room.

I hardly even register the slight pinch as it glides inside—still reeling from the pleasure of my orgasm. Wave upon wave of lusty heat crashes over me, while another sensation slowly takes hold: a delicious pressure writhing deep inside me, even deeper than the tentacles swirling into my g-spot.

This one radiates deep into my stomach. A pounding, hot ache that drives me mad.

Yep. This is the hottest sex dream I've ever had. Hands down.

The other arms wrap around me, stroking at my wet lips, sliding in and out between my folds, rubbing back and forth against my swollen clit. All the while, the pressure in my stomach builds hotter and hotter, as sucker after sucker grinds against my ass.

Oooooooooh Goooooooood... The moan that comes out of me rumbles from deep in my chest. It's entirely unrecognizable from any sound I'd ever heard myself make.

The coiling sensation deep in my belly pulses stronger, and

suddenly, I feel my hips buck back of their own accord, forcing the tentacle inside my ass even deeper.

I need more. I'm going to come again. I'm going to–

Deeper! *I scream, mouth opening soundlessly while my mind tunnels on that one thought. My only wish, and it comes true.*

The monster impales me. In and out, pulling itself from me before ramming back between my legs, filling my deepest spaces, and curling into my stomach as it utterly wrecks me from the inside out.

A second orgasm rips through me, and that rough low voice I didn't recognize rumbles from my throat. It almost seems to multiply, like two voices are moaning and crying out in unison, until the tremors slow, and cease, and I float back from whence I came.

CHAPTER 7
ERIK

Guilt wracks my body.

I scared her, she ran, and she drowned.

How could I be so careless?

No, not careless... impotent. Frozen. I knew the monster could help her, could curse her like he did me, but I could not fathom damning someone to the same fate. Surely being saved, at the cost of living forever tied to an evil sea god, is a fate worse than death?

And now that she is gone... she will no longer have to choose.

You fool. She lives.

What?

Can you not sense her presence? Different, yes, faint... but it is she.

Disbelief consumes me. I leap into the water, propelling myself with powerful strokes to the spot where she disappeared. Once there, I dive into the depths, shifting as I allow my captor's senses to overtake my feeble human once.

As a man, I am not powerful enough to smell her. But my monster is. He opens his beak and the scent of her flaxen hair envelops me. My heart rushes against my gelatinous ribcage. *Alive!*

She is alive. She is breathing.

Breathing? But how—

I watch the gills along her pale neck flutter as she breathes. Gills. As impossible as it would seem, despite the fact that I stayed away, kept my monster from her... she was still cursed.

Cursed like me. Forever.

It doesn't need to be forever. You both can still be free.

I shut my eyes, trying to block out the voice of the monster in my head. He tricked me. This must be His doing. There is no other explanation.

He never intended to free me of the curse. He just wanted to capture a victim for his perversions.

They are not perversions. Or if they are, we are so intertwined by now that they are as much yours as mine.

I wince. I hate it. The monster inside me. Hate how its lust boils through my veins, how its pleasure weaves through me at the sight of her. How it drives me to seize her in my arms...

And now, she too is cursed. Any excuse I had to stay away is gone, and I...

The loch monster has ruined me for anyone else. I have to have her for myself.

But if this curse would ever break... I need to know she would be with me on the other side. Need her understanding. I must not force myself on her. Whatever I give, she must want it as badly as I want it.

Want to feel her soft skin against mine. Weave my fingers through her beautiful hair. Hold her to me as she squeezes around me, taking me into herself, surrendering to the pleasure...

Over and over and over again.

She stirs in her sleep, and I panic. Should I be here when she wakes? Should I take care of her? Feed her?

It is not safe for her to be floating in the open waters. She should be somewhere safe when she awakens. Somewhere where I can keep an eye on her and the monster together.

I gather her gently in my arms, careful not to disturb her rest. Her eyelids flutter rapidly as she tosses and turns against me, making it more difficult to swim to the spacious underwater cave that I call home.

Whatever dreams haunt her cannot be entirely unpleasant, though, as the noises she is making do not seem to be ones of pain.

In fact... she seems to be enjoying herself.

Her lips part on a gasp that has bubbles drifting from her soft mouth and an ache forming in my gut. Her legs twist together, rubbing as she clenches her thighs, and the scent of her becomes overwhelming. It saturates the water around us, until my face heats with the headiness of it.

Gods... just what is she dreaming?

Those visions aren't all her own.

What?

The voice of the monster ringing in my head deflates the swelling of my manhood. Confusion fills the void left behind.

What do you mean? Is this your—

It is not my doing. None of this is my doing, despite your assumptions to the contrary. There is another presence here. One I haven't felt for many seasons...

My chest tightens. Another?

Another monster?

Phorkys. I address him by name. That terrible, powerful name that sparks with a magic far more ancient than humans. Even without speaking it aloud, I can feel its power as I command him. *Tell me who did this to her.*

He does not answer right away. Instead, he pushes our limbs more quickly to our cave, transforming my lower half to aid in the propulsion. On the way, he snatches a walleye for me to prepare for dinner. Another, he shoves noncha-lantly into his beak, as if he needs to prepare his strength to have this conversation.

At last we reach the cave. I lay sweet Lillian against the smooth rock of the wall, covering her modestly within a patch of lake weeds. She sighs soundlessly, and I feel my heart ache for her.

It is then that he speaks.

I am not the only god who dwells in these waters... there is another.

Fire twists in my belly at the confession. *How dare you keep this a secret all these years!*

I believed her to be gone. Along with the last of our brood.

Our?

You... you were family?

Lovers. For many moons, we ruled the seas to the east. Had many magnificent children. Witnessed the death of too many. The Grecians... they were a cruel people. We left their shores to find a more accepting home.

Grecians?

Long forgotten memories, stories my people would tell around bonfires, of a people far to the south. Beautiful scholars, less fearsome than ourselves, and strange. But many: their civilization was rumoured to stretch across continents.

We sought to grow as they had. Built ships. Sailed west, to lands they would never dream to explore. Further and further we sailed, past many islands and settlements, through rapids, until...

We crashed here. Where the lake monster destroyed our ship, leaving only me...

I was not the one to destroy your ship, human. It was my lover. My Keto.

Unbidden, the scene flashes before my eyes. A towering creature, female, with hair like eels and innumerable tails that coiled and crushed our wooden ship from bow to stern. Her awe-inspiring body, curvaceous and proud, wrapping our entire lives in her fearsome embrace, and then...

Phorkys, approaching the ship. Discovering me, my family. Attempting to reason with her. Her explosion of fury.

What few members of my people that may have remained perished in the ensuing lover's quarrel. I was the lone survivor, but even I would have died if not for...

Yes. I saved you.

Why?

Useless tears dissolve into the lake around me as fast as they form in my eyes. An all-consuming sadness over-whelms me as I remember that horrific day, through his eyes. A memory I had long repressed.

My family. My wife. Our children. Gone.

Because of *Her*.

Why would you save me? *Why could you not save them?*

So much of our magic was hers. She was my world, my

source of power. Without her, I was nothing more than a shell. I needed you as much as you needed me to prevail.

You used me. I try to summon my ever present anger, but the sense of loss is too great. Instead, I merely weep. *I would have rather died.*

I understand this now. But alas... one such as I has only ever had one prevailing drive. To live, and to multiply.

Lillian cries out in her sleep—a haunting, lascivious sound—strong enough to echo even throughout the watery cave. I flinch as my body responds with an unnatural excitement.

You are an abomination.

I am a god.

You used me!

And you, me! Hot rage burns through my sorrow, and Phorkys fills my head. **You would have perished without me! First in the wreck, and thousands of times over from your incompetence! Without me, you would have starved. Without me, you would have drowned. Without me, you would have frozen. A hundred thousand deaths I've saved you from, and still you curse me!**

I never asked to be saved.

His tentacles reach out, and I do not stop them. Caressing Lillian's face, her breasts, and down further to–

Stop, I beg him. *Please do not use my body for this.*

The limbs pause, then retract. I feel the monster consider my request, and a long moment passes before he speaks to me again.

I need you for one more task, my unwilling human. One more, and then I will set you free.

Using every last reserve of mental strength I possess, I

search his words for any hint of dishonesty. Any tell that this is another one of his tricks.

I have never tricked you. And I've no reason to lie. My Keto lives, and she calls to me through this human female.

My eyes widen. *What did she do to Lillian?*

You will not like the answer. But you can use it to free you both.

I should resist. Find some other way. I have been better at repressing him, at keeping him at bay. Certainly, if I only try harder—

Erik.

There has to be another way.

You are not strong enough to fight a god, boy.

Lillian's breathing slows. Her breasts rise and fall in a steady, gentle rhythm. My body slowly transforms back to my human self as I watch her, my cock swelling once more as I take in her beauty.

You have my word as a god, Erik. Do this one thing, fulfill my purpose, and then you and your female will be free.

WHEN AT LAST she opens her eyes, any hope I cling to crumbles away. Their inky blue depths swirl and sparkle with the magic of the curse.

She jumps when she sees me.

"Who–?" She tries to speak, but only bubbles escape her. She gasps, then panic lights her features as the mouthful of water chokes her lungs, only to relax into an expression of confusion when she does not drown.

She frowns at me, a line etching her strong brows.

We cannot speak down here without much effort, I telepath my thoughts to her. Her eyes widen.

How did you– she blinks. I smile.

It is one of the curse's many... gifts. I grimace.

The curse? The crease between her brows deepens. *What curse?*

I shrug my shoulders in a breathless sigh, then gesture to the fish I prepared for her. *Let us eat. I will explain.*

CHAPTER 8
ERIK

You're the homeless man from the beach! Lillian telepaths to me, and I cannot help but smile at her picking up the new way of communicating with such ease.

It is refreshing and beautiful to hear another human in my mind in this way. Her voice is as distinct and bell-like as it was on land. Rich and lovely, and so different from the voice of the monster that has slithered in the back of my mind for so, so long.

Homeless? I chuckle, and I can hear her surprise as my laughter rings in her head. No doubt, it is less rough and hoarse than my physical voice must have sounded on the island. *I suppose...I have not seen my homeland in many years.*

She tilts her head. *Where are you from?*

Far away from here.

I gesture with my hands to the cave around us. She follows with her eyes, as if seeing her surroundings truly for the first time. But instead of fear, resignation fills her features. Her shoulders droop, and she returns her gaze to me.

Am I dead?

No, Lillian. But you will wish you were. The words burn to send themselves to her, but I hold them back. *You are not dead. You are like me: cursed to survive in this place, at the whim of gods who do not think highly of humans.*

Where are they?

Her hair swirls about her as she spins, hunting for the monsters as if they are hiding in the shadows around us. Her movements are so graceful. She clearly is a talented swimmer, as comfortable in the water as she is on land.

The corner of my mouth tilts up as I watch her, and she scowls at me.

Erik! What are you laughing at? Where are they?

They are within us.

I hold my hand to my heart, grimacing at the truth in my words. But Lillian looks confused.

Oh. Like, a metaphor?

Now it is my turn to tilt my head.

Metaphor?

Like, figuratively. We've been cursed to live underwater, and that makes us monstrous. Not physical monsters. Not real—but it's like a bad side of ourselves.

I shake my head. *No. The monsters are very real.*

She frowns.

And they're... inside us?

Not you, female. The voice echoes hauntingly around us, and I see her shudder at the new voice. The one I would do anything to hide from her. **Only him.**

Her eyes become saucers as she backs away from me, hiding away in her long, flowing hair.

Lillian, please! Let me explain!

Who... who are you? The question is a quivering whisper, piercing my psyche like a knife. *Tell me the truth this time.*

Opening my fingers, I spread my arms to my side, in an attempt to show her I mean no harm. It is too late to attempt to hide any of this reality from her. Now that she is here, cursed with the same misfortune as I am, it would be cruel to keep it a secret. *Yes, I will tell you everything, from the beginning.*

I take a deep breath through my gills, and then launch into my story.

I was not born in this land. My village is—was—far away from here, in the northlands across the sea.

Long ago, my family and I set off with a large crew of our brothers to explore this new land. Our ships were long and thin, and fast. Nimble. We sailed inland on rivers, braved rapids and unfamiliar waters, between many northern islands and through many forested riverlands, before eventually spying the shores of this giant freshwater sea.

It was beautiful. Not unlike our homeland. We decided even before reaching land that we would settle here.

But a storm engulfed us before we could dock. Rough winds, giant waves of ice—terrifying conditions, yes, but we were a sailing people. We had braved the arctic oceans before; this was no different from what we were used to. But we could not have known that there were dangers here we had never seen. Cruel and powerful. Giant and mighty.

I feel a hand on my arm, and realize that Lillian has come closer to me. Strands of her golden hair weave with mine as she looks up at me with concern in her eyes.

What happened?

I do not wish to tell her. Even now, it is painful, to speak of the community I once loved meeting its horrific end. I feel the monster stir within my belly as His part in the tale draws near.

I have tried to forget, I admit, letting out a torrent of bubbles from my lips in a sigh. *But He will not let me.*

Who?

*The monster. One of them—*I correct—*there are two. The one who destroyed my people's ship was as giant as a mountain, with a woman's torso and the legs of a massive squid. She wrapped herself around our vessel as if it were a child's toy. Crushed it with her massive limbs, while her gaze petrified our crew into ice and stone. Sailors fell heavily from the deck into the frigid waters. If they did not die instantly from her glare, they soon froze to death in the lake's unforgiving depths.*

Her fingers tighten around my forearm, and her warmth seeps into me. *I'm so sorry.*

My family was killed.

Oh, Erik…

I turn away, unable to look her in the eyes as the most unbearable part of the story approaches. Yet, she stays, stroking one comforting hand up and down my arm as I tell it.

I fell into the waters, and it was so cold. My lungs turned to ice within my chest, until… He found me. The one who destroyed our ship, my people: she is the one named Keto. An ancient goddess and mother of all manner of evil creatures. And her lover, Phorkys, He… He saved me.

The words taste bitter on my tongue. My resentment of the monster still overwhelms what small amount of pity I feel for Him and His struggle to survive. *He lives within me; I can resist him to a point. But I have been cursed to live a double life for many years.*

The confession, once put forth, sends my thoughts into a spiral, as I seek to soften the weight of it.

I have tried to keep it at bay, protect the many humans who have ventured to these waters as my people once did, I plead to her, *but I have not always been successful. I let my guard down when you appeared in the water. Your form, your body, it is...* My face heats. I look up, meeting Lillian's deep blue eyes, and even in the throes of reliving my worst memories, I can feel her effect on me. *It is very pleasing to me. To me and the monster. When it sees you, it also...He burns to make you His. To mate with you.*

Lillian's cheeks burn a lusty red, and I break eye contact.

Well that explains some of the crazy dreams...

What? Her entire face floods with color, and I quickly back away from her. *I am sorry, I do not mean to presume your trust—*

No! She shakes her head, and in my mind I hear a soft, shy giggle.

She is... laughing?

When I was asleep, I dreamt... well, let's just say my dreams were a lot spicier than I'm used to.

Spi-ci-er? I am unfamiliar with the word.

There were... tentacles involved. In... positions. I thought it was just the smut I'd been reading, but...

The red of her cheeks darkens impossibly. My entire body grows uncomfortably hot.

I underestimated its lust for you.

I swim away from her, terrified to hear that she has already suffered in her dreams as the object of the monster's perverted desires. Disgusted by my own body's reaction as I realize what she means. As I imagine what it might feel like, to take her in such a way.

Again, I feel a hand on my arm. Her beautiful voice rings clearly in my head once more, and I wish I could simply listen to it like music. I want to hear her in my mind forever, that lovely, human sound.

You're embarrassed. Her fingers trail up the sensitive skin along the inside of my elbow, and my body shivers. *You don't have to be. You've been like this for... God, it must be close to a thousand years, right?*

My tone is bitter. *I have lost count.*

Her thumb brushes my waist as she reaches for my hand, and my cock jumps impatiently. I try to quiet the monster, but his drive is so mixed with my own conflicted feelings toward this woman that I cannot quell the stirring. I am humiliatingly hard, so much so that even the light movement of the water across the skin of my shaft is like torture.

Surely, she sees it all. Is revolted by it. By me.

Why don't you ask her?

Ask me what?

Her hand stills as Phorkys speaks once more, ruining our intimate moment with His presence. I shudder, this time from frustration, and turn on her.

He wants to know if you are as disgusted by me as I am of myself! I snap, crossing the cavern with a petulant kick. I am behaving like a child, I know, but I cannot find balance in these hot and cold flashes of emotion. I do not even know what is me and what is the monster anymore.

Lillian is quiet for a moment, and my breathing settles. The silence stretches long enough that I lift my head to hers, to see if she has given up on me after all.

You are only a man, she says at last. *A man with a monster inside him. And I'm... I'm still coming to terms with the fact that I may have a monster in me, too.*

She cannot possibly mean that.

Lillian, you are perfect. If I asked Odin himself to craft a maiden explicitly for my afterlife in Valhalla, he could not do better than to simply grant me you.

A strange, hiccuping sound bubbles from her throat,

and she coughs. *Well, fuck me. You know how to compliment a girl.*

My cock bobs in anticipation. *You wish for me to–?*

Oh, God, no, I'm sorry! I didn't mean—I mean, it's not like... She waves her hands before her and flaps for a moment. I suppress my excitement, turning away.

Of course not.

No! Erik, that's not what I meant. I'm not—fuck, I'm really screwing this up, aren't I?

She drifts to the rocky ground and groans in her hands. I long to wrap my arms around her, comfort her, but I know it is best that I keep my distance.

Erik, trust me. You're gorgeous, okay? If I even thought I stood half a chance with someone like you in the real world, I wouldn't hesitate. But I...this... Ugh, what's even going on right now? I feel like I've been thrust headfirst into one of my monster romances!

Monster...romance?

Interesting.

A growl not my own rumbles from my throat, and Lillian's face jerks up in shock. Her eyelids droop as the sound continues, and a heady scent fills the cave. Pink blooms across her pale chest, and before I know what's happening, I have crossed the cave to hover over her. Our eyes lock with each other, and my tentacle caresses her chin—

No!

I jet away, propelling as fast as I can and retracting the monster's control. *How dare you. How dare you take advantage of her like that! Of me!*

We are running out of time.

You gave your word!

I merely said I would not harm her.

So you will simply use her body?!

Um, guys?

The fight between us pauses as Lillian, wide-eyed once again, eyes me with flushed curiosity.

Yes, Lillian?

Shouldn't I get a say in this?

CHAPTER 9

LILLIAN

Deep breaths, Lillian. Just like your therapist taught you. In, two three four, hold two three four, out two three four.

And again.

Okay.

Alright.

This is...fine.

I drowned in Lake Superior. I was rescued by some ancient god monster in the depths of the lake. I've got *gills* now, that's fun.

And I'm apparently the smokin' hottenest thing this sexy Viking octopus shifter has ever seen.

Cool.

Cool cool cool.

In, two three four...

Cool.

You're quiet.

I'm thinking, I snap, and then immediately regret the anger in my tone. Isn't this square breathing thing supposed to calm me down? Hack my central nervous system or something?

Maybe my central nervous system is different now that I have *fucking gills!*

Ah, fuck. I'm losing it.

I just—I need a minute to process, okay?

Erik, supposed gentleman that he is, nods and steps back a bit to give me some semblance of privacy in this dark, spooky underwater cave.

I drift back to my little nest of weeds and try to hide myself behind the drifting flora.

This is fine. This is cool. I just got into a fight with my best friend in the whole world and swam myself into some cursed existence with Erik here. I'd say this is some weird sex dream, but I already had one of those, and I'm pretty damn sure I woke up from that to find Mr. Tattoos and Golden Hair staring deeply into my eyes.

Which means this is real. And I'll likely never see Tiffany or Dean or anyone from my old life ever again.

Are you hungry?

I peek out from my weeds to see Erik floating there, still naked as the day he was born, offering me a flat rock with some sashimi on it.

It's Walleye. My favorite. I find that sometimes assuaging my hunger helps my mind clear.

Amazing. Not only is he muscly and deep-voiced and dreamy and well-spoken and is obviously attracted to me (if his *still* rock-solid dick is any indication), but he also cooks.

Cooks!

I shuffle out of my makeshift corner and give him what I hope is a look of gratitude. *Thank you. I don't remember the last time I ate.*

Or how much time has even passed since I left the shore. How long was I out? Did I actually die? Do I have brain damage? Is all of this really some elaborate hallucination, and I'm actually in a coma right now in some hospital in rural Michigan?

Eat, human. You will need your strength.

Erik flinches at the voice of what I can only assume is the monster. That rumbly, heady voice that makes my insides clench and wriggle at the same time, like some kind of sexy cramp.

Sexy cramp? Yeesh. Maybe I *do* have brain damage.

That's the last time I let myself read monster romances before a swim. I swear, a minute ago, when that... *thing* took over Erik and hovered over me while growling like some feral animal, it was like *I* turned into a monster. Like he was pulling something out of me that's been dormant my whole life, and now that it's awake, wants to devour everything in its path.

Okay, so let me get this straight. I start shoveling fish into my mouth as I telepath my thoughts. That's one nice thing about this new fancy way of speaking: no worries about talking with your mouth full! *You're human, like me, but you have a monster inside you that sometimes takes over your body?*

My companion shifts uncomfortably. *Usually, I can keep Him under control, but yes. He can inhabit my body and change my form.*

How so?

There's a slight pause while I finish up the fish on my rock plate. I've never been one for sushi, but it's shockingly good. Fresh and clean tasting, with a texture that doesn't have any of the chewiness that I usually associate with California rolls. I consider licking the rock clean for a second before thinking better of it.

Just because I'm a cavewoman now doesn't mean I have to act like one.

I've never seen His true form, but I have felt it. He is squid-like in nature, but I am unsure whether or not he has a human torso of his own. Although he sometimes leaves my top half intact. It is often easier to navigate the lake waters in his form than my own.

So like, a mermaid but with tentacles? I clarify.

He winces. *Yes. Tentacles.*

I take a minute to imagine what he must look like half-transformed. Like Ursula, from The Little Mermaid, but with a young, blonde King Triton on top.

I don't hate it.

That's kinda hot.

Erik ponders this. *There is a warm sensation in my stomach when I shift, I suppose, although I have never really thought about it.*

I feel myself blush. Fuck. This guy really has been alone for a millennia, hasn't he?

Alone and tormented. Poor guy lost his family, his whole village, in a terrible monster attack, and has been forced to live with the lover of the thing that killed everyone he knew.

I don't think there's enough square breathing in the *world* to fix that kind of trauma.

So what exactly does He want with me?

You are to be my mate.

Fuck. So I did hear that right the first time.

Erik closes his eyes and furrows his brow, and I can see his chest rise and fall as he works to suppress the other voice. I've seen him do that a few times now. Whenever the monster speaks, his eyes flash an unnatural blue. Then, they flicker back and forth between that haunting glowy cyan and the familiar gray, before he eventually gains back control.

The curse requires that He fertilize a brood before He can leave my body. For as long as He doesn't breed, He is stuck with me. And I, Him.

Oh.

I have tried to find another way. I have even tried to starve myself in an effort to break this awful connection, thinking that perhaps in death I would be free. But it is impossible. He says this is the only way.

I blink as his words sink in. This isn't just for some ancient monster with a breeding kink. This is for Erik, too.

Erik, who's been stuck in this cave for a thousand years at the mercy of some all-powerful sea monster, unable to move on or even die.

My lover and I traveled here eons ago to avoid destruction. In the waters where we originated, there were humans who sought to destroy us. So we fled.

I saved this human. I believe my lover saved you. But for some reason, she has not returned to me since I inhabited this body.

Wait a minute, I interrupt. *How is it that She was able to save me without taking over my body, but you needed to take over Erik to save him?*

The man's eyes flicker back to gray for a moment, and I assume he's also interested in the answer. Is it even possible for me to still be human after all of this, or is that goddess—Keto—inside me after all?

Simple. I was weakened in the battle in which Erik's people perished. Compared to Keto, I have always been less powerful. Her influence is subtle, yet mighty. And her

physical form is a magnificent force. We have both grown weaker with time, but she is still fearsome in her abilities. When we escaped, she was carrying our brood. She was protective of them. As was I.

She saw the human ship as a threat. She attacked. The humans attacked back. I protected her.

I suffered many wounds from the battle. I needed a new body to recover. Erik's body. But this form is incompatible with hers.

The time approaches that her eggs will die, without a proper mate to carry them. We need you, Lillian.

To be your...surrogate?

A low rumble, reminiscent of a hum, fills the cavern as Phorkys considers. **Yes, I believe that is the most appropriate word.**

So, you need me to—what, put her eggs inside my hoo-ha somehow and heat 'em up for a few months? I shake my head incredulously. *How would that even work?*

The glowing blue of Erik's eyes intensifies, and suddenly his lower half is changing. His legs elongate and split into multiples of four, and even his penis shifts into a long, suckerless tentacle that reaches towards me.

My eyes widen as I take in his half-shifted form, his piercing cyan gaze locking onto mine as the monster's voice whispers into my brain.

Would you like me to show you?

No!

Our staring contest is broken abruptly as his eyes clamp shut and Erik shakes his head. When he opens them again, they are that clear, human gray, and they look at me pleadingly.

You do not know what you are asking! He insists. *The monster wants to breed. He wants to fill you with his eggs, needs you to incubate His children in your human womb. To be a mother to a pack of monsters! We cannot know what we will release to the world, Lillian...*

My heart clenches as I see the salty tears form on Erik's lashes, only to dissolve into the water around us.

He's fought for thousands of years to keep these gods from unleashing their young. If I agree, it would be against his wishes. Against everything he's worked tirelessly to prevent.

You would rather live like this, forever? I ask him.

The electric blue flickers feebly in his eyes, the muscles in his neck tensing as he struggles to maintain control.

We're closer now, close enough that I can cup my hand to his cheek. Feel the clenching of his jaw again and again beneath my fingers.

His hands grasp at my back, and he pulls me flush against him. My chest touches his, and a soundless gasp pushes past his lips in a flutter of bubbles. His fingers flex against my back, digging into my flesh, while his still-transformed bottom half explores my ankles and legs tentatively.

I wrap my other arm around his neck, and I can feel the struggle inside him. His hips jerk unnaturally, and I look down to see his human form slowly wrestling control back over his body.

His fingernails sink deeper into my back, so hard I can feel the half-moon indentations his nails are making in my skin. I gasp, and that seems to be enough to snap him to attention. In a flash, he's human again, pushing me away and breathing heavily through the gills flaring across his neck, his chest rising and falling rapidly with the effort.

You are not safe here, he says, and I can hear the straining in his voice.

Erik—

Go!

The command bursts like a gunshot in my mind, and instinct takes over. I kick off from the cave floor and push out the entrance, seizing what could be my only chance to escape.

CHAPTER 10

LILLIAN

Just keep swimming, just keep swimming…

It's amazing how your brain will spin up the most unhinged commentary when you're frightened for your life. I bolt out of the cave like a cannonball, stroking through the cool, deep water faster than I've ever swum in my life. It's like the "curse" that Erik talked about made me a better swimmer in addition to letting me breathe underwater.

Eventually, the lake floor rises, and I find myself close to land. I surface without thinking, trying to get my bearings for a minute.

The sky is inky black, sprinkled with white stars. The moon is barely a sliver in the sky—which means that I've missed a whole day in this weird magic-induced coma. The night Tiffany and I fought was a wide crescent, so I must have been out for over twenty-four hours.

I shiver.

Wherever I passed out, I seem to have traveled or been carried far away from there. The land of the UP is just a black line against the dark surf way out in the distance. The strange little island I stumble upon appears to be miles from the mainland, nothing but pebbles, sand, and evergreen trees.

Fuck.

To make matters worse, my stomach growls, and I realize that one plate of sashimi wasn't nearly enough to make up for a whole day of not eating.

I rise from the water and test my ability to breathe. It takes a minute, and more coughing than I'd like to admit, but eventually I get the water out of my lungs and my land-based respiratory system sputters to life.

I touch the side of my neck gingerly, and feel the little closed-up slits quiver beneath my fingertips.

Holy shit. I really do have gills.

And I'm still completely naked.

Welp. That'll be fun to explain to Tiffany when I get back. And Dean, I guess. My family...

I scramble up to my feet and walk the rest of the way onto the shore. The temperature, while well above freezing, is chilly on my wet skin, and I start gathering twigs and sticks to start a fire for the night. Which gives me plenty of time to reflect and regret how few people in my life would be bothered by me returning from vacation with gills.

My family only sees me once a year, over the holidays. We keep our visits to a strict three day, two night protocol, from Christmas Eve to Boxing Day, just long enough that we don't end up at each other's throats and ruin next year's annual visit.

They never approved of me moving to Chicago. But then again, they made it clear they weren't going to let me be one of those millennials who moved back into their childhood bedroom after college. You know. One whose parents love and support them.

Tiffany has been my only true family for close to a decade.

And now, she's starting one of her own.

Work is work. For years, I've been one of three assistants to an overpaid lawyer at a fancy commercial firm. The three of us rarely interact: only speaking enough to make sure we keep the boss well-caffeinated, his email inbox orderly, his calendar up-to-date, and his dry-cleaning picked up. I keep my head down. Put in my forty-five hours a week. And then...

What then?

What *now?*

The sticks in my arms poke and scratch at my exposed skin as I gather what I think is enough to start a fire. Of course, even if I stack it perfectly, I still need to start the dang thing, which is going to be interesting. At the cabin, we've always had matches or one of those stick lighters to catch the kindling. But as I dump the pile of damp wood down on the beach, I realize that I don't even have so much as a newspaper to help get a flame started.

Exhausted, I plop onto a large driftwood log by my sad stick pile, and think for a second.

What am I going to do?

Even if I did have the energy to swim back to shore tonight, I can't see well enough in the dark to know how long that could take. I have no sense of direction aside from the north star, which does *not* give me the Google Maps-level analysis of my surroundings that I'm accustomed to.

Besides, I've never even *seen* this island. How the hell am I supposed to know how to get back to the cabin, when I have no idea where I am in relation to the campsite?

I don't cry. It isn't worth wasting the tears.

Instead, I let out the mother of all sighs, find the two

driest sticks in the pile, and start rubbing them together in hopes of getting a spark.

Fun fact: if you want to get the worst night of sleep in your life, try lying naked on a pebbly beach in the 40-degree cold with a bunch of smokey twigs by your face.

Oh, and bonus points if you can get your stomach to growl so loud it wakes you up. Multiple times.

It's the *fifth* such time that my own hunger rings its alarm that I finally decide I'm done tossing and turning for the night. Shivering so much I can barely feel my fingers, I attempt to rekindle the smoldering pile of ash and sadness that is the fire.

I fail. It's not surprising.

I'm so hungry my stomach is twisting in knots. I'm also still exhausted, to the point that it's difficult to focus my vision. The glare of the morning sun on the lake is blinding. My eyes water every time I look out to better triangulate my location.

"What do I do?"

My voice is hoarse, likely from dehydration. Desperate, I trudge to the edge of the lake water and cup my hands to take a drink.

It's no Fiji, but it is cold and surprisingly clean. I drink more, and more, until my stomach starts to cramp.

Weirdly, that pain doesn't feel as bad to me as the gnawing emptiness I woke up with.

"Okay, well, that's one necessity off my list. Now it's just food and shelter."

Two far more difficult tasks, if my ability to manage a fire is any indication.

A shift in the trees catches my attention, and it takes a moment before my brain can process it's a squirrel.

Squirrel. Squirrels are edible.

Digging through my kindling pile, I find a still-green split twig that has some give to it. Then I fumble around the shore until I find some weeds strong and flexible enough to tie around the ends of the stick, and a little more searching yields some good-sized rocks.

A little bit of trial and error, and I've got a somewhat serviceable slingshot. I wouldn't get any Girl Scout badges for it, I'm sure, but it's a weapon.

And I guess I'm a hunter.

The sun is high in the sky by the time I feel confident enough to take this thing out for a spin. But luckily for me, the rodents of the island seem fairly confident in their safety around here. They don't skitter away when I approach, which makes it easy to at least attempt to shoot them.

Of course, that ends after the third time I launch a rock at them, and they realize I *am*, in fact, trying to hurt them.

They rush back up into the high branches of the endless evergreen trees, where the canopy is dense and impossible to see through. Even if I could make out where the bark ends and squirrel begins, my aim wouldn't be good enough to take one down from the forest floor.

My stomach growls again, and my shoulders sag in defeat. *I wonder if I'd have better luck with fishing.*

I graze a hand across my neck, where the closed slits of my gills pucker the skin. It's all like some horrible nightmare.

The last thing I want to do is go back into the water, where the monster waits for me. Even now, I can still feel the way He hypnotized me down in the cave, flooding my body with unnatural urges.

Because it *is* unnatural, right? To be attracted to the idea of getting impregnated by a giant, ancient squid? Monster smut and Japanese brush paintings notwithstanding, coitus with a tentacle monster is a *fantasy* ideal. It's fodder for dildo manufacturers and horny auteurs like Guillermo del Toro.

It is *not* something I agree to on a whim on summer vacation.

It isn't something I sacrifice my actual, physical body over to out of curiosity.

No matter how curious I might be.

Looking down at the sad slingshot in my hand, I examine myself. After an entire afternoon of hunting down squirrels, my skin is covered in tiny scratches and dirt. My shoulders and chest are an angry shade of pink from the hot sun, and the soles of my feet ache from trouncing over rocks, pine needles, and sticks all day.

I venture deeper into the shade of the forest, switching gears to the idea of building shelter instead of hunting for food. After all, I'm a bigger girl. What are all my fat deposits for if not fueling me during my unplanned stint on a deserted island?

I can just picture my colleagues at the office now. *"Oh, Lillian, you look like you lost some weight! What's your secret?"*

"It's this new fad I tried over vacation. I call it the "Naked and Afraid" diet!"

I snort to myself, even though it isn't all that funny. My coworkers don't even look up from their laptops long enough to notice my existence most of the time. I doubt they'd spot me losing a couple pounds.

Will I even make it back to the office?

No. No, no, no. I'm *not* going to go all existential crisis in the middle of the woods. Pretty sure that's Rule Number One in surviving in the wilderness. Focus on the positives, Lil. Like... mosquito season is over! That's something to be grateful for, yeah? I could be starving, sunburnt, and *itchy* right now, and instead I'm just starving, sunburnt, and chafing from the sand in my crevices!

So much to be grateful for.

As I stack a bunch of pine branches into a pile to build with later, something catches my eye. Only this time, it's way bigger than a squirrel.

Deer.

And as luck would have it, it's a female deer. Which means it shouldn't try to attack me, right? And even if it did, it doesn't have any horns. So I could probably take it, right?

It takes a few steps into the small clearing where I'd been planning to set up camp. So far, it either hasn't noticed me behind my pile, or doesn't care, because it seems perfectly calm as it bends its neck, sniffs at a young sapling, and starts chewing at it.

I must be suffering from hunger-induced insanity, because in that moment, I swear this doe was sent directly from God to save me. I am woman, the fiercest and most dominant of this planet's species, and I will devour this prey like my ancestors before me!

I straighten my arm and aim my slingshot for its eye. Of course, I miss, and the rock sails right past the doe's nose, startling it. It bolts from the clearing.

And in its wake, just barely hidden in the trees beyond, I see the *actual* apex predator of this forest. With its glowing, yellow eyes.

Eyes that are now focused entirely on *me.*

CHAPTER 11
ERIK

For hours after Lillian leaves, I stare at my hands. My wicked, evil hands that carved crescents into her soft skin when I could not control the monster's influence. Hours, and I am still shaking. Still clenching my entire body, using every muscle to wrest myself back, until I am sure that every bone, tendon, and muscle is completely mine.

But that is the rub, is it not? It will never be mine. For as long as I resist, I will always have to. And there is no guarantee that I will continue to succeed.

One woman already died because of me. Am I doomed to condemn another? When will it end?

Your self-flagellation grows tiresome, Erik.

What would you know of guilt? Anger burns in my wordless throat, and I thrust my clenched fist against the cave wall. Bits of rock and shell float mockingly around me, drifting lazily to the lake bed, and I tremble at my own impotence. *Why did you do this to me?*

The burden of repetition should not be on me if you are unable to listen. I saved your body in a moment of weak-

ness. It is done. I have told you how to undo it, and you refuse. I have no pity for you, human; the continuation of this curse is on you and you alone.

How can you expect me to—

I, too, would love nothing more than to retreat into myself and mourn the loss of my lover. But an eternity is a long time to dwell in self-pity.

I want to protest, but his words give me pause. I forget that Phorkys is a god, and as such, he has lived many lifetimes longer than me. Even with my unnaturally extended lifespan.

Defeated, I return to my hunting grounds to find fish for the night. And then I retire fitfully.

THE NEXT DAY, it feels as if the monster has, in fact, retreated somewhat from my mind. His voice is more subdued than usual as I gather firewood for my shelter on the lagoon and hunt for the day's meal. Summer is approaching its end; the nights already grow too cold to pass comfortably on land. It is time once again to prepare for winter: killing game and drying meat for energy reserves, stacking plenty of wood for the weeks I will spend on the surface. While I know I shall lose many nights to my other form in the depths of the lake, it comforts me to have the option of a log edifice and a crackling fire when homesickness strikes.

This land is so very beautiful when it snows.

I work up a sweat splitting logs to cure for next year, and I dip back into the waters to wash myself as the sun passes midday. It is then that a wave of unease laps at my stomach.

Erik!

The monster's voice is different—a note akin to panic creeping into its deep rumble as it warns me.

She is in danger!

Who? I ask, an uncomfortable symphony of confusion and dread swirling in my mind. It is impossible to know just what is mine and what is the monster's.

Lillian!

Though the water is not cold enough to warrant it, my shoulders tense as an icy shiver runs down my spine. *What is happening? Where is the danger?*

North... north of here. On the other end of the island. I can feel her fear.

Lillian's?!

Keto's. The voice pauses, and another flash of confusion spikes the flurry of words and thoughts. **Erik, you must save her!**

Certainly you *could simply save her yourself without my permission?*

My powers are weak on land. My control of you cannot persist there. Erik! Please!

Please?

You would beg me?

My Keto is afraid, Erik. I do not have a choice.

But I do.

I hesitate, ignoring the pleading terror gripping my heart, and instead pan for what remains of my conscience.

Lillian is in danger. Phorkys's mate fears for her life which means she too, believes that Lillian is necessary to break the curse. These two have never been closer to unleashing their brood onto the world, and her death would delay that.

I feel an unexpected pang at the thought of Lillian dying. But I know first hand just how devastating it can be to survive, only to be a puppet dancing on the strings of gods. What life could she possibly live after this? The only fate that would be left to her would be the same as mine, destined to wander the small islands of this inland sea, hunting for game and prowling the waters.

Unless she is unable to resist the pull of Phorkys after all, and lets her body be used for his unnatural ends.

I am about to refuse, when a scene flashes before me. Yellow eyes, predator eyes, and a vicious growl as a coyote stalks toward me, baring its teeth...

Erik! Save her!

And in that moment, it is not Phorkys's fear I feel, but Lillian's. I know, because it is littered with unfamiliar exclamations like, "fuckingfuck!" and "holyfuckingshit!". Words that are odd and fuzzy in my head, but nonetheless filled with terror.

Lillian!

I dive forward, and my lower half unspools into its many-tentacled form as I blaze through the water, heading north. Praying I am not too late...

CHAPTER 12

LILLIAN

"Fucking shittenass cocksucking motherfucker!" I scream as I run for my life, scraping the bottoms of my feet against rocks and fallen debris I'm too terrified to avoid.

Behind me, the coyote barks, tearing its way through the clearing. I can hear its approach hot on my heels. *Fuck fuck fuck!!!!*

This is it.

I'm going to die.

Eaten to death by a coyote in the middle of a deserted island in Lake Superior, of all places.

And no one will care. No one will even know whatever happened to me. I doubt there will be enough of my body left to identify the remains...

Crack!

I tumble ass-over-teakettle as a fallen branch snaps under my bare foot, twisting my ankle unnaturally as it catches in the brambles. I manage to free myself, but when I try to get back up, my leg collapses under my weight.

"Ow!" *Fuck fuck fuck!!*

91

The coyote slows at the sounds, but I can see its furry body inch closer, sniffing all the way. Its wild, yellow eyes spot me sprawled out on the forest floor, and I swear drool drips from its jowls.

Yep. I'm going to die.

"Lillian!"

I snap my neck in the direction of the voice, tearing my eyes away from the predator's at just the wrong moment. The coyote leaps, and I burrow my face into the brush and cover my head with my arms like a fifth grader hiding under their desk during a tornado drill.

I know it won't save me. But I'd rather the last thing I see *not* be the rabies-infected jaws of a wild animal.

Our father, which art in heaven...

Oh God, am I praying right now??

I must be *really* fuckin desperate.

My body shakes as the seconds of my demise stretch out further and further, and I think this must be it. The moment where my life flashes before my eyes. The final reckoning before I see the light at the end of the tunnel...

Only, none of that happens.

Instead, a *swoosh* sound slices through the air above my head and a strangled, animalistic cry rings out through the forest. Footsteps run past me, followed by a little scuffling, and then a dull, sickening *crack* before all goes silent.

And I, miraculously, am still alive.

I peek from behind my fingers, raising my head just enough to get a line of sight from behind the fallen branch. And there, standing over the unnaturally bent corpse of a dead coyote, is Erik.

His chest rises and falls rapidly as he maneuvers a long wooden handle. With a gross *squelch* that will absolutely haunt my nightmares later, he frees a sharpened spear tip from the hide of the coyote.

Oh. My. God.

Erik saved me.

With a fucking *spear.*

Um... is it the adrenaline talking, or is that the hottest thing any man has ever done for me?

Laughter bubbles through the trees, and my shoulders start to shake. I look around disbelievingly, trying to see who on earth would find this primal display funny, only to realize...

It's me.

I'm the one laughing.

Ah, fuck.

And I can't stop.

I try. God knows I *try* to close my mouth, take a breath, regulate my body in any way I can think of, but the hysteria won't stop. Tears stream down my cheeks and I wipe at them uselessly, gasping for air as the laughter turns manic, and my chest starts trembling, and I–

"Lillian! Lillian, please. Speak to me."

Erik is holding me now, his sweaty arms sticking to the burnt, clammy skin of my back as he tries to calm me down. It hurts, but it also feels like the only thing in the world that I want right now: to be held, to be protected, to be cared for.

"E-Erik, I—I..."

"It is alright, Lillian. You are safe. Breathe."

As if my lungs were waiting for his permission, I suck in a massive gulp of air. So big I cough a little as I regulate my breathing, trying to remember what my therapist used to say when I'd start to get anxiety attacks after my miscarriage.

"Your body thinks it's real, Lillian, but you can trick it. You

can convince it that you're okay. Count with your breaths: in for four seconds, hold for four, out for four, hold for four. Can you do that? With me..."

His large, calloused hand weaves through the tangled mass of my hair and cradles my head. Slowly, he hugs me, holding my head to his as he breathes with me, matching my inhales and exhales and pauses like it's the most natural thing in the world.

Like this is totally normal.

Like *I'm* totally normal.

But nothing about this is fucking normal! The tears are pouring like faucets now, drenching my face, and snot is dripping from my nose and making it even harder to regulate my breathing. The raw skin of my shoulders rubs against Erik's embrace and through it all, he holds me close. Breathing with and soothing me like only he can, speaking mind-to-mind, as our gills lay flat against our necks.

No Lillian, his voice soothes in my head. *Nothing about this is normal.*

A fresh sob breaks forth, and he squeezes me tighter, massaging his fingers into my scalp. It feels so nice, such a glistening silver lining in this absolute shit show of a cloudy situation.

I just wanted to get some food, I reply. *I was trying to hunt a deer, but then the coyote...*

He pulls back to look at my face, a sparkle lighting in his light gray eyes. "You were hunting?"

"Yeah," I mumble. "I'm so hungry."

He takes in my surroundings, looking down at the brambles around us and taking in my ankle, which is swollen now, and bleeding lazily from a few shallow scrapes.

"You do not have a weapon."

"I had a slingshot."

"A slingshot?" His face screws up tight, and it takes me a second to parse out his expression.

"Are you... are you *laughing* at me, Erik??"

"You cannot hunt large game with a slingshot!"

"You can if you shoot out its eye!"

He's laughing in earnest now, and I'm sure my blotchy, tearstained, sunburnt face is an even deeper shade of red as his grip on me loosens. He tries to catch his breath, but I shove him away.

"I'm serious! I've seen in the movies that if you shoot a deer in the eye..." I start off strong, indignant, even, before the stupidity of my words sinks in and I trail off. "What do you know, anyway?"

He gestures to the spear lying a couple feet away from us. Gives me a knowing look.

"I hate you, you know that?"

Actual hurt crosses his features, and the laughter leaves his eyes immediately. "Perhaps you should. It is my fault–"

"No! No, Erik, I didn't mean that literally!" Guilt grips my stomach as I take in the pain in his expression. "I was just embarrassed. You saved me! How could I hate you?"

"It is my fault you needed to be saved. All of this could have been prevented, if I had never seen you bathing naked in the lake."

I let out a breath, and it fans a few hairs into my face. I swipe them away with a shrug. "By that logic, it's my fault for going swimming naked in the lake."

"Lillian–"

"We could go back and forth for hours like this, Erik. It doesn't matter. The fact of the matter is, I'm stuck here, and I'm probably going to die now that my ankle is broken. I can't hunt deer if I can't fucking walk."

And, sure, I'm a little sulky as I admit it. And I understand that a sour attitude isn't going to help my situation right now. But the last thing I want to do is play the blame game with the only person who's offered me any sympathy in the past week.

Erik's lips flatten in a stern line, as if he wants to argue more, but then his brow relaxes and he nods.

"Then I will carry you."

"Erik–!" His name turns into a squeal as he manhandles his giant, muscly arms underneath my knees and ribcage and hoists me into the air. I'm literally on the ground one second, and then the next I'm getting up close and personal with my boobs smashed against this Viking's blonde chest hair.

Breathing in his scent.

Wrapping my arms around his neck.

"Th-this isn't necessary," I stutter, my face scorching from more than just my sunburn. But he's already walking us back towards the clearing.

"I have a shelter not far from here. I can tend to your wounds there, and you can recover safely."

I open my mouth to protest when he hoists me higher. I end up squeaking again instead, and decide it's best I keep my mouth shut until we get to his shelter.

CHAPTER 13

ERIK

Lillian is sleeping peacefully in my arms by the time we arrive at the small shelter I built years ago on the north edge of this island. The isolated bit of land is large and crescent-shaped. My cabin is located on the widest wedge of the crescent, across the wide lagoon sheltered within its curve. Here, the winter winds blow in from the northlands, which keeps most of the animals sequestered to the southern half nearer to the shore during the cold months.

The shelter is not much: a cone-like structure made of thatched pine branches. But the overlapping needles take the bite out of the wind, and the hole in the center of the roof allows the heat of the fire to siphon through the top, which keeps the inside warm and free of smoke.

A bed of needles and furs makes up one side of the shelter, and the other is stacked with logs from the last time I stayed here. I am sure to prepare and store supplies throughout the spring and summer when I am able, so I always return to a stocked camp at the beginning of winter.

Sadly, there are no stores of dried meat in this particular

lean-to, so I will need to scavenge for some while Lillian rests.

I lay her on the nest of furs, being careful of her ankle as I arrange her legs. Scanning the space for anything I might be able to wrap it with, I come up empty.

I will gather supplies while I catch dinner.

The sun is low in the sky when I return to the shelter, several squirrels slung through a belt about my waist. I skinned them by the lake, where I also filled a skin with water for the evening. I set to building a fire and roasting dinner while I cut strips of hide with which to wrap Lillian's ankle. She sleeps through all of it, clearly exhausted from her earlier efforts.

Or, perhaps, still recovering from the shock of it all.

I vaguely remember the early days after the shipwreck, when I was alone and hopeless here in the western wilds. But I, at least, was a warrior, with decades of hunting, fighting, and training at my back.

From what little I have observed of modern humans, they seem to live a life separated from its daily chores. Families visit the lake for a short while, with large colorful boxes filled with ready-made food. Fresh vegetables and fruits I have yet to locate in the local flora; fluffy-looking bread with nary a wheat or grain field to be seen.

Despite the lack of farms or animals, there are spiced sausages and ground meats cooked over iron grills (one of which I stole for myself to use at my main shelter by the lagoon, along with several shiny tools which make turning and cooking meat much easier). They play with vibrant, reflective toys, painted in colors I had never seen before.

But most amazing of all is their music boxes. Silver, black, blue, red—they come in a myriad of colors. And all of them can recreate the sound of an entire ensemble of musicians, with a seemingly endless collection of songs.

I hum one of the tunes I heard many times this summer from the campers' music boxes as I turn the squirrels on the spit. I am not loud, but Lillian stirs at the sound.

"Are you...is that *Cruel Summer?*"

"You know this song?"

"Uh, yeah, everyone knows that song. It was all over TikTok this year."

"What is TikTok?"

"Nevermind," she says quickly, sitting up and taking in the surroundings. "Did you build all this?"

"Yes."

She starts and winces as it shifts her ankle. "How long was I asleep?"

"Not long." She looks at me blankly. I tilt my head, until I realize the cause for her confusion. "Oh! I built this shelter years ago. I remembered it, and brought you here to recover. Are you hungry?"

Lillian's eyes dart from me to the meat cooking above the fire, and licks her lips. It is a lascivious movement. I look away quickly and gesture to the meal. "I was not sure how long it had been since you had eaten, so I prepared extra."

"I am *starving*. Is it ready to eat?"

I smile at her, plucking the spit from the stand and handing it to her, before replacing it with another. "It is ready. And hot."

"Fuck yeah." She pinches the ends of the long stick between her fingers, and tears into the steaming flesh with a vicious bite before I can stop her. Instantly, she regrets it, fanning her mouth with her free hand and chewing open-mouthed while chanting, "Hosh-uh, hosh-uh, hoshhhhhhh!!"

"You should let it cool for a moment!" I say helplessly, as more tears spring to her eyes. Good gods, I cannot bear the sight of this woman crying. It tugs at the very core of me.

I find the water skin and hand it to her. "Here, drink!"

She grabs it, chugs from it gratefully, and then heaves a sigh. "Thank you."

"You are welcome."

A moment passes in silence as she blows air onto the meat to cool it before taking another, more tentative, bite. Watching her plump lips part, the slow and cautious movement, causes a heat to rise to my face. I look away, allowing her to sate her hunger in privacy.

Instead, I observe my own dinner, a second spit that I slowly turn over the crackling fire. She draws closer, warming her pale legs as she chews.

"How did you know I was in trouble?"

I do not answer immediately. My focus is concentrated on regulating my body's reaction to the nearness of her, her scent, her soft vulnerability. Phorkys was honest in his warning; I can feel how much weaker his influence is the further I am from the shore.

Yet I know from experience that his pull is strong enough to keep me locked to the water's pull. While he has less physical influence over my body, he can still command my consciousness. Still speak inside my head. Drive me to insanity.

"He told me."

Lillian chews on this for a moment. Then, "How did *He* know?"

I turn the spit with my other hand as I stretch a shoulder. "Keto told him."

A shiver rolls down her spine and I know it has

nothing to do with the cool evening outside the shelter walls. Her voice is barely a whisper when she admits, "I wondered if she was in my head. I can't hear her, but..." she sets her now empty spit on the packed dirt floor and hangs her head in her hands. "There's a... a *drive* there that wasn't there before, you know? Like a compass pointing me toward something. And I can't seem to veer away."

"Like instinct."

"Yes!" she shouts, eyes wide. "Like instinct."

My gaze blurs as my eyes swim out-of-focus, the spitting fire transforming into overlapping orbs of white and orange. "That is how it begins."

I feel it before I see her stretch out her leg and test her ankle, bending and rotating it gingerly. A slight wince crosses her features, and I hold out my hands.

"Here, let me wrap it. I did not want to wake you before."

She tenses briefly, then nods, her shoulders slowly relaxing away from her ears. I reach behind me to the pile of straight sticks and strips of hide I reserved to make a splint.

Taking a small piece of fur I cleaned earlier in the lake, I douse it with a pour from the water skin and carefully wipe her wounds clean of debris. Despite my gentle hand, she winces, and my chest clenches in response. I raise my eyes to hers in apology, some wordless whisper falling from my lips in place of an earnest remark.

There is so much I want to say to her, that the words form a pile in my mind, blocking passage to my throat. A shipwreck of intentions and platitudes, blocking any current of conversation. I close my mouth, feeling utterly impotent, and instead focus on keeping each swipe of her skin with the cleansing fur as light and effective as possible.

Her breathing steadies, thankfully. I examine the tender ankle, taking in the swollen skin and angry red scrapes.

No sign of infection. That is good. Still, I reach behind her in the pile of furs for the herbal poultice I store in all of my shelters. An ancient recipe, brought from home. While I have little fear of dying (quite the opposite), festering wounds are quite an annoyance I do my best to avoid when preparing for the long winters on land. Cuts and bruises are an inevitability, but prolonged discomfort need not be.

As I locate the small clay pot, a relic rescued from the shipwreck, my arm brushes her hip. A tiny gasp skitters over my back, raising the small hairs on my neck.

I pull it back quickly, reorienting my position so the stirring in my lap is less visible to her. I have since donned some hunting furs to protect myself, but they do little to hide the quickening of my flesh as it tugs against its wrappings.

Lillian, of course, is tantalizingly bare before me.

"This–" I clear my throat– "will prevent infection."

"Right," she answers, her voice almost as hoarse as mine. "Totally. Thanks."

I nod, not trusting the air in my lungs. Slowly, I apply the crushed herb paste in dabs across the scratches that mar her legs. I shift her ankle this way and that, examining her injuries closely in the firelight, before deciding that I am satisfied. Then I apply the splint.

A small hiss as I set her joint to rights. Then a sigh as she adopts a more comfortable position, exposing more of her front to the fire.

Gods, I bite my cheek to keep from moaning. Her ample chest sways as she takes it upon herself to rotate the spit for me, saving the downwards-facing side of my dinner from charring to a crisp. The tender flesh of her belly seems to bounce in the flickering firelight, and it takes all of my willpower to keep from imagining her jiggling beneath me, making more of those delicious sounds: gasps and sighs and hopefully cries of delight with that bell-like voice of hers...

"Erik? I think it's done." She removes the spit from the fire and hands it to me.

"Thank you," I croak, my throat drier than a sandpit in a drought. Her cheeks flush.

Beautiful.

Beautiful, and damned.

CHAPTER 14

LILLIAN

Not everything about being cursed on a deserted island in the middle of Lake Superior is bad.

Sure, it's not the fate I'd personally choose for myself. But the squirrel is tasty.

The fire, cozy and warm.

And the company is...

Okay, the company is *distractingly* attractive. He's put on some clothes since the last time our paths crossed underwater, but even the heavy furs tied around his body can't stop the hotness from emanating from this guy. As he stokes the fire, his triceps bulge, tattoos shining with sweat. The gold in his hair and beard positively glisten in the flickering light, making his eyes sparkle everytime he looks at me.

The way he tears at his dinner, just digging in with his teeth as he rips the meat off the kebab? *Fuck* me. It's animalistic. Primal.

But then, his touch is so gentle when he wraps my ankle that I can hardly feel it. I shiver more from the slight tickle of his fingers brushing the arch of my foot than I do from any actual discomfort, but he looks at me as though I'm some precious, fragile thing.

Me. Precious. *Fragile.*

No one, but especially no man, has ever looked at me like I'm someone who should be *protected.* I got so used to it that I started to wear my self-sufficiency like armor, until one day I never took it off.

And the further Tiffany and I drifted apart, the more independent I had to become. The heavier the armor became, until eventually, my personality was just as heavy as the rest of me.

But the way Erik looks at me? It doesn't feel like the way men look at heavy, independent women. It feels like the way someone looks at someone they care for. Someone they *love.*

But that's crazy. Right? I mean, "lust after" might be more accurate, given the situation. The guy's been stranded out here for literally a thousand years. I bet any pair of boobs would make a man salivate after that long by himself.

Still, though. I'm not oblivious to his body's response. And he's yet to be a creep about it—he does his best to hide it, prioritizing my comfort always. I'm even teasing him at this point, leaving myself uncovered and letting my boobs hang free, crossing my legs so my kitty is on full display, and *still.*

He catches himself whenever his eyes stray below my chin, redirecting his gaze to my face, my ankle, checking on me. Interested in me. Listening to me, even when I ask him stupid questions about the shelter like, *"Did you build this?"*

Duh, Lillian. It's not like the coyotes did it.

And it's so fucking cute the way he's trying to hide his boner. My God, this guy is harder than the Hope Diamond and he's acting like if he just shifts his knees to the side I'm not gonna notice the Sears Tower pitching a tent in his loincloth.

I should just put him out of his misery.

But then I'd have to deal with the rejection when he pushes me away. Again. Despite the fact that I'm the only woman he'll ever actually get a chance to sleep with. That I'm the only one that can break his curse.

He still would rather suffer for all eternity than sleep with me.

But then, why wrap my ankle? Why save me at all? Wouldn't it have been easier to just let me die?

"I don't get it."

"Get it?" Erik swallows another bite of dinner, blinking at me. "Do you need something?"

"No, I'm just...trying to understand."

"Understand what?"

"Why you would save me."

He tilts his head at that, and studies me for a moment.

That's another thing about Erik; he's not impulsive. He thinks: a lot and deeply, before answering a question.

"I wish for you to know, Lillian, that I would never seek my fate for another human. To outlive one's family, one's children, one's entire village and culture...it is immensely painful. I have been stripped of everything that made me a man except for the basest of survival instincts, and that is a pitiable creature to be."

"What do you mean? We're talking, aren't we? You need more than instincts to be able to hold a conversation."

"Ha," he barks, and in that moment he does sound more animal than man, his voice hoarse and growling. It's like the more cynical he is, the more his humanity is buried. "Hardly more than grunts and snarls. Nothing like your beautiful voice, or the delighted shouts of children I hear playing with their siblings along the shore. Nothing like *Cruel Summer,* or any of the other haunting melodies that tease me from your music boxes."

"You were literally just humming that twenty minutes ago," I argue. "How long has it been since you've tried to actually sing? I bet you have a lovely voice when it isn't gravelly from not using it all millennium. Come on, what's your favorite song?"

"Favorite?"

"The one you like best. Or one of the ones you like best, it doesn't have to be a contest or anything."

He concentrates for a moment, his gaze shifting to the fire as he thinks, taking another bite of meat and chewing before answering me.

"I do not know the words in your language," he admits. "I have learned English by absorbing bits of thought and conversation from vacationers through Phorkys, and scavenged texts from abandoned campsites. The words of your people are shorter, livelier, and your songs are spirited. They are unlike the songs of my people."

"Would you sing me one? From your life before...?"

I'm leaning forward now. It's so hard to believe that this man, a literal Viking from who knows how long ago, taught himself English through eavesdropping on campers all these years. Taught himself to *read.*

Granted, I guess he had some supernatural help. Being able to read people's thoughts and intentions like Phoryks can would be helpful when trying to learn how to communicate.

But all of that evaporates from my head the second Erik's beautiful baritone voice floats from his lips.

"Þat mælti mín móðir, at mér skyldi kaupa

Fley ok fagrar árar
Fara á brott með víkingum, fara á brott með víkingum
Standa upp í stafni, stýra dýrum knerri
Halda svá til hafnar
Höggva mann ok annan, höggva mann ok annan."

His singing hits me like a freight train. The melody is dark and keening; the language is unlike anything I've ever heard. Rolling r's and glottal stops, both deep and lilting in an ancient and powerful way. My heart stops in my chest as I feel the strength of Erik's voice slowly increase, the low notes vibrating my very ribs.

By the time he finishes, there are tears in my eyes. I wipe them away before he notices, his gaze still a thousand yards away as the fire flickers in his pupils. The last note drifts up and away with the smoke before I speak.

"That was *beautiful,*" I breathe. "And so... sad."

A moment passes, long enough that I think he might not have heard me. But when he finally responds, I have to strain to hear him. "There was a time it was inspiring to me. A story of a great adventure, something to aspire to. But now... yes. I would say it is very sad."

His vision clears after a moment, and he claps his hands. The noise jolts the still air in the shelter, and I jump, pulling the furs around my waist up to cover my chest.

I feel exposed all of the sudden, and the flirty, teasing attitude I started this conversation with seems naive and inappropriate all of the sudden.

"Now it is your turn, Lillian. Sing a song for me."

"Uh, yeah right," I snort, shaking my head at his insistent grin. "I didn't start this with plans to sign up for a sing-along."

"Do you know other songs like *Cruel Summer?*"

"You know T Swift has a whole discography, right?"

"I do not know what those words mean."

I sigh, his boyish expression painfully adorable. "I mean, the singer who wrote that song. She has literally hundreds of others."

He gasps. "Do you know them? Have they played on the music boxes? Could you sing them for me?"

I can't help it. Shaking my head and holding back a laugh, I do the most ridiculous and unimaginable thing I could possibly do in this moment.

I sing *Shake it Off* for my Viking hero at the top of my lungs.

I SLEEP LIKE A BABY, cozy and warm in the bed of furs in Erik's makeshift shelter, while he huddles in a fur of his own on the other side. I wake a little after sunrise, and he's already cooking some fish on a metal grate over the fire. I wonder for a second where he got it from, before shaking the thought out of my head. I reach for the water skin and take a sip before greeting him, attempting to ignore the pressure in my bladder until I know I can walk somewhere to relieve myself.

"Good morning!"

He nods and tilts his head towards my feet. "How is your ankle?"

I test it, wiggling it a little in its splint. Despite it being made of cleaned branches, fur, and sinew, it's surprisingly strong.

"A little stiff, but not screaming at me like it was last night. I might want to soak it in the lake for a bit today to help with the swelling."

He stiffens, but nods. "Perhaps that would be good for it."

There is a long pause while neither of us meet the other's gaze.

"Erik, I–"

"Lillian, it would be–"

We both stop abruptly as we talk over each other, and I look away at the same time he does. I reach one of the furs up to my chin to cover myself.

He nods to me. "You first."

"Thank you for all of this!" I blurt out. "I don't think I really said it yesterday, but you totally saved my life back there with the coyote. I would be dead meat if it wasn't for you. Even now, it's gonna take me, like, ten minutes to get to a good spot to go to the bathroom with my leg like this but you're still here and taking care of me and I—I don't even know what to say. I thought I was good at camping. That maybe I could handle myself. But I was so, so wrong. You know what you're doing out here, and I'm...totally out of my element."

I'm out of breath by the time my rant ends. He is so patient throughout the whole thing, taking in my words with an open and serious expression. After a moment, he swallows.

"I do not mind taking care of you," he says quietly. "I am... I have been alone for a very long time. You are a lovely distraction."

His gray eyes meet mine as he says that last bit, and I can feel the blush rise to my cheeks.

"Lovely," I mutter, shaking my head. "I don't think I've ever been called *that* before."

"Then you have not known many honest people."

It's almost a good thing when my bladder interrupts my thoughts to let me know I *really* can't ignore it any longer, because I can't even begin to respond to his compliments. "I gotta pee," I mumble, and crawl—*crawl*—out of the shelter to avoid having Erik help me walk to a pee tree.

It isn't glamorous, but I get the job done. Then take a quick dip in the nearby surf to rinse off the couple of days' stank from roughin' it. I couldn't really smell how ripe my armpits were in the lean-to, with all the roasting wildlife and woodsmoke smell filling the air, but let's just say a quick whiff in the great outdoors was enough to let me know why Erik wasn't keen to snuggle up last night.

As I wash my face, a wavy reflection blinks back at me in the lake surface. A frizzy halo of blonde circles my head, and my features look blobby and unbecoming in the waves.

But the water takes some of the weight off my foot, making it easier to move around. If only for the time I'm in the water.

Lillian...

My shoulders tense as I hear my name, almost like a whisper on the breeze. It isn't Erik; it's a lighter, more feminine voice. I swear I've heard it before, but I can't place it.

Our conversation from last night replays in my brain and Erik's words come back, making me shiver.

That is how it begins.

As fast as I can with my injury, I hightail it back to the shelter. Along the way, I pick up a few extra twigs to toss on the fire to distract myself from the unsettling mix of fear and arousal swirling in my gut, trying to filter out the emotions that don't feel wholly my own.

"Here," I say, tossing them onto the blaze when I let myself in. The wet sticks hiss on the embers, and Erik makes a face. "Oh fuck, I'm sorry, I didn't think they'd be wet!"

But of course they were. They were on the beach. Where the water is.

Great job, Lil.

"It is alright. We will let the fire burn down a bit for now, until sunset. Please eat, there is plenty."

He points to a few charred whole fish on a plate. An actual *plate*.

Wait—what?

I take the offered breakfast, along with a metal fork that sits beside it. "Where did you get these?"

"Vacationers leave them sometimes. I have quite the collection now, at my cabin by the lagoon. I hiked there for supplies this morning when I caught breakfast."

I sit cross-legged (or, half cross-legged, as my injured foot sticks out a little at a weird angle) and hold the plate in my lap. As I do, Erik reaches back and grabs some fabric.

"And these I gathered from your cabin."

"My clothes!" I practically throw the plate aside as I reach for the soft, modern clothing, more grateful for this teensy convenience than I've ever been for anything in my life. "Oh my gosh, thank you so much! How did you find these?"

"They were drying on the railing. I thought you might like some protection from the sun." He gestures to my chest and shoulders, before quickly correcting himself. "People often leave clothing. I only had some furs in this shelter, but I also retrieved some modern short pants for myself."

As he says this, I realize that he is, in fact, wearing something other than the kilt-like getup he pulled on the night before. He's now in a pair of neon orange swim trunks that contrast blindingly with his sun-kissed skin. I'm amazed it wasn't the first thing I saw when I woke up this morning.

The V of his hips disappear into the waistband, framing

his gorgeous abs that flex as he bends and twists to gather up all the supplies he brought back while I was sleeping in.

Of course. The grill. The plates, the silverware... all of them are totally the standard Walmart-issue camping supplies the average midwestern American family would bring on their summer lake vacation. He even has a couple of those plastic-y reusable grocery bags that someone must have left behind at the end of the summer.

He walks over with one of the bags next, dropping it by my lap as I pull on the loose sundress I use as a swimsuit cover-up. Unfortunately, I didn't leave a bra hanging to dry on the porch of our cabin, because I can already feel the sweat beading in my underboob.

Ah, well.

"I brought you something to entertain you while you recover."

I smooth the fabric down my thighs and look over at the bag he's holding out to me. It's filled to the top with *books*.

But not just any books. These are–

"*The Highlander's Pirate Bride!*" I can hardly believe my eyes as I pull out the well-worn paperback at the top of the pile. "My God, I used to have this book! I brought it to the cabin years ago to reread on vacation..."

My mouth hangs open as I put two and two together. "You *didn't*."

Erik blushes. "I told you that I learned your language from books that summer visitors left behind. I find more every year. That is one of my favorites."

He smiles as I dig through the bag, pulling out book after book, although no more that I recognize as my own.

It's a whole library of old Harlequin romances, some

dating back as far as the 60's, with cheesy titles like *Crimes of the Vicar* and *Vivian's Secret.*

I want to read them right now.

"Erik, this is amazing! You," I look up at him, at a loss for words. Taking in the mix of old and new, of hunter-gatherer know-how combined with his present-day resourcefulness. "You're incredible."

A shadow passes behind his eyes. He looks away, the smile fading from his lips as if I'd just insulted him. "No, Lillian. I just didn't want to leave you with nothing to do."

My heart sinks. "You're leaving?"

"I will be back with dinner. But I need to gather more supplies. And it is best if I stay away. The monster is quieter on land, but his voice still rings in my head. Now that you are safe, it is best if I do not put you in more danger."

"Erik, you're not–"

"Enjoy the books. I will be back with dinner in the evening." He hovers for a second at the doorway, his hand twitching at his side, before he nods once and turns to leave. "Goodbye."

Stunned, I watch him go. It's only when my stomach growls that I'm reminded I have breakfast waiting for me.

Breakfast, and a fuckton of paperbacks.

"Well at least *these* hunks won't leave me with blue-balls," I mutter, stuffing a forkfull of fish into my mouth and cracking the spine on *Vivian's Secret.*

CHAPTER 15
ERIK

You do not need more supplies.

My chest heaves with breath as I swing down my axe, splitting log after log to store for the long winter ahead.

I always need more firewood.

We winter in the lake.

"I do not want to winter with *you* in the water any longer!" My voice rings out into the forest of birch and pine, causing the squirrels and birds to scatter. Silence follows, and Phorkys's chiding tone is the only thing I can hear, grating the inside of my mind.

You could be rid of me forever if you would only–

Stop! Stop it! Why can you not accept that I will not mate her! The axe clatters to the ground as it slips from my hands. I reach up to my temples, fingers grasping at my hair as if I could physically remove him from my head if I only tugged hard enough. *Let me go! I beg of you! Find another body to molest, I cannot bear it any longer!*

Eight hundred seventy four years since I lost my family in the shipwreck, over ten thousand lunar cycles of this madness. And now, even in my island solitude I cannot escape from him.

Because I cannot escape from her. Lillian.

In my heart, I know that is the difference. The final weight upon the scale of my conscience that topples me over the edge. Alone, I could withstand the torture. But knowing that my fate is shared by one as delightful and lovely as Lillian, knowing what I must *do* to her to escape it, I...

I cannot.

But you want to.

I whip the axe back into my grip from the sandy ground and perch a log atop the chopping stump. *Whack!* I will not listen to him. *Whack!* I will not admit to those unnatural urges. *Whack!* No matter how much I yearn for her—*whack*—soft, swaying breasts to—*whack*—jiggle as I—*whack*—hover over her and—*whack*—fill her with my–

Thunk!

The axe wedges deep into the stump, fractionated bits of wood scattering across the beach as I abandon the task.

"No, no, *no!*" I scream in fury, running now, as if the faster I carry myself away from the beach, the further I could get from my own lust.

It is not merely my own desires that I imagine. I am not ashamed of wanting to pleasure a beautiful woman with my cock. To suck upon her swollen nipples, or lick her lower lips and bury my face into her sweet musk.

No, it is the *inhuman* images that make me shudder: twining my tentacles around her legs, burying my hectocotylus inside of her and fertilizing my lover's eggs until Lillian's stomach bulges with my seed...

The familiar strain in my loins, spurned on by those unholy thoughts, infuriates me. *Why?* "*WHY?*"

You will never be free of these desires. Not until you realize them.

Have you not tormented me enough?

I am on my knees now, kneeling in the soft bed of pine needles deep in the quiet forest. The hot sun is hidden by the forest canopy, and the rivulets of sweat cool rapidly on the back of my neck and my arms, making the fine hairs covering my body stand on end.

I dig my fingers into the soft, dark earth for any comfort it might offer. But in the end, it is only rocks and grubs and fungus. It cannot cure my agony.

The monster does not answer, mocking me now with its silence instead of its miserable words and mind-pictures. But even without his urging, my mind circles back to Lillian. Lying in her nest of furs. Availing herself of my library, my little tote of treasures.

I remember the look on her face as she read the title of the first book: my favorite, with the European sailor who captures a sassy pirate lass and her crew at sea, only for her to win him over in the end, earning her people's freedom with her love. While it is difficult for me to parse through all of the texts I gave her—many of the words I skip over because I cannot discern their sound or meaning—I often find myself filling in the story myself from the context of the scraps of text I _am_ able to absorb and the salacious artwork on the cover.

The way the smile lit across her lips when she saw it! The way her toes wiggled in unrestrained glee—even the ones on her injured foot, albeit less energetically—filled me with an emotion that I have not felt for centuries.

Joy.

All I want is to return to the lakeside shelter with my arms full of firewood, build a blaze to last the night, and curl up beside her soft curves while she reads to me. Listen, until the sound of her voice hitches when she reaches the scene in chapter nine where the heroine seduces the stoic captain, stripping herself of her wet clothes after a storm. Watch the heat rise in the apples of her cheeks as she stumbles over the part where he grabs the maiden by the waist and carries her to the captain's quarters, throws her onto the bunk, takes the peaks of her breasts into his hot mouth and–

"Ah–!"

A wet and sticky mess plasters the rough fabric of my modern short trousers. I had been palming myself through my clothing without realizing, allowing my daydream to become a... *wet* dream.

I shake my head. Pathetic.

Not wanting to return to the water, where Phorkys's influence is bound to flood my consciousness with even more shame, I strip myself of the cumbersome shorts and wipe off the remaining evidence of my prepubescent fantasy.

While I would love nothing more than to cozy up to Lillian for the entirety of the cold months, filling our days and nights with reading and lovemaking, that is entirely unrealistic. Irresponsible. Cruel.

She has a life in the modern world. A life she could, perhaps, return to—if I can only keep my lust at bay for long enough to nurse her to health and see her back to the mainland, before Keto's influence becomes too great.

She is not yet hearing *Her* voice, after all.

And as long as that is true, then mayhaps she stands a chance.

• • •

It is my favorite time of day when at last I return to her, dragging a convenient thick-wheeled wagon behind me stacked with reserves of dried meat and firewood. At my waist, a belt of freshly skinned squirrels obscure a fresh pair of shorts.

"It's about time you got here!" Lillian whines. "I was about to die of boredom!"

Her tone is sharp, but her eyes sparkle with humor. The expression takes me off guard, particularly the devilish smirk tilting her full, pink lips, and my heart quickens in my chest.

"I wanted to make sure I gathered enough supplies."

"We have more than enough supplies," she says, the echo of Phorkys's earlier scolding ringing in my brain. I hold back a wince. She peers behind me at the wagon. "Although, if that's jerky you're packing, then I'll hand it to you—that was a good call. If there's one thing we're low on, it's handy snacks. I refilled the water skin, though!"

She holds up the skin, beaming with self-satisfaction. I cannot help but mirror her joy.

"I am impressed! It could not have been easy to walk on the sand with your ankle." She nods in agreement, raising her eyebrows and pushing her lips up in such an adorable, self-satisfied expression that I have to stifle a laugh.

What a woman!

"How is it?"

"The ankle? Meh." She shrugs. "I mean, yeah, it hurts, and yeah, I'm not going to be entering any 5k's anytime soon, but I'll live." I frown at that, not fully understanding her answer apart from the fact that it is still causing her pain. She tilts her head at me as I remove my belt to begin preparing our dinner. "Are those new shorts?"

My face heats as I clear my throat. "Uh—yes, I dirtied the other ones while preparing fuel for the fire."

No need to tell her the details of *how,* exactly, I soiled them.

"Better take good care of those, then. I can't imagine you have too many extra pairs lying around. Although, if you have to run around naked again you won't hear me complaining."

The nonchalant tone she uses is once again in conflict with her salacious words. I almost drop the squirrel carcass I am holding as I attempt to spear it onto its spit. "I am sorry you had to see me at my most...natural earlier." I mutter. "I hope I did not scandalize you."

"Uh, are you forgetting you left me with a pile of Harlequin romances? Pretty sure *that* would scandalize me way more than seeing your morning wood."

I glance back to the wood pile. "It is dusk, not morning."

She shakes her head. "Nevermind. Can I help with dinner?"

She favors her left side as she scoots closer to me, securing two squirrels onto a waiting spit. While she handles the food, I stoke the embers in the fireplace back to life.

It is comforting, setting about these domestic tasks with another human. Visions of my distant past come back with a bittersweet ache, as I remember my former wife and children. Lillian hums while she works, songs that are at once familiar and strange to the scene: a mix of modern and timeless.

"Erik," she begins, and I lift my face to hers. "I've been thinking."

"What about?"

"About this whole…" she waves, gesturing about the shelter. "Situation."

My hands still in their task, and anxiety builds in my throat as I wait for her to continue.

"Obviously, this is weird. Right? God-monsters in Lake Superior, immortality, *gills*… it's a lot for me to process. And seeing as I've been sitting around all day with a bum ankle, I've had plenty of time to think. And I'm doing my best to take it all in, but like I said, it's a lot."

She pauses, as if expecting me to cut in, but I do not speak. I have little to add to her analysis. Her words, though simple, are wise.

It is, as she says, "a lot."

I merely nod in response, hoping she will continue.

"When you went to the cabin to get my clothes, did you notice—I mean, was anyone else there?"

"No."

A wrinkle forms between her eyebrows. I long to reach over the fire and smooth it away. "Was there a sign of anyone? A car, or other clothes or anything?"

I do not know what she is talking about when she says "car." It is a word I have heard before but have little context for, aside from the fact that it is something modern. Regardless, the cabin appeared abandoned when I went there to gather her things.

"I am sorry, Lillian. There was no one."

"Damn. So she's really gone."

Lillian looks down at her hands and fusses about with the stakes for the roasting spits. The first batch of meat is cooking over the hot embers before she speaks again.

"I didn't come to the lake alone, Erik. Every year, my best friend—well, *former* best friend, Tiffany—and I, we come up to the cabin for a girls' trip. This year was supposed to be our last one."

"If you come every year, why would this be your last?" I ask, confused.

"Because she's having a baby with her fiancé, Dean."

"She is engaged to be married?"

She lets out a breath, heavy with sorrow. "Yeah. Yeah, she is."

I toss another log on the flames and dust off my hands before crawling nearer to her. "This makes you sad. Are marriages and babies not happy things? In the books you like–"

"I'm happy for them!" She says, loudly and quite *un*happily. Again, her tone and words are in conflict, and it makes my nose scrunch. She glances at my expression and sighs, spinning the spit as she continues. "I mean, I'm happy for her, that she's found someone she loves. She deserves that. But ever since she and Dean started dating, we've been growing apart. It's like… the things we used to connect on, the stuff we always used to do together, it just isn't clicking anymore, you know? She hardly ever makes time for me anymore, she barely texts me back. Like, this vacation, right? It was supposed to be our last one, but she wouldn't even go swimming with me! And Dean came along. He was staying in a tent right down the beach from us!"

I nod slowly, still confused, but beginning to see why she sounds unhappy when she speaks of her best friend. "Even when you were with her, she was not wholly with you. You were lonely."

"Yes!" She nods emphatically, her deep blue eyes sparkling with recognition. "It was like when we were hanging out she was there, physically, but not with me mentally, you know?"

"Hanging out?"

"Like, spending time together," she explains.

"Ah."

There are so many phrases she uses that are new to me. I want to ask her to slow down, but before I can she begins speaking at a rapid pace.

"And like, I get it, right? She's got other stuff on her mind with the baby coming and the wedding and her in-laws sounds like a whole lot and I know I should be supportive, but I really just wanted this last vacation to be about *us*, and our friendship, and a chance for everything to be like it used to be, you know?"

I nod, trying to keep up.

"But she couldn't let any of that go. Dean had to come with us, and she wouldn't go swimming, and everything kept coming back to the baby this, and the baby that, and she wouldn't want to hurt the *baby*, what if something happened to the baby? When she should *know* how much saying those things might hurt and be triggering for me…"

She looks up at me, and my eyes must be wide with confusion, because she allows the words to fade on her tongue. "I'm sorry. I know you don't understand the situation, and I'm totally ranting now, but I do have a point."

"I believe you."

She smiles then, a small curve of her lips, the joy of which does not reach her eyes. Not knowing what to do, I reach out my hand to place it over hers.

Her fingers twitch beneath mine, before she shifts her weight so she can grasp my palm.

"What I'm trying to say is, we grew apart. We were probably always going to, you know? It happens. Our paths diverged, and that's just fate. It's sad, yeah, but with her wanting kids and me being—well, *me*—it was bound to, eventually."

I empathize. As she speaks of the cruelty of fate, I squeeze her hand. But there is something in her words that does not make sense to me, beyond just her modern euphemisms.

"When you say that you were bound to grow apart because you are *you,*" I ask, speaking slowly to make sure I do not mince my words. "What do you mean?"

Her throat bobs, and moisture gathers in her eyes. My chest aches to see so much emotion building inside her. I do not understand. She is Lillian; she is beautiful and funny and lovely. What about her could cause such a rift in her friendships?

"I lost a baby. Years ago," she says. A single tear spills from the surplus clinging to her eyelashes, and once it falls, more follow. "And the doctors said—well, they told me that there's something wrong with me. I get these polyps, I guess, and it makes it really hard for pregnancies to be viable. So."

She shrugs and lifts her sad eyes to the sky, as if to punctuate her sentence.

"So... what?"

She sniffs. More tears fall from her eyes, and I squeeze her hand harder. She pulls it away to wipe at her face, and I instantly regret my attempt to comfort her. But before I can back away from her and give her space, she grabs my hand again and sighs.

"I can't have kids, Erik."

"Because of the–" I try to remember the word she said. "Pollies?"

"Polyps, yeah," she corrects. "Or something like that. I

mean, I've had PCOS my whole life and my periods are awful, so like, I've always known I'm probably not especially fertile or anything, but like, I wanted the option, you know? And when I found out I was pregnant, there was a part of me that was really excited. Even with my boyfriend leaving me and my job being boring and all the other crap in my life, there was something *there*, you know? Something that made it worth it. It felt like something I could do. Something I would be good at, raising a child. I—I wanted to meet them. Him or her. Be a better person for them.

"But clearly, it wasn't meant to be. I'm not supposed to be a mother, I guess. It's not in the cards."

The meaning of her words strike me, and I believe I know what she is attempting to communicate. "A cruel whim of fate."

She nods, wiping at her eyes again. I grasp her hand again, and reach my other to her face, wiping away the errant tears for her with my thumb.

She gives me a watery smile. One that I return.

"Lillian, I am sorry that fate has been so cruel to you. You are so beautiful, so lovely, so..." I clear my throat. "So *perfect*. It is an excruciating injustice to see what fate has done to you."

She abandons twirling the meat over the fire and leans her face into my hand, holding it with hers. Her words are just above a whisper when she replies, "You, too, Erik. You've also been fucked in the ass by fate, and it's stupid and dumb and it just fucking sucks."

I startle at her language, and a wave of heat rushes to my cheeks. I clear my throat and pull away from her.

"Your words are very—ah—*graphic*. I do not...I have been alone many years, and while I have been curious to explore certain pleasures in my loneliness, I do not believe–"

Her responding laugh is loud and raucous and honking, and it breaks the sad, weighted air of the shelter. I feel it shatter the tension between us as she wipes her face again, new tears bursting forth as she gasps for air.

"No, it's an expression!" She continues to laugh, and I tilt my head. "When something fucks you in the ass, it's like saying it's screwing you over. Beating you down, ruining your life."

"Oh!" I heave a sigh of relief, my chest also shaking with laughter. She has so many strange sayings! "I do not agree with that expression!"

"What?" She's wheezing now, water pouring from her eyes faster than she can smooth it away. "What do you mean?"

"Fucking in the ass," I clarify. "Your meaning for it is silly. Why should that mean ruining one's life?"

"I mean..." There is a pause as Lillian thinks about my question. "You know what? You have a point! It's a pretty prudish expression, isn't it?"

"Prudish?"

"Like sheltered, or insecure. A prude is someone who thinks sex is bad."

I chew on her explanation for a moment. The heavy mood from earlier has lifted. Lillian's face is ruddy from her tears, but far less sad. Her expression grows thoughtful as she watches me.

"Erik, what are your feelings about sex?"

The question takes me by surprise. For the past few days, my priority has been to hide all of my sexual feelings and urges from her. Knowing that if I were to give in, I would be putting her in danger. Placing her in the path of my monster's destruction. Potentially ruin her life.

Fuck her in the ass, as it were.

The phrase seems infinitely more appropriate in the context of my curse.

I resume cooking duties, stoking the cooking fire to a healthy blaze and tossing on another log. I take over the rotation of the spit while Lillian looks on, expectantly.

"Perhaps I am a prude," I say at last. "I do not believe that sex is bad. But the monster within me... he has desires I cannot abide. And I believe that, for me, sex can only lead to damnation."

For several minutes, the only sound in the small space is the crackling of the fire and the *swish, swish, swish* of spit on stake. I let my vision go hazy, the light of the fire blurring into a pulsing pastiche of orange and brown.

A soft pressure rubs my shoulder, and I blink to see Lillian kneeling behind me, her hand brushing my back. "That's awful, Erik."

A lump forms in my throat. I swallow, the sensation of her touch feeling at once wonderful and uncomfortable, and nudge her away. "It is the only way."

She bends at the waist, pushing her head into my field of vision, just above my shoulder. "Is it?"

The heat of the blaze is stifling. My palms are hot and clammy with sweat. I remove myself from the shrinking space between the woman and the fire, scrambling out of the lean-to and grabbing the water skin as I go.

"I am going to get more water."

"Erik, I just filled it up—"

"I will return soon," I shout over my shoulder, running towards the shore as soon as my feet hit the ground.

CHAPTER 16

LILLIAN

A list of things Erik likes: Taylor Swift, spicy romance novels, and buttsex (question mark)?

A list of things Erik clearly *doesn't* like: me.

For a minute there, he really had me going. With the listening, the comforting, squeezing my hand, bringing me jerky, etc. And for a guy who seems to want nothing to do with me sexually, he sure does deliver a great pickup line.

"You are so beautiful, so lovely. So, so perfect."

Cool! Thanks, dude! Beautiful, lovely, and perfect, until I try to broach the topic of actually *doing* the dang deed.

What the hell, guy?

"Perhaps I am a prude." Chyeah. Ya think?

"Fuckin' tease," I mutter, turning the fucking squirrels on the fucking spit above the fucking fire. Ugh, I'm supposed to break bread with this guy after he rejected me *again?*

I shift on the ground, my thighs aching—not just from kneeling and squatting more than I ever have in my life (and on a bum ankle, at that), but also from spending all day being a wet, horny mess from reading all those books he brought me.

Is he trying to punish me? What, he can't have sex because of this stupid curse, and he's tired of suffering alone?

They say misery loves company...

I poke one of the carcasses with my finger, gauging how done it is. The flesh is firm, barely yielding, so I push the meat onto one of the plates and start the next spit spinning.

I don't know what to do. He can't expect me to just read for the next week as my injury heals, can he? I look down at my foot, the skin mottled with purple and swollen. I assume it isn't broken, but who knows how long it'll take to get better?

I tried to cool it down in the lake earlier, but I heard the whispering again. I was so freaked out and confused from the morning's interactions with Erik, I couldn't figure out if all of the feelings I was having were mine, or if some of them were...

No. Nope. Not going there.

It's one thing to grow gills overnight. But hearing voices?

Okay, maybe that isn't the most convincing argument. But it does make some sense that I would be conflicted and paranoid given the past few days. I'm in a new environment, in the *wilderness*, for Christ's sake—of course I'm going to be a little jumpy. I'm on high alert; I'm hearing all sorts of noises that I would usually tune out—snapping twigs, scurrying rodents, bird calls—because I'm in *survival mode*.

That's a perfectly normal response to the trauma I've endured in the last 72 hours.

A completely understandable, *human* reaction.

Erik shuffles back inside, and I turn my face away from him. Ugh, right. And then there's all *that* extra stress on top of it all.

I stab one squirrel with a fork for myself and shove the other one towards him while I dig in, food-on-a-stick style. It reminds me of chicken wings: not a lot of meat for all the fussing with the bones. Same with the fish we've been eating.

I'm grateful that Erik came back with some dried venison earlier. It was good of him. Smart. Kind.

"You are mad at me."

"I'm not mad at you," I huff. He pokes at his dinner, but doesn't eat it. "What, are my cooking skills not good enough for you, either?"

"What are you talking about?" He asks, looking far too innocent.

"I just don't understand you."

I want *him* to be mad. I want him to get angry at me for being obtuse, yell at me, tell me I'm being too emotional, so I can blow up and give him a piece of my mind. I want him to give me a reason to make him the target of my anger so I won't feel guilty about lashing out at him the way I want to.

So much of me is angry right now. At Tiffany, at Dean, at my ankle, at this whole fucking situation. This is *stupid*, it's the stupidest, most ridiculous thing that has ever happened, and yet I'm stuck here. I'm stuck on my ass in this pile of leather and fur, eating squirrel meat with a so-hot-it-should-be-illegal hunk of man muscle that refuses to sleep with me because he has a literal monster inside him, and is afraid that unleashing his forbidden lust will release a literal monster in *me*.

Like, what the actual fuck?? Why does the world seem hell-bent on making me suffer like this?

I'm tired of it. I'm tired of being a good sport about this, trying to be a good, contributing cavewoman while pretending I'm not annoyed that he keeps running away from me. Convincing myself that he doesn't want me, despite him getting a *raging* erection whenever he's around me, just because the world has told me that girls like me aren't supposed to have guys like him.

I'm just so fucking *exhausted* of taking every single punch that life throws my way and trying to be chill about it. It isn't fair! I didn't *ask* to be stranded on this island! I didn't *ask* to be cursed. But since I'm here, I should at *least* get to bang the sweet, hot caveman I'm cursed with, shouldn't I?

I want to scream. I want to terrorize this entire forest until one ounce of it makes sense. And seeing as Erik is the only one who's here right now, *he's* the one who's gonna have to put up with me while I do it.

But he doesn't deserve that. Not yet, anyway. So instead, I resort to being pissy and passive aggressive until he does something to deserve my anger—*then* I can let it all go.

But instead, what does this motherfucker do?

His crystalline eyes shine at me with sympathy. Sympathy!

Then he gives a defeated nod, curling in on himself in what I can only describe as all-consuming shame, and he says, "If you cannot understand me, then no one on this earth will ever be capable of it."

And *fuck* me.

It hurts. It hurts so much to see him embodying such hopelessness over our situation. Especially when he's the reason I'm still here. He's the reason I'm *alive* right now—and if *he* can't find the strength to carry on, well.

What possible chance do I have?

This strong, amazing man, who can kill a coyote with a spear and build a fire with his bare hands and carry a full-grown woman halfway across a forest, has been broken by life and fate in just about every fucking possible way. And he's just... giving up.

"No."

He blinks up at me, and his eyes widen with surprise. Probably because I'm shaking. My fists are clenched so tight to my sides that the muscles and tendons running up and down my forearms are trembling of their own accord.

And I snap.

"You don't get to do that! You don't get to be sad, Erik! You don't get to pull at my fucking heartstrings—you don't get to make me *like* you, only to decide that you're hopeless. That you're destined to be alone!"

I stomp my injured foot, and searing pain shoots up my entire side. *When did I stand up?* He reaches to catch me, but I push against his arm, fighting him while simultaneously using him for balance.

Erik's back is grazing the side of the shelter as I lean into him, cornering him, away from the fire and the small opening that points to the beach, blocking off his exit. I push in closer, until I can feel his pulse speed up from the puffs of breath that ghost over my face.

Balancing on my good leg and bracing myself with one hand on his arm, I poke him in the chest as hard as I can with the other, punctuating each word.

"You! Aren't! Allowed! To give! Up!"

He has the audacity to look hurt by that, confused. And it makes me even angrier. So I get even closer, until my nose is practically bumping his chin.

"How dare you take care of me! How dare you rescue

me, and feed me, and hold my hand, and bring me fucking *books,* only to reject me like every! Other! Fucking! Man!" I take a shuddering breath, and of *course* I taste salt on my lips. Because of *course* I'm crying again. "I was *vulnerable* with you, dude! I tried to relate to you! I told you my deepest, darkest hurt in all the world, and you... you..."

You listened, I want to say. *You cared.*

Only to run away from me the second I let myself care back.

"Lillian, I never meant—"

"I know! I know you didn't mean to. That's the worst part! You're not even *trying* to hurt me, you're not even being callous or shitty or creepy, you're literally trying to *protect* me, and that makes it even worse! Because you care so much about keeping me alive that you don't even want to try to be *happy*!"

Suddenly, my arms are so heavy I can't summon the energy to poke him anymore. I can't even lift my hand. My leg is shaky from holding all my weight, and I stumble forward, right into his firm, beautiful chest.

I gasp in a shuddering breath through my tears, and my nose fills with his warm, manly scent. It melts me. His arms encircle me, and the bastard squeezes me so hard my ribs crack, burying his face in my hair. I feel him breathe me in, his arms pulling me in tighter as he does.

A shiver runs down my entire body as the pressure of his skin on mine *does* something to me. A wave of desire overcomes me, making my whole body shudder against him.

His whole body stiffens, and in that instance I know he can feel it too. The pull between us, that isn't just because we're the only people on this island, or the only two people in the world cursed to live under the thumbs of two primordial god monsters.

This is the pull between a man and a woman who've seen each other for who they really are, for all their faults and scars, and are still crazy enough to want each other.

"Lillian." He sounds choked as he says my name, as if he's holding back a groan. "I am sorry I have not been honest with you. I did not mean to reject you. I am not afraid of your vulnerability. I am not dissuaded by your past. If you only knew how I truly felt..."

"Then *tell* me. Tell me how you feel."

His arms squeeze me tighter, as if he's afraid that if he lets even the tiniest molecule of air between us, he'll lose the courage to speak.

"I am drawn to you like a moth to a flame. From the moment I first saw you, I have *longed* for you. I have only stayed away from you to protect you from the monster. He wants you for himself, to use you, and I worry that if I let myself give into my feelings for you that He will... that I will... Lillian, I cannot *fight* desire like that!"

"Then don't," I breathe. "Why fight your own feelings? Why fight fate? Erik, don't you get it? We can't win a fight against the gods! We can't change our fate. We can't control our destiny. It doesn't matter! None of it matters! The only thing we can control in this world is our own happiness, and no one will give that to us. No one is handing out stickers and get-out-of-fate-free cards for being 'good.' So why should we deny ourselves?

"You *know* what you want, Erik. What will make you happy. Why won't you just let yourself take it? Don't you want me? Don't you want this??" I reach my hand down between us and squeeze the throbbing bulge that's been pressing into my stomach. He hisses, his whole body buck-ling as I grind him through the fabric.

"We can't! Lillian, if I give in..."

I pull away from him abruptly, emboldened by the lust pounding in my veins. I need to see his face; I need to know why he's fighting, what he's thinking. If he truly wishes for me to get away from him, or if he's denying himself the thing he wants most just because he thinks it will protect me from something neither of us can control.

His hands are claws digging into my shoulders, and I wrap my arms around his to steady myself. He's shaking now, hanging his head, hiding from me; his wavy hair a shivering curtain obscuring his face.

Gently, I slip my fingers through and part his locks, cupping his cheek and tilting his chin until I can meet his eyes. The pure, light gray sparkles in the firelight as he battles with himself, his gaze darting up and down my entire body before settling onto my face.

His expression is full of desire, awe, and a gut-wrenching humility as he takes me in.

"Lillian...*please.*"

I remember the electric blue stare that burned into me in the cave. The inhuman glow that accompanied that terri-ble, awe-inspiring voice in my head. But there's none of that here now. The clear, pale eyes that bore into mine are wholly human. Wholly Erik.

"There is no monster here, Erik," I whisper, gripping his face and willing him to listen. "This feeling between us, this desire: it isn't Phorkys. It isn't Keto. This is entirely *us.*"

"How do you *know*?"

"Because of your eyes!" My own dart between his, tears streaming down my face as I will my words to sink in. "I can *see* when the monster is taking over. Your eyes glow. But right now? They're perfectly clear, perfectly human. It's *you*, Erik. Just you."

"Just me..." He repeats, the words barely audible on his cracked lips.

"Just you."

He blinks for a moment, and I feel another shudder pass through his body before he opens them again. "Even now?"

Nothing has changed, but his voice is desperate. I nod. "Even now."

A slight pause, then he squeezes my shoulders. "Still?"

"Erik," I hold back a giggle as he moves his hands down, exploring my body and passing his rough fingertips down the sides of my breasts and over my ribs, making me gasp. My eyes flutter closed as his thumbs brush my nipples.

"Answer me!" He demands, and my eyes fly open.

"Yes! Still you!"

He exhales a disbelieving laugh and explores me more. Moving his hands lower, to my hips. My thighs. The curve of my ass.

"Now?"

I sigh with pleasure, smiling at his perfectly gray gaze. "No glow."

Now it's my turn. I snake my hand back down to the waistband of his shorts, eliciting a pained gasp from the Viking. I raise an eyebrow and wait for him to give me permission.

He nods, wide-eyed. I slip the knot of the drawstring free before dipping my fingers under the fabric.

The lowest, most primal moan I've ever heard rumbles from his throat in response and his eyelids flutter closed as I wrap my hand around his rock-hard shaft. I work the heavy cock out of its prison, pushing down his shorts until it springs free between us. Then I curl my fingers around the base, letting my palm cradle the underside.

His eyes spring open. In a panicked gasp, he asks, "now?"

I raise on the tip-toes of my good foot, pressing myself into him so I can graze his jaw with my lips. His fingers twitch on my ass cheeks as he draws me closer. "It's you, Erik. *This–*" I give him a squeeze and he groans, fingers sinking in tighter, but his eyes stay gray, "–is *all* you."

Suddenly, my legs are in the air. A growl fills the shelter as Erik scoops me into his arms, and before I realize what's happening my back is flat against the furs I've been using for a bed and there's a muscly, long-haired hunk kneeling between my legs. My bad ankle is cradled against his shoulder and he's licking a trail of hungry kisses from my heel to my hip, pausing only to sniff greedily at the apex of my–

"Oh *God,* Erik!"

"Look into my eyes, Lillian," he murmurs into my core, his facial hair tickling me right where I'm aching and sensitive. "Who am I now?"

"You're—*uh*—still—still Erik," I pant, just managing to keep my eyes open and trained on his face as his breath whispers against my clit.

His eyes—gray as the day I met him—crinkle in the corners as a triumphant smile splits his lips. He lifts his face away from me, but before I can whimper at the loss (just when we were finally making progress!), he runs his fingers up and down my slit. My hips jolt at the contact, and his face grows serious.

"I have longed to do this since the moment I laid eyes on you, sweet Lillian." Slowly, he delves the tips of his fingers between my lower lips and finds my soaked, waiting cunt. I'm so wet from an entire day of reading smut and pining after this man; he doesn't meet any resistance. His smile widens as he traces languid circles through my folds, gathering up my slickness, working me up into a writhing, squirming mess. Then he brings his fingers to his lips and sucks.

Fuck me. It's the hottest thing I've ever seen.

His eyes flutter closed on a *very* lewd moan, so low and dirty I can feel it in my stomach. The want, the *need*—it's there in full stereo, and it only stokes the embers of desire burning in my core. He opens his eyes again and pins me down with his stare, removing his fingers from his mouth before speaking.

"I need you to promise me, Lillian."

"Anything," I whimper, dying for him to finish what he started. But he is all business as he cups me with his hand.

"You are to look into my eyes the whole time I am pleasuring you. No matter how much you want to close them, no matter how close you are to your climax, you will keep them open and trained on me. If you see any sign of the monster, you will tell me."

"Okay," I breathe.

"Promise me!" He says, thrusting two fingers inside me once again and swirling them, faster and faster and driving me crazy with pleasure. It feels so good after being empty for so long, and I roll my hips into his hand, crying out as he hits that spot inside me that makes me see stars.

"I promise!"

"*Look at me!*"

I lock onto his gaze, his still-gray eyes boring into mine with an intensity that has me shaking. But it isn't just his eyes, it's his fingers. He's pulsing them inside me, spinning them in tiny circles that push against my inner walls. It's so good, *he's* so good—his fingers thick and rough and relentless as he brings me closer and closer to the edge.

Wordless, keening noises are already leaking from my lips, mixing with the sloppy sounds of my sopping cunt, when he adds another finger to the mix and bends down to tease me with his mouth.

"*Fuck!* Erik, ah–" my voice breaks off in a high-pitched scream as he thrusts his tongue between my folds.

The whole time, he maintains unbreaking eye contact, driving me crazy as I watch his face. Normally, I would have my head back on a pillow when someone goes down on me, but with Erik, I can't look away. He made me promise.

But that means I see *everything*.

I see how he swirls his tongue under the swell of my mound, sucking on the sensitive skin of my inner lips before lapping at my clit. I see the moisture gather on his beard as his fingers pump inside me, my juices spilling onto his face and glistening on his lips. I see the fat of my thighs jiggle when my legs shake with every wave of pleasure, the hunger in his expression, and the way his eyes roll back into his head when his fingers frantically pump into that perfect, aching spot inside me and a stream of clear fluid gushes onto his face.

But I don't just see it. I *feel* and *hear* the guttural moan of pleasure from him when it vibrates against my core. I feel the scream claw its way out of my throat as the building wave of ecstasy crashes into me, I hear him slurp down every last drop of my release.

And I watch him through the entire rollercoaster. His eyes stay gray the whole time.

They shine with delight and arousal as he slowly licks me through the aftershocks, holding my thighs on either side of his head and letting me grind my pussy against his face while the tremors slowly ease.

When the final pings of pleasure fade away, he lifts his chin from my center. "No monster?"

I shake my head, allowing myself to finally relax my head against the ground for a moment as I catch my breath. "Not even for a second."

"That is good," he says, and he lowers my hips to his lap, lining up his shaft with my entrance and rubbing it lengthwise against the slick skin. His cock is impossibly hard, leaking precum from its thick, flushed tip, and it feels so good rubbing against me.

It twitches with impatience. "I wonder if he will stay away while I seek my pleasure."

I wiggle my hips against him. "Only one way to find out."

CHAPTER 17

ERIK

Lillian's words echo in my head, a glorious respite from the usual voice that dwells there.

"It's you, Erik. Just you."

Her eyes, as deep blue as the lake in the bitter heart of winter, bore into mine as I rub my aching cock at her hot, wet entrance. My heart is hammering harder in my chest than it ever has. I am watching for any spark of fear or surprise, the smallest sign of recognition that might light in her face as I drive myself to the brink of insanity, teasing myself with the feel of her. Every now and then, her focus flits from my eyes, hungrily darting lower to the place where our bodies grind against each other.

"Do it, Erik," she pants, contracting her stomach muscles to urge her hips upward in my hold, her legs trembling against my chest. "Please."

I breathe in slowly, scouring my brain for the faintest hint of the monster's voice. Even the slightest murmur of his alien instincts flaring like emotion in my gut.

But it is silent. So mercifully, beautifully silent.

I am afraid to trust it. I have wanted this woman since I

first saw her bathing in the water. Wanted to fondle her sweet breasts, kiss her plump lips, delve into the fuzzy folds between her legs. But I am afraid—terrified—knowing that if I give in, if I turn over control to my desires, it could all go wrong at any moment–

"Erik!"

Her pleading voice snaps my attention back to my beautiful Lillian, and there *is* something in her eyes now. A fire. The deep blue sparkles like sapphires as desire burns from her soul into mine. Aching. Desperate.

Human.

"Do not look away," I grunt, truly on the edge of pain as my balls swell with days of unrequited lust. I have not touched myself since the day I first spoke to her on the beach, not on purpose, so fearful that any sensation against my shaft would summon Phorkys's hunger, would put her in danger. I can hardly speak through the haze of longing. "I need you...*ungh*...to watch me. For any—any sign..."

Her blonde hair flies in staticy wisps against the bed of furs as she nods frantically. "I will. I promise. Erik, please."

The plea falls from her lips like a prayer as her eyelids hood, turning her expression sultry.

I nod, not trusting my voice, hardly trusting my body. I maintain eye contact while I line up the head of my cock with her dripping entrance, wet from my earlier attentions, relying solely on the feel of her folds to guide me.

The bittersweet sensation stretches on for eternity until I suddenly feel my tip notch at her channel, tucking into its firm embrace, and the pressure on my sensitive head draws a keening sound from my throat.

"Please, Erik, *please,*" she answers my cry, her brow scrunching as she struggles to keep her eyes on mine. "I need you."

Need. If only she knew. How deep the need for her runs through my veins, terrifying and all-consuming.

He needs you too, I think, and it is the only thing keeping me from thrusting myself inside her until my balls bury between her cheeks. My resolve is the only thing protecting her from him.

"I—I cannot–"

"It's only you, Erik!" Her hands grasp onto my forearms, gripping so tight I can feel her nails carving crescents into my skin, her eyes blazing wildly. "It's just you and me. Make me yours!"

"Augh!" I growl, the pain of her grip connecting me to her as our gaze sizzles, burning away my fear until the only thing that remains is the points where our bodies connect. Her fingers on my arms. Her thighs against my stomach. Her plump ass on my thighs.

And my shaft, at last, sinking into the tight, perfect embrace of her core.

"Fuck!" She moans, head thrown back into the scream, hips jerking up as her body attempts to straighten.

"Eyes!" I order, and her neck snaps up, locking back in. The pleasure of her squeezing around my cock is ecstacy, and it is unlocking a possessiveness inside me that I did not know existed. I dig my hands into her ass, gripping its supple flesh with claw-like fingers.

If it did not feel so good, so all-consumingly *perfect,* pulling out and sliding in to feel her tight flesh welcome me back, perhaps there would be room for fear. Perhaps I would worry that my hands *were* turning into claws, that my lust *was* unlocking something dangerous, something possessive and greedy.

Something monstrous.

But I cannot. In this moment, losing myself in this

magnificent woman, I can only ask her to warn me before I give in completely. Can only trust that she will hold my gaze to hers, and with the power of her perfect eyes and voice and body, I will not fall apart. That she will not let me.

I thrust my hips forward and pull her hips in, burying myself inside her again and again. Her breathing quickens to match my relentless pace, her face flushing, lips parting, but her eyes hold steady.

"Yes, yes, *yes,*" spills like a mantra from her lips, and it draws my attention down to the plush, pink flesh of her mouth. I slow, allowing myself to take in the rest of her beautiful body: round red cheeks, pale full stomach, soft heavy breasts. "Erik," she gasps. "Look at me."

"I am."

Everything inside me protests, but I manage to withdraw from her wet heat, not wanting to spend myself just yet. I open her hips to spread her legs on either side of me. My cock aches without her touch, but I suppress the urge to plunge back inside her or stroke myself. Instead, I lean forward, hovering over her, posting my weight on an elbow while I brush an errant, golden lock of hair from her lower lip.

"I have to kiss you," I confess. "I need... I need to feel you everywhere, Lillian."

A new emotion crosses her face as she reaches up to cup my cheek with one hand, wrapping around and tickling up my spine with the other. I shiver from her gentle touch, letting out a shuddering breath as her nails trace the definition of my shoulders.

My whole torso relaxes into her until our chests brush. I run my free hand from her scalp, down behind her ear, over her collarbone to the side of her breast, where I push the kneadable flesh in between us, plucking at her pink nipple with my thumb until it pebbles beneath me.

She gasps, a sweet intake of breath that inspires my cock to twitch against the soft skin of her belly. I groan, grinding slowly against her, as I squeeze and finger the lusty globe.

The entire time, I fight to keep my eyes on hers. She is relentless, holding my gaze like our lives depend on it —*knowing* that they do. She understands what is at stake here, understands what I need from her. The realization catches in my throat, and I cradle my arm behind her head so I can hold the base of her skull like a pillow to ease the strain on her neck.

And then, holding her gaze, I draw the firm, rosy peak of her breast into my mouth.

A tortured sound dribbles from her as I trace the pebbled skin of her areola with my tongue, drawing smaller and smaller circles until I flick the tip over her nipple again and again. I wrap my lips around the sensitive bud and suck, pulling it into my mouth and hollowing my cheeks like a babe in her embrace, rubbing the underside of my shaft against her to the tempo of her moans.

The hand that had been holding my face falls away, and I see her take up administrations of her own to her other breast in my peripheral vision. Her fingers clench and tease, her thumb plucking and rubbing, her hand even cradling the entire mass at one point to push it against the side of my face. I chuckle.

"You wish for me to lick the left?"

"Both," she pants, and frees both hands to press her tits together. My mouth goes dry as I see the two mounds distort in her grasp, the line between them lengthening as she pushes her nipples closer together.

My cock twitches again; an image of my seed spraying across her neck and face while I fuck her jiggling tits springs to the forefront of my mind. I swallow, pleading with her with my eyes. "You want me to..."

"Suck them both. At once."

I do not need to be told twice.

I replace her hands with my own, shifting my weight so my torso presses into her hips while I dive face-first into her perfect breasts, squeezing and licking and sucking, drawing both tips into my mouth and laving them with my tongue until I feel her squeeze her thighs around me.

"Oh, *fuck*, Erik—that's so good!"

Losing myself, I close my eyes and waggle my head back and forth with my tongue out, flicking the pink peaks relentlessly while I push them together with my hands.

"Eyes!" She gasps, and I pop them open at the same moment I drop my hands to her hips.

"I cannot wait any longer, Lillian. I need to be inside you."

"Thank god!" She says, the humor in her voice warming my chest.

I center myself between her legs and she locks her thighs around my hips, my arms supporting her at her lower back. I rub against her entrance again, feeling more human than I have in centuries.

"Am I still... myself?" I check, one last time, before I give myself over to her pleasure.

"Still Erik. Still *you*." A look I have never seen before crosses Lillian's face, open and kind and caring and...

Loving?

Could it be possible? Could Lillian love me?

Could any woman, as broken as I am?

The mystery emotion flickers between us for only a

moment, before desire burns hot enough to consume every-thing else.

I notch myself at her entrance, and slide home.

She cries with pleasure, taking all of me in that first, slow thrust. Her channel is hot and wet and wanting as it welcomes me in, the sweet friction making me shudder from head to toe. We both gasp at the rightness of it, the pure perfection of our bodies locked together and becoming one.

I try to resist the pull deep in my lower belly, but my cock has been aching for this for too many days. I drag my length against her inner walls, back and forth, and the pres-sure builds too quickly.

"Lillian," I breathe, "I will not last long–"

"You've got me on the fucking edge, Erik," her voice is reedy and thin, and little noises sneak out between words as she struggles to keep her eyes open. "Harder, please, I want you to just fuck me!"

A primal urge bursts forth inside me at those words, and my hips snap forward greedily. Lillian cries out, and I do not need to confirm whether or not it is a good sound. Her eyes are wide as saucers as she wails beneath me, my stomach pulling tighter and tighter with every snap of my hips.

I pound into her, my own gaze growing frantic as I fight the urge to give into my most base desires. I see my plea-sure mirrored in her face as her eyes roll back with every thrust, only to return to mine as I pull back: a crazed dance between bliss and duty as she struggles to obey my demands.

She feels so *good*. The pleasure, the pure ecstasy, is a feeling I have grown to associate only with the monster's machinations. The way he would toy with and torture me at the slightest hint of lust, the unnatural swelling in my loins and the pictures he would plant inside my head. It is inseparable from the agony and guilt I feel at my cruel fate, and yet...

To feel this good in my human form, inside this human woman—*Lillian*—it is excruciating. It is euphoric. It—

I feel my balls tighten, and it is as if something within me cracks open. A barbaric cry rends itself from my throat and tears burst from my eyes as I explode inside her, pleasure uncoiling from the base of my spine and pouring itself from the very depths of my soul.

Lillian is screaming too, a frantic chorus of, "Yes, yes, Erik—yes!" as I thrust forward once, twice, and three more times, feeling my release mix with her own as it surges inside her.

We freeze, joined together, her legs twitching around my waist and my final spurts of seed trailing down the curve of her ass. Panting. Shaking. Unblinking, as we hold each other's gaze.

"Still human?" My voice is a hoarse whisper, hitching as the last tremors of my orgasm shudder through me.

"Still human," she assures me. Then she lets out a contented sigh, finally resting her head back and allowing her eyelids to flutter closed.

AFTER, we lay together, her body cradled against me and her soft hair fanned over the furs beneath my chin. I tickle my fingers over her spine and shoulders, tracing the subtle lines of her vertebrae through the smooth flesh, enjoying the sound of her contented hums as my nails move up and down.

"That was so good," she purrs. My stomach flips happily. I squeeze her tightly.

"I am glad."

"Was it good for you, too?" She tilts her head up and I cannot help but laugh at the concern wrinkling her forehead.

"Lillian, my treasure," I sigh and press my lips to the furrowed skin, kissing her worry away. "It has been hundreds of years since I have felt the pleasure of a woman in my bed. And *you*—Odin's beard! Your body holds within it more pleasure than one man could ever hope to enjoy." Certainly a man like me.

She squirms in my hold, embarrassed by my compliment, and I lift my finger to her chin. She stills when I tilt her face to mine. "You are perfect, my treasure. I feel as if I have died a warrior's death, and been rewarded Valhalla."

"You don't have to make it weird," she murmurs, but snuggles closer to me, wrapping her arms around my waist. "You could just say my pussy game is on point and move on."

I pause, attempting to translate the unfamiliar words in my head, but surrender the battle. "Your pussy game is on point."

She snorts into my chest, and then I feel her lips press a kiss against my sternum. It is not long before her body sinks more deeply into my embrace, and her breathing slows into a steady, even rhythm.

And for the first time in centuries, I drift out of consciousness without the voice of a monster whispering me to sleep.

CHAPTER 18

LILLIAN

For once, I wake up before Erik, deliciously sore after our enthusiastic session the night before. A sheen of sweat covers my skin despite the early morning chill in the air—no doubt a side effect of Erik's furnace-like warmth snuggling up beside me under our furs.

I long for a shower, but I linger beside him. Taking in the smooth lines of his face, the relaxed set of his shoulders against the soft pile of bedding. I wonder how often he sleeps on land. Is it easier to let the monster take over at night? Prowling the lake waters, drifting in his rocky underwater cave? Does he even truly let his body rest, or does he simply hand over consciousness while he clocks out for a few hours?

I stroke the stray locks of wild hair away from his face, careful not to brush against his skin lest I wake him. He's such a beautiful man. Strong-featured and square-jawed, not to mention his arms are bigger than my calves—with the gentlest demeanor.

He's had such a rough life. The loss of his family alone

would have crushed a man with a stronger support system. But he had nothing. No one. Except a terrifying voice in his head attempting to control his every thought.

How much willpower does it take to keep a god like Phorkys at bay?

The image of his heated gaze boring into mine, desperation squeezing his eyebrows together like a vice, while he begged me not to let him fall into the abyss...*fuck,* the very thought of it makes my nipples hard. That was, without a doubt, the hottest fucking sex I've ever had in my life, and yet...

It was that edge of danger. Of destruction. Knowing that at any moment, it could all be taken away by a cruel twist of fate. But still, I trusted him.

He's fought those urges for longer than I've been alive. Shit, for longer than my oldest ancestor was alive, and then some.

But I can't help but wonder why.

What good does it do him to fight so hard? To cling so vehemently to some predefined moral compass that was formed without the slightest inkling of just how cruel the world could be to a man like him?

My hands wander a bit over his scalp, his chest, his arms. Super light touches—not nearly enough to wake him, but enough to appreciate his gorgeous body. I hold back a snicker as his morning wood tents the fur covering his body, rising a good five or six inches without even standing at full mast.

Wowza. And I had that inside me last night.

Not that that's hard to believe, given the slight pinch and ache that zing up my crotch when I sit up, testing my ankle with a few rolls before I attempt to stand. It's still pretty tender. It might be worth it to craft myself a pair of crutches today so I can get around without stressing the tendons anymore than I already have; two days walking on the sand between our shelter and the water's edge is not the best therapy for a sprain.

I drain the last few sips from the water skin and crawl over my Viking, before quietly slipping out of the tent to freshen up.

"So what's on the docket today?"

Erik tilts his head questioningly at me, eyes lifting from the speartip he's sharpening. It's a gorgeous, sunny day on Lake Superior. We spent the morning outside, roasting some fish on a small cooking fire he prepared in a circle of rocks custom-built for that very purpose. Our sleeping furs are drying flat in the sun, stretched out on some large boulders and a driftwood log. Cleaning them became imperative when I re-entered the shelter with a fresh nose and just about fainted from the sex stank all over them. Cleaning Erik was the task of penultimate importance, which he thankfully agreed to without much prodding, skipping off to wash in the lake while I gathered the bedding.

Our clothes are also drying in the midday sun, hanging from a makeshift clothesline I fashioned from birch branches. It's oddly domestic.

My Viking, naked as the day is long, asks me: "Docket?"

"You know, the day's agenda. I'm sure there's plenty of prep to do to gear up for winter. What's a typical day look like for you?"

"That is a curious question, seeing as today is anything but typical." He smiles at me, then purses his lip thoughtfully, twisting the speartip and eyeing it while he comes up with an answer. "On a day like today, I would prepare to hunt at dusk. That is when the deer are most active and least likely to sense my presence."

"Okay. How do we prepare for a hunt?"

He gestures to the pile of sharpened sticks and arrowheads beside him. I let out a sigh.

"Yeah, alright, caveman, I get it. Og hunt big game with pointy stick. But what about after you catch the thing? Do we chop it into steaks, dry it into jerky? It's not like we have a cooler we can stick it in."

"We skin it and hang it by the hide, slit its stomach to drain the entrails. The organs we leave for carrion. We can dry the rest."

I wretch a little in my mouth. "Oooo-kay. Cool. Cool cool cool. So uh… what do we need for that, a drying rack?"

"We can smoke it over the fire. A net across the roof of the shelter will do."

"Say what now?" The image of a bunch of rotting meat hanging over my head while I sleep at night makes my stomach turn. "Uh, no. We can build, like, a box for that or something, can't we?"

The corner of his lip twitches. "Why would we do that?"

Is he laughing at me?

"Because it's gross to sleep under a bunch of rotting meat??"

He's absolutely laughing at me. I can tell because he honks out a hearty guffaw at my disgust. "It is not rotting meat, my treasure, it is *drying* meat. The same as the snack you enjoyed mere moments ago."

Yeah, the same snack that's threatening to come back up at the thought of carrion nomming on a bunch of deer entrails.

He notices the blush that colors my cheeks—the source of which is definitely the nausea I'm fighting and *not* my reaction to him calling me his 'treasure'. It's a nickname he's used a few times already today, and it totally doesn't twist my stomach into butterflies and knots every time it comes out of his mouth.

"Why do you ask?"

I hobble over to his spot by the cooking fire, leaning on the cane I discovered during my morning potty break. Okay, it's just a big-ass branch that hasn't started rotting yet, but it's strong enough to support my weight and thick enough that it doesn't sink completely into the sandy shore.

I plop down beside him on the driftwood branch, letting out a small "eep!" as the cold, damp wood makes contact with the bare skin of my ass.

He watches me sink down with heated eyes, paying particular attention to the way my boobs bounce as my ass hits the log.

"I can help, you know. There's plenty I can do without my ankle. Not everything requires the ability to run away from coyotes."

He lowers the spear to the pile and rubs his rough palm against my thigh. The contact sends a zing up my spine, and I bite the inside of my cheek as he turns his full gaze on me.

"You have helped me more than you will ever know, sweet Lillian. Please, rest. You have already helped enough for the day." He gestures to the clothesline and the drying furs. "I can hunt for dinner. Perhaps you can read more books."

He presses a kiss to my cheek, then bends down, plucking a dull stick from the ground and setting back to work with his hunting knife.

"I'm not going to sit around all week and read while you

do all the hard stuff," I argue. He may have set the topic down, but I'm gonna pick it right back up.

Lillian Desmond doesn't just let someone take care of her, even if he is a strong, capable warrior like Erik. I may have been weak in the past, but I can't afford to let my guard down now that I live in the wilderness with coyotes and lake monsters. I need to learn how to take care of myself without modern-day conveniences like Walmart and microwaves.

It's great that Erik's pussy-drunk and thinks he can take care of the "man's work" while I just sit around reading smut and fantasizing about dick all day, but I'm not about to let myself be vulnerable again. I almost died: first when I drowned in the lake, and then again when I tried to hunt my own dinner.

If I'm cursed to be some urban-legend Yooper Cryptid with gills and a Kraken shifter boyfriend, then you better believe I'm gonna learn how to hunt for myself, sprained ankle or no. Starting today, Lillian Desmond earns her keep.

He tilts his head at me. Again.

This is something I'm noticing about Erik. He doesn't just leap into arguments willy-nilly. He thinks before he speaks. And fuck, if that isn't almost as sexy as the way he eats me out.

Almost.

Ladies, find yourself a man that goes down on you with the enthusiasm of Naruto sucking down a bowl of ramen noodles.

"You do not want me to take care of you."

The sadness in his voice knocks me out of my lurid daydream, and I refocus on his face. Confusion furrows into the ridges in his forehead, and my heart squeezes.

Ah, fuck, I didn't mean to offend the big guy.

"Hey, I *love* the way you take care of me," I assure him, leaning into his hard, sexy arm. "You spoil me. And that's amazing! But..."

I blow a hair out of my face, brushing it away and wishing for the twelve-thousandth time today that I had an elastic hair tie. Erik watches me, more curious than hurt now, as I struggle to find the right words.

"Look, you aren't the only one stuck on this island anymore. I'm cursed too, remember? So I need to start learning this stuff. How to hunt, how to skin a deer, how to–" I suppress a gag– "leave entrails for carrion. I wasn't raised by Vikings like you."

"Lillian," he cups his hand to my face, and he's so big that his palm spans the entire width of my cheek from nose to ear. He pushes his fingers back into my scalp, tilting my head back a little so our eyes connect. "You will not be trapped here like me."

"Huh?" I blink at him. What is he talking about? "Uh, I have gills now, dude."

He shakes his head and touches his forehead to mine. "You must not stay here any longer than you have to. I believe, if we can nurse you back to health and return you to the mainland before Keto's influence is too great, we can spare you my fate. My treasure, I will not let you suffer here."

I breathe in his sun-kissed, musky scent, wanting to nuzzle into him and the rumble of his voice, but I break away. "It's not that simple. I can't just go back. I have *gills*," I repeat the sentence slowly for emphasis. "What aren't you getting about that? Chicago is cold, sure, but I can't wear turtlenecks year-round. I'm just as cursed as you are!"

The image of Erik in a turtleneck springs to mind. Mm.

It *is* a curse that I'll never see this hunky Viking wrapped up in a sweater.

"You aren't yet hearing Her voice in your mind, Lillian. She may have saved you, but she is not inside you. You are free of Her influence for now. But it will not be that way forever. We must get you back to the mainland before She digs Herself into your mind."

My heart skips a beat. "What?"

"We need to get your strength up so we can swim back. And then you can go back to your other life."

"But–"

"I cannot linger on the mainland, but I am sure *you* still can. Long enough to sever the ties that bind you to Her. Once you are free of Her influence, your powers will surely fade. They must." He kisses my forehead, then turns back to his whittling.

"Erik..." I hesitate, warring with myself. There's so much hope in his voice when he talks about sparing me his fate. The way he talks about it, it almost makes me believe it. "Ke–"

"Do not speak Her name!" He snaps, thrusting his arm out in front of me like a mother would her child when she slams on the breaks of her car. "I have been blissfully free of His voice for a day, my treasure. Do not summon Them here. Our sacred space."

He softens, bending his arm and drawing me to him, cradling my head into his warm, muscled chest. He breathes deeply, burrowing his face and his fingers in my hair as he does, combing through the tangles as he scratches at my scalp.

Maybe he's right. Maybe that voice I heard earlier was just a symptom of my shock. Still me trying to process it all. I was so lonely then, before Erik and I connected and—

"But wait," I murmur into his skin, and he allows me to lift my head. "Erik, if I go back to the mainland, what will happen to you?"

And that's the moment I know that Erik is the strongest man I ever met. Because there's something that takes way more strength than carrying firewood or splitting logs or killing coyotes.

Facing a future alone.

It's so quick. I could almost convince myself I didn't see it: the flicker of all-consuming despair that flitted past his vulnerable, human eyes. Because it's immediately replaced by so much gratitude and love, that my heart catches in my throat.

"I will be forgotten, Lillian. And you will be free."

CHAPTER 19

LILLIAN

"**N**o!"

I'm sorry, *what* did he just say?

I smack his chest. It's entirely ineffective, but he does look down at my hand on his chest and back to me before tilting his head. "Why do you hit me?"

"Because you're an *idiot,* that's why!" I smack him again. He looks down in confusion, but not nearly enough confusion to knock some sense into him, and I'm not having that. So I smack him a third time. "How *dare* you say that to me!"

"I am confused–"

"Yeah, ya are, ya big oaf! Not just confused, but fucking insane! If you think I'm just going to let you waste away here on your own–"

"Lillian!" He grabs my hand, which has been flapping against his immovable chest like one of those big long noodle clothes in a car wash. I resume the ridiculous attack with my other hand, and he instantly grabs that one too, drawing our hands between us. "Why are you tickling me with your palms?"

"Tickling??" I attempt to yank my hands free, but his grip is too strong. Because of course it is. He's a fucking badass who literally spends his free time chopping down trees. And I'm a plus-size paralegal. If he wanted to, he could crush me like a bug.

But he doesn't want to. He wants to rescue me. Protect me.

Even if it means cursing him for all of eternity.

"Calm yourself, my treasure. You are breathing too fast. Please, tell me what is wrong?"

"You! *You're* wrong! I'm not going to leave you here alone for all eternity!"

Sadness crosses his features again, but this time it carries an edge of pity. He shakes his head. "Lillian, it is too late for me. You do not understand–"

"I understand what Pho–sorry, what *He* said to us in the cave. I remember it crystal clear. He said that there was only one way for us to get out of this situation, and that was to–"

I'm cut off when Erik covers my mouth with his in a crushing, bruising kiss. My hands are trapped between our chests as he maneuvers me like a rag doll, surrounding me in his embrace with one hand locked around my back and the other securing my head against his. He sweeps his tongue into my open mouth and devours me with everything he has, fighting my lips like a war until I succumb.

How could I not? Jesus Christ, this man makes me *melt*. In an instant, I'm returning his affections with gusto.

But as quickly as it started, it stops, and I'm left panting when he wrenches our mouths apart. His eyes are wild when his fingers sink into my shoulders to the point of pain.

"I will *not* let him use you! *Never,* Lillian! Not you. Not anyone, but never—never *you...*"

Tears flow from his eyes as he chokes on his own words. The bruising grip falters, sinking down my arms to my hands, which he squeezes with wordless affection. His head dips, forehead falling to my chest, and the man sobs.

Earth-shaking, heart-wrenching sobs.

For the second time in twenty-four hours, Erik soaks my lap, but this time it isn't my thighs clenching. It's my throat, as I work to swallow down tears of my own.

Fuck. It's tragic. Absolutely tragic. And I have no idea how to fix it.

I bend over him, resting my head on his back and holding him, stroking up and down his spine in long gentle scratches, soothing him in the only way I know how. I flash back to the days that Tiffany held me like this after my miscarriage, when I would just cry for hours and hours as hormones and guilt and fear and who knows what cocktail of emotions swirled endlessly through my brain.

But that was nothing compared to this. I can't even comprehend living a month without Netflix, and this man has lived hundreds of years completely alone. With only a couple of stolen Harlequins to offer him the slightest distraction from the literal monster clawing for dominance inside him.

"Let it out, Big Guy," I coo, my mouth squished against his trapezoid. "Just let it out. You're not alone anymore. You don't have to be."

The muscle under my cheek tenses and stretches as he shakes his head. "No... no, no..." is all I can make out.

I ALMOST FALL ASLEEP SCRATCHING Erik's back, folded over him on the log by the cooking fire as the sun shifts westward in the big, open sky. But eventually, he shifts himself up from my lap, eyes red from crying a thousand years worth of tears.

"I must hunt," he says at last, gathering the sharpened sticks and arrowheads by our feet.

"I can hel–"

"No. I will do this. You will read," he says, tone hard. I just nod. My legs are numb from holding our position for as long as we did, and it's going to be a bitch to get the blood flowing back into my ankle. I lean back on my walking stick and straighten out my legs and posture, and by the time the pins and needles finally ease away, Erik is gone.

I guess we're back to this.

I'm not used to a man being so... emotional after sex. Even my boyfriend of five years never acted this attached to me. He certainly wasn't protective. I remember once we got a flat on the highway on our way back from a concert, and he didn't even help me change the tire. He made conversation with an unhoused man on the sidewalk of the corner gas station while I cranked the carjack, *after* said unhoused man cat-called me while I loosened the lugnuts.

Real winner, that guy. Really shouldn't have been surprised that he peaced out after knocking me up.

I can't imagine Erik doing that. No way. He's the kind of man that would drop everything to take care of his baby mama. Even if they drifted apart. He'd still be there, providing for the kids, helping them with their homework, picking them up from soccer practice...

Picturing Erik in the modern world is wild. At once completely insane and totally natural.

I bet he'd be an amazing father.

I cradle my stomach, scolding myself as tears prick my own eyes. It doesn't hurt nearly as much as it did those first few months, of course. After I had time to process, and honestly, after Tiffany forced me to come out here for our annual girls' trip like always, I was able to see that life *does* go on.

And I haven't cried about it since. Not once, oddly enough. It was like once we came back from vacation, the grief lifted. Enough for me to get back to my life. To move on.

Of course, there will always be twinges. When Tiffany and Dean found out she was pregnant, I had a little twinge of jealousy. A few more, when he crashed our vacation this year.

And now, thinking about Erik and the life he could have, as a normal guy, with a normal wife, and two adorable little kids…

All within the realm of possibility.

My hand freezes on my lower belly as fear skitters down my spine.

It's just the tide, Lillian. Making swishing noises. It's all just a shock to the system; you're fine. Totally not hearing voices.

I get up from the log and drag myself around the campsite, shaking out the furs to the best of my ability as I lean on my walking stick. They're basically dry now, so I gather them up and arrange them back into their comfy nest in the corner of the shelter.

I debate making two. Will Erik still want to sleep next to me after this afternoon? He seemed pretty distant when he went off to go hunting.

He cannot resist you. You are his treasure. His perfect mate.

My spine snaps straight as the voice rings in my head again. Crystal fucking clear this time.

Fuck. Fuck fuck fuck.

Sweet Lillian…

Every hair on my body is standing at full attention as the familiar voice fades as it says my name. Casually, almost, like a "see you later," but creepy and powerful.

I collect the rest of the laundry as quickly as I can, slipping into my own skimpy cover-up because being naked feels too vulnerable. Using a metal scoop that Erik brought from his other cabin, I carry in some embers from the cooking fire and use them to breathe some life back into the shelter fire. Once it's lit and flames lick the little pyramid of logs I've built, I curl up under one of the fresh furs with a book, taking Erik's advice after all.

I hope it warms up soon. The shelter's got a bit of a chill all of the sudden.

CHAPTER 20

ERIK

The next morning, I wake holding Lillian tight to my body. Her breath fans across my shoulder, her hair sticks to the inside of my mouth, and her luscious curves embrace my body lovingly.

Her form is so inviting. I cannot get enough of the way we sink into each other, how holding her feels like everything is right in the world.

I have yet to hear the monster since she and I copulated. And the quiet is...peaceful.

How long has it been since I have known peace?

I bend my head into her scalp and breathe the scent of pine, sunlight, and woman. Her warmth envelops me. Her legs unconsciously tangle with mine.

Is it possible to love this woman? Someone I barely know, yet has changed me so completely?

How could she keep the monster at bay if it were not a spiritual connection between us? Something divine, holy— destined, even? Perhaps she is the salvation I have been waiting for.

Our fight the day before rings in my head. The things she almost said, before I silenced her with my lips.

But I will not think of that. Instead, I will make her breakfast and make amends for my outburst yesterday. She expressed a desire to learn the arts of survival. This is something I can teach, for as long as it takes her ankle to heal. I will enjoy her company to the utmost for every second I have her, and then when she is well enough to swim to the mainland...

I will say goodbye.

And I will not think of a day beyond that.

She stirs in my hold, and I try to shift my hips in a way that will not alarm her. I have always been virile, but in her presence my drive for sexual activities has increased immensely. My cock is at a constant aroused or semi-aroused state, particularly when she is close enough to touch and smell. My body craves her like water after a day of chopping firewood: an endless thirst that I cannot describe.

"Mmmm," she moans, and her hand moves between us. I stiffen, both my upper and lower body, as she strokes my thickening shaft. "Somebody's ready to make up."

I swallow the dry lump in my throat. "I am sorry for abandoning you yesterday."

"You came back," she mutters, still teasing me with her soft fingers. "You had a lot on your mind."

"I should not have snapped at you."

"No," she agrees. Then she tilts her head and stares at me with molten eyes. "But I can think of a great way to apologize."

She turns my body so I am lying on my back, and she straddles me, her generous ass and thighs spilling to the sides of my waist. I huff out an exhale as the split between her cheeks cradles the tip of my cock, and she scoots back until my whole shaft is lined up with the seam of her backside.

"You—your ankle–"

"Is just fine for now," she finishes my thought while shifting her weight forward and wiggling her feet to either side of us, showing off her flexibility. "Besides, I don't need my ankle to do this..."

She slides down my body, every inch of her soft front caressing my torso as she positions herself so that her face lines up with my pelvis. My mouth is bone-dry, now, as I see the plush pink pillows of her lips part as she eyes my cockhead with a look that I can only describe as *hungry*.

Her tongue darts out and swipes across her mouth, and my body reacts of its own accord. My manhood twitches beneath her chin, as if seeking out the warmth of her breath. Or perhaps–

"How long has it been since you've had your cock sucked, Erik?"

For a moment, my brain is completely and utterly blank. My vision whites out for a fraction of a second, and when I come to, Lillian is eyeing me with a devilish expression.

My shaft jumps again, and this time the vixen catches it with her tongue, curling it to graze along its notch.

I groan, bending at the waist involuntarily as a jolt sizzles up my spine. I post on elbows, watching her. "I—I do not..."

"You don't remember?" She sits up a little, pushes her breasts together under her chin and around the base of my shaft. My whole body shakes as the soft cushions embrace the sensitive skin, and I hiss at how *lewd* a picture she paints: my treasure, with the peaks of her tits staring at me like doe-eyes beneath her own sparkling blue gaze, my cock twitching and bouncing between them like an eager child.

I shake my head. Even in my youth, I have never experienced a woman between my legs in this manner. With her breasts pushed around me and her mouth–

"Ah!" I gasp as she parts her lips in an *o* and lowers herself onto me. Wet heat envelops me while the rough texture of her tongue runs up and down the underside of my shaft, and it has my whole body clenching with pleasure.

And then she does something very, very lewd indeed.

She arches her head back, opens her tits, and spits on me.

A rumble echoes in the shelter as she uses her saliva to lubricate her breasts and proceeds to swallow my cock whole—slickening the length with her slutty mouth until she kisses her breasts at its base, only to pull back and repeat the agonizing slide again.

It is demeaning. Disgusting. *Captivating.*

And I am *growling* for it.

"Mmm, you like that, don't you? I can taste your cock leaking for me."

She proceeds to speak the dirtiest things to me as she works my cock with her mouth and breasts, the words sloppy and distorted by the way she has to mold her annunciators around my erection. Somehow, the sloppiness makes it headier, more pleasurable, and she works me up until I am practically writhing on the furs.

"Lillian, please, I am about to–"

"Are you gonna come in my mouth, Erik? Fill my slutty, wet mouth with your–"

I do not know the next word she says because I explode, pleasure peaking in an unbearable lurch of my core. My hips thrust upwards, seeking their instinctive end, and I can feel the head of my cock reach the back of her throat as I spill myself inside of her.

My balls shove in between her breasts, and the pressure adds to the spiraling sensation. They draw up even harder, and another burst spurts forth, so much that I feel Lillian begin to cough and sputter around me.

"My—treasure–" I grit out through my teeth, trying to pull myself back from her, but she clamps her lips down harder around me, squeezing another spurt of seed from my cock. I shudder beneath her, a full body wave this time, and feel her nails clench my hips as she pushes her breasts even closer around me with her arms.

She hollows her cheeks, scraping her tongue around my head and poking it into the sleeve of skin that surrounds my shaft. I jolt, the uncovered length so much more sensitive than its collar.

And when she is done, she pops her mouth off of me and opens it wide so I can see that she swallowed my entire load.

I am panting when I ask, "How... does that... count as an apology?"

She gathers her hair off of her neck and rises to a seated position. "Oh, that was my apology to you. You can pay me back later. But right now, I need some water and a cut of that deer jerky we started last night."

FOR THE REST of the morning, Lillian is distant. After our breakfast, she announces that she is going to read on the beach and rest her ankle. I set about processing the rest of the doe I hunted the day before, stretching its skin upon a birch frame to cure and boiling its bones for broth and tool-making. Perhaps I can carve a comb to present to her as a parting gift.

I look over towards where she is sitting, among a pile of boulders that she was somehow able to climb, despite her injury. It is a fair distance away: visible, but far enough that she looks small and I cannot make out the details of her face.

It is difficult for me to understand why she was so affectionate this morning, only to avoid my company so wholly for the rest of the day. When I asked her if she needed anything from me after breakfast, she shrugged her shoulders, saying that she assumes I have more important things to do.

How can she say that, when I have tried to make it clear that she is the most important to me of all? I do not know how I can explain it to her in a way that she will understand. How can she say she wants to spend eternity with me on this island, when she has so little concept of how long eternity is?

She does not want eternity.

My spine straightens like a bolt at the horrible, familiar voice again. No, no, *no!* He has been so mercifully silent in the last two days!

I cannot leave you, Erik. Not until–

Silence! I will not hear of your perversions.

There is a sound of amusement in my head, a crackling hum that chills me to my very core.

And yet you allow yourself to fulfill every fantasy with your human lover outside of my influence? Interesting, interesting…

That is different. Lillian and I–

Are mates? How is that different from my divine joining with my own mate?

I shudder. It is pointless to argue with a god. He cannot possibly understand what Lillian means to me, when He is the very reason I am eternally unlovable.

Unlovable? You believe this to be true?

What other word could I use to describe myself? How could any woman subject herself to be with me? With a monster?

But you have found someone who loves you, have you not?

I search across the beach to see my sweet Lillian soaking her feet in the surf as she reads upon a large rock. My chest squeezes as I take in her delicious form, more bronze from the days we have spent in the sun.

She has barely spoken to me all morning, since our dalliance in the shelter.

She does not love me. She cannot. It is not her fault.

Interesting, interesting...

His voice fades away, and the loneliness He leaves behind is all-consuming.

And now that He is back, it is too dangerous to reach out to Lillian for comfort. It would be too great a risk.

I can never let the monster have her.

Never.

CHAPTER 21

LILLIAN

I am about to lose my fucking mind.

It's been a week since Erik rescued me from the coyote. Six days since we had sex—the most mind-blowing sex of my *life*—and started sleeping together in the shelter. Five days since the argument about me staying on the island, and four since I woke him up to what I thought had to be a pretty fucking amazing titty blowjob.

You'd *think* after all that, the dude would have caught the hint that maybe I like him? Maybe he doesn't have to be all macho-hero-save-the-girl, and maybe I could actually help *him* out?

Sure, I get it. The whole "let a Kraken knock you up and we can be free of the curse" thing is a lot to take in. It would be for any woman. But the longer I have time to sit on the idea (and the more romances I read), the more I'm like... would it really be that bad?

And who knows? Maybe my infertility will actually render the whole process moot. Maybe Phorkys will *try* to put his eggs in me and my body will be all like, "Nope! Psych!" and then everyone will realize what a disappointment I am. But instead of just ruining my life like it did the first time, my miscarriage will set Erik and me free and the gods won't release their evil babies onto the Midwest and we all can just go on with our lives.

We can't know until we try, right?

But that's the other problem. I don't even know if Erik would be willing to try anything with me anymore. Since that blowjob, the guy hasn't even *touched* me. Sure, he still snuggles up for warmth at night, but he doesn't get handsy. He doesn't go in for a kiss. He doesn't even nuzzle me and sniff my hair anymore (which, granted, is a little weird, but like, sweet, once you get used to it), except in his sleep.

He still wakes up with a giant erection, though. The second morning after our fight, I tried to give him a little relief—if you know what I mean—but he just slithered away from me to start making breakfast instead.

It's like he's afraid to get too close to me. Again. Even though we clearly demonstrated that we're compatible.

Or maybe he's more of a prude than I realized. We joked about it that first night together, but I assumed that meant that he *was* interested in sex. Maybe even some light pegging. I thought his comments about being a prude were all because of the curse.

Didn't we break past that, though, when he didn't go all Ursula Magical Girl Transformation when we had sex?

I'm so confused, I don't even know how to bring it up to the guy. So I just end up spending most of the week making my way through his bag of Harlequins, until I finally finish the last one. It only took me five days to devour a bag of books.

When I say there's nothing to do on this island except eat, read, and fuck, I mean *nothing*.

"Alright," I say at last, getting up from my reading rock

and limping over to what I now call the 'working fire,' because it's where Erik sharpens all of his spears and arrows. "I need something else to do."

The giant of a man looks up at me from his easy crouch, where he's testing the strength of some deer sinew to use as a bowstring. Which is both gross and badass.

"I thought you were enjoying your books."

"I'm out of books."

"You have read all of them?" His eyebrows raise in surprise, and it's such a vast departure from his permanent scowl of concentration that I have to hold back a snort. "How is that possible?"

"I'm a fast reader. Even with a full-time job, I usually get through three or four a week. But out here, I have nothing else to do."

He shifts his posture, examining my ankle as I talk. The bruising is all gone by now, and I can walk fairly easily where the ground is hard. On the beach, where the shifting sand is constantly testing my tensile strength and stretching the ligaments it's a little rough, but I'm better enough that I abandoned my walking stick yesterday.

His eyes are hopeful when he catches my gaze. "How are you feeling?"

"I'm..." The word 'fine' catches on my throat. If I tell Erik that my ankle is feeling better, well enough to try out a swim, he's going to want to take me back to the mainland. The last thing he said to me before this weird stand-off began was that I was to focus on recovering so we could 'put this nightmare behind us–' a phrase that felt *real* good to hear less than an hour after sucking his dick.

But despite his distance, in lieu of the unspoken tension that's stretched between the two of us for the past four days, I don't want to leave just yet.

By now, the PTO that Tiffany and I had claimed for this vacation has run out. If my calculations are correct, I was supposed to be back at the office yesterday. A no-call, no-show is a pretty unforgivable offense in any legal firm, but considering the one I work at is one of the most competitive in Chicago? I doubt I have a job waiting for me when I return.

I bite the inside of my cheek. At the thought of work, the whole reality of my situation comes crashing down on me.

I'm on a deserted island in the middle of Lake Superior. My best friend abandoned me, and maybe hasn't even cared enough to report me missing. I haven't seen any rescue crews or even vacationers in boats anywhere near us the entire time I've been recovering from my sprain. And the only human I have any contact with wants nothing to do with me.

Before I even realize there are tears in my eyes, wet trails are running down my sun-kissed cheeks, and Erik is standing before me.

"Lillian? Lillian, what is wrong? Why are you crying?"

A sob wracks my chest, and then his arms are there, wrapping around my shoulders, and I feel positively tiny in his grasp. This is more physical contact than we've had in days, and I can't resist the comforting weight of his muscled chest pressing into mine. I return his hug, smushing my face into the smooth divot between his pecs and cry, wordlessly.

He rubs his fingers up and down my back, alternating between cradling my head with one hand and running his fingers through the seemingly endless tangles. When I shift my weight, he adjusts to lift me off the ground entirely— hugging me to his chest and carrying me into the shady forest, where the tips of the canopy of foliage are just beginning to turn yellow.

There is a giant oak that's fallen and covered with soft moss a little ways in, and he sits upon it, nestling me in his lap and arranging me so I've got one arm draped over his shoulder and the other woven with his. A giant hand supports my back in a splayed grasp.

It's the closest thing to comfortable I've been since swimming away from the cabin.

"I have been cruel to you," he says, so quietly I almost can't make out the words over the sound of my own sniffling. When I do, though, I shake my head.

I mean, he hasn't been the easiest guy to be around the last few days, but that wasn't what brought me to tears.

"It isn't you, Erik," I sniffle, wiping my nose when my voice comes out all stuffy and warbled. "It's... everything else."

He holds me steady as I try to regulate my breathing, which still gets broken up every few seconds with a stuttering sob. Eventually, though, the tears slow, and I can breath through my nose without getting a mouthful of snot.

Hoo boy, I bet I look *great* right now.

But when I'm calm enough to meet Erik's eyes, he's not looking at me like I'm disgusting or ugly. His gaze is far away, as if he's looking past me instead of at me, and his lips are tilted down in a slight frown.

When he realizes I'm looking at him, he refocuses, and the overwhelming affection in his eyes is enough to set my lungs stuttering all over again.

"Please tell me what is wrong," he says, and as he does, I feel his fingers tremble against my back. "I wish to help you anyway I can."

I let out a sound that's something between a huff and a cough. "You can't help me. I mean, not with this stuff. You've already been helping me this whole time. But it's not exactly like you can write me a recommendation for a new job, or a doctor's note to my boss to make up for me not showing up to work."

"Work? What work are you talking about?"

"I have a job on the mainland. I'm a paralegal—someone who does all the actual work for a team of lawyers in the city. You know, people who argue over who's right and who owes who money when there's a big disagreement between companies."

He nods as he takes this in. "Do they disagree often?"

"Oh yeah," I snort. "Constantly. It's a big job. We're always super busy. This vacation was the only time off I had for the year; they hardly give us any vacation because they need us in the office to handle reading all of the cases and client forms and filing paperwork."

"I am sure you are very good at it. You are smart, and you read exceedingly fast."

I can't help it—I laugh. "I mean, sure, yeah, but the reading I do for work is very different from reading the books you gave me. It's not exactly something I can skim most of the time; it's exhausting. Takes a ton of focus."

"Skim?" He tilts his head. "What do you mean?"

"You know, like when you scan over a page to get to the good stuff."

He shakes his head a little, scrunching his eyebrows. The movement is surprisingly boyish, and it makes him seem younger than his 800-odd years. I try to control my face.

It's hard to stay mad around him when he's trying this hard to understand.

"That is not how I read. It is still difficult for me. My sessions are few, with many days between them, and the rarity makes it challenging."

As he says this, a blush creeps up his cheeks, as if this embarrasses him. I reach up to touch the place on his face where his pink cheek gives way to beard, the coarse hairs dotting the transition from soft skin to hard jaw.

"I could teach you." The words come out breathy, even though I don't intend for them to. He starts to lean into my fingers, then shakes his head.

"We should not..." he begins, trailing off when I let my hand trail down to the firm muscle of his pec. Dark, tribal ink swirls in patterns across his chest and arms. It's striking, and when I think about the primitive tools he would have used to mark his skin in such a permanent way in the middle ages, I shudder.

"How about this?" I shift a little in his hold, straightening my back so we're more eye-to-eye, less cuddly. "Every day, you teach me a little about hunting, and I teach you a little about reading. A trade."

He considers this.

"A trade."

"Yeah. After all, I don't have much else to do on this island while we wait for me to get strong enough to swim to shore. But I still need to get some exercise, stretch out my ankle some, otherwise the muscles will atrophy."

He hums, tilting his head at the last word, but seeming to piece it together with context clues.

"What lesson would you like first, my treasure?"

The endearment surprises me a little. He hasn't said it in a few days—hasn't said much of anything, honestly—so the sweetness in his tone gives me pause.

"Well... you were working on making a bow just now, right?"

"Yes. I have made many arrows, but my best bow is at my other shelter."

"How about we start with that?"

He slowly inclines his head, before speeding up into a true nod as he thinks it over.

"I believe this is a good way to spend our time together. We will prepare for the hunt while the sun is high in the morning, engage in exercises to strengthen you after mid-day, and then study books by firelight after dinner each night until you are well."

"What book would you like to start with?" I ask him, curious. He mentioned that he'd read every one of the stories in the bag that he gifted me, but now that I've read them all, I'm dying to know which one is his favorite.

"*The Highlander's Pirate Bride.*"

CHAPTER 22

ERIK

L illian is a very quick student.

After we walked back to our worksite on the shore, I assisted her in sitting onto the logs by the curing fire and began to explain the process of twisting sinew for the making of bowstrings.

I have a tightly woven basket of ligaments that I have already pounded into threads. She marvels at the collection, then asks about the others soaking in a carved wooden bowl of water from the lake, and listens with rapt attention as I explain how to wind three or four of the wet strands together until they bend back upon themselves, before stretching them and tying their ends on the frame that I have built.

"They dry together, which tightens their bond and locks them in the spiral shape," I say, holding up a three-ply cord that I made earlier in the day. Then I add more threads from the basket to the bowl, before offering it to her.

She nods, eyes sparkling with the desire to try it herself. I cannot help but admire her as she carefully separates three threads from the bowl and spins them deftly between her soft, gentle fingers.

"It's like spinning wool, almost," she marvels. "I had no idea ligaments were thin like this."

"They are not. You must pound them with a rock until they break apart."

Her face turns slightly green at that, so I quickly change the subject.

"The fibers are very strong. Plant fibers can also be gathered and spun in a similar way, but those are far better for static objects like baskets and shades. But for hunting, a more flexible material is better."

She has finished her string by the time I am done speaking, and she stretches it over the frame easily, despite the stiffness in her legs. With the two of us working together, we complete an entire army's worth of strings before the sky has even settled into the orangey-pink of pre-dusk.

"Well that was fun," she says, slapping her wet hands to her thighs and making the flesh there jiggle enticingly. Her lips curl up into a grin when she asks me, "what's next?"

By the time I return from the forest with dinner, my unlikely companion has whittled and quilled an entire quiver's worth of arrows. I highly underestimated her abilities. Upon seeing the pile beside her, bone-straight and well-feathered, surprise and something else—pride, perhaps?—fill my chest.

"That is so many!" I praise.

"Is it too much? How many do you need?"

Her face flushes with embarrassment, and I grin to reassure her. "It is always good to have more. This is enough for today."

Without thinking, I stoop down to kiss her pink cheek, freezing when my lips are a hair's breadth away. I hear her breathe in, and I realize my mistake.

I straighten. Then I turn and carry the skinned squirrels to the shelter for cooking.

I hear a cough from outside, before the tell-tale sound of shifting sand that lets me know she has gone for a walk.

That is good. It is important she stretch her legs and build up her muscular endurance. I am not sad in the least that she is gone.

I do not long for her. I do not desire to kick myself for making her feel unwanted, like I do every morning when I pull myself from her arms.

Liar.

I do not need to justify my actions to you.

What about her?

What about her? She knows the reasons I cannot submit to my desires. I have explained what is at stake.

Hmm.

"Why do you insist on being so cryptic?" I shout, banging the cooking spits against their supports and almost snapping the thin wood. My anger is all the more fiery for the despair that saturates it. I resent the voice for coming back more than I ever did for it existing in the first place. Its crimes are far more abhorrent when juxtaposed against their absence. I stare at the heavy, iron pot in the corner of the shelter, the one in which I boil bones for broth and skins for leather-making. I consider bashing it against my own head, if only for a moment of silence.

You call me cryptic, but it is you whose actions are without logic, human.

I scoff. "I do not expect a monster to understand. What do you know of protection? Of affection?"

I know a great deal. More than you.

What makes you say that? I revert back to mind-speak as I worry that Lillian may return to hear me talking to myself.

My lover and I communicate. Even when we quarrel, separating for centuries at a time, I am still honest with my feelings. I do not know another way to be.

I have been nothing but honest with Lillian.

Is that so? Were you honest when you denied her affections? Honest, when you made her feel as though she were undesirable?

My self-righteous indignation turns to ash in my mouth. I reach for the water skin, only to find that it is empty.

I stand and leave the shelter, heading to the lake shore to refill it. When I emerge from the forest, Lillian is standing at its edge, watching the horizon over the water.

Her face is slack and unreadable. She has not noticed me, and I do not want her to.

So I slink away like the detestable creature I am, unable to face my own companion for fear of seeing my sins in her eyes.

CHAPTER 23

LILLIAN

"Alright. Here's how we're going to do this."

Erik's been quiet all dinner—even more than usual, which is saying a lot, considering he's barely spoken to me all week. I thought we may have gotten over the whole "stay away from me, temptress," phase of our relationship when we decided to teach each other life skills earlier today, but that must have just been a fleeting fancy for my Viking camp counselor.

I'm beginning to think that's all he is. Hot one minute, cold the next. I wonder which came first: the Kraken possession or the mood swings. Would he be less contradictory if the curse was broken, or was he broken before?

It's hard to think he's a bad person, not when it's obvious how much he doesn't want to hurt me. He winces whenever our hands touch, and then winces at the wincing, like he feels bad for letting his regret show when he can't stick to his own strict no-touching policy.

He faces me full-on when I speak, and for the first time in hours I make eye contact with the man. He has circles under his eyes, something I've noticed has gotten worse the longer we've been avoiding each other.

"How we are doing what?"

"Teaching you to read," I answer. *Duh,* I want to say, but he didn't have TV during the 90s and likely wouldn't understand the slang.

His language is so proper. I haven't heard him use a contraction once the entire time we've been cozied up together. I'd like to teach him some more modern speech, but sadly all of the books he's got in his collection are from forever ago, like he started collecting them in the 1940's. I'd kill for a book that came out in the past decade, but I'm pretty sure the newest volume in his collection was published in 1978, and it's a historical romance. So we're out of luck.

I wave the worn mass-market paperback of *The Highlander's Pirate Bride* at him, the faded, oil-painting cover of a dark-haired Fabio type clutching a skinny, big-breasted, raven-haired beauty in a peasant shirt, her back bowed over his muscular forearm like he's dipping her in a tango. The red-tinted sky glows in the flickering light of the cooking fire, which I just freshly stoked to give us more light to read by.

It's the light that I'm worried about. Out here on the shore of Lake Superior at night, the water sucks every ounce of light from the sky like an inkblot. With the fire, we can see well enough to eat and drink and avoid bumping into each other, but it's not ideal for reading. Especially this old, tiny print.

While I'd initially thought we could sit side by side and sound out the words one by one, my fingers cast shadows over the text whenever I try. So I had to come up with a new plan.

I pat the furs beside me, laying down so my hair (which is still wet from my evening bath) can dry closest to the fire, with my feet brushing the angled wall of our teepee-like shelter. "Come on over and lay down. I'm gonna hold the book up like this–" I demonstrate, straightening my arms and tilting the open paperback so it catches the full force of the fire's light above my head– "and we're going to read together. You'll follow along with your finger as I read aloud each word."

I tilt my head back, squinting at him sitting behind the glow of the flames.

"I am to... lay beside you?"

"Yes."

I figured he'd have a problem with that. I'll admit, the light source is not my only reason for choosing this position. I want to force him to face his hypocrisy a little bit. I'm tired of being treated like some teddy bear he's trying to grow out of.

I know he likes me. He's said as much. And I'm going to force him to start *showing* me he's not disgusted by being close to me.

I suspect this has something to do with the monster, which is why he hasn't said anything about it. He seemed so happy, so relieved when we had sex and it didn't draw out Phorkys. I want to remind him that it's possible for us to be close without triggering the monster inside him. That we can be friends.

Maybe more than friends.

At least friends-with-benefits.

Because, let's be real, I'm not about to read this steamy pirate fucking novel again without getting a little physical relief. And, considering Erik and I are rooming together for the foreseeable future, he's going to have to rein in the monster long enough for me to get off in his presence.

Finally, he rises from his seat on the other side of the lean-to and lays himself down on the fur beside me, his long hair fanning out next to mine. I wasn't sure how I felt about his 80's rock band hairdo when I saw him on the beach that first day, but I've gotten used to it now, and it's actually kind of a turn-on. I like that I was able to grip it when he was eating me out, and the way it fell over us when he pushed himself inside me, tickling the sides of my face and my chest as he moved, was pretty hot.

It reminded me of when some of my past boyfriends used to tell me how they liked my long hair. I thought it was just because they liked to hold it like a ponytail when I'd give them a blowjob, but I'm beginning to think there's more to it than that. It's not just a convenient handle. There's something sensual about the strands falling around your lover's face, framing their eyes and the curve of their jaw...

"What now, Lillian?"

I blink, Erik's expectant face swimming into view as I refocus on the task at hand.

I clear my throat. "Right! Um... let's start with chapter one, I guess." I flip past the title page. "Here we go. I'm going to read aloud slowly, and I want you to move your finger to point to each word as I say it. Okay?"

He nods wordlessly, and raises his index finger to the pulpy, cream pages and points as I read the heading.

"Chapter One. Boarded by the Pirate Queen.

"The water's gentle waves were red on the night of the attack. The glow of the sun's yellow light was hazy behind the smoke of cannons..."

My pace is glacial at first. With every word, I take a little pause, indicating to him that it's time to scoot his finger forward. At first, Erik furrows his brow in concentration at the end of each word, waiting for me to stop before moving to the next one. Eventually, though, I'm able to increase in speed as he adjusts to the cadence of my voice and is able to match the sounds more quickly.

We're a few paragraphs in when he stops me.

"What is that word?"

"Lieutenant?"

"Say it again."

I sound it out, more slowly this time. He scrunches his nose, and I suppress a smile. The fact that his face can look so cute when he's confused is ridiculous. If I weren't holding a book, I'd want to pinch his cheeks.

"There are three letters between the L and the T," he says, "and none of them make the "oo" sound. Why do you say them like O's?"

I explain that sometimes, multiple letters together make different sounds, and we spend the next few minutes finding more examples that I sound out for him. Shore. Cruel. Waist. Through. Breathe.

"Why does the letter E sometimes get spoken, and sometimes not?"

"That's called a silent E," I explain. Although, as I say it, I realize it doesn't actually answer the question. "I'm not sure why, exactly. English can be weird sometimes."

I chuckle to myself when I say "weird," remembering that it's one of the words I'd always misspell because it breaks the "I before E" rule we were taught in English class. When Erik raises his eyebrows in question, I shake my head.

"Nothing, nothing. It's just funny. I guess I haven't thought about how tough reading and writing can be since… well, since I was learning. It's been a while." I turn on my side a little, until it's easier to meet his eyes. I let the book fall to my hip, holding the page with the thumb of my right hand while I prop myself up on my elbow. "You said you read these books before."

His cheeks turn pink, and it makes me want to pinch his cheeks all over again. How can someone so undeniably manly look so boyish in certain lighting?

"I can understand some of the words. The simple ones. I have other books at my more permanent shelter… ones I believe are intended for children. On long summer afternoons, when I was too tired to work or had completed all of my preparations early, I would go between practicing on my own and attempting to read the stories that were more appropriate for an adult."

"That's really impressive, Erik."

"People have lived and campled on these lands for many years, Lillian. I have overheard many conversations, and witnessed many children learning from their parents. It is not *impressive* that I was able to glean the meaning of some words in so long a time."

"But you were alone," I argue. "Anything is hard to learn without a good teacher."

He swallows, and a shadow passes behind his eyes, almost like he's keeping something from me. I wish he wouldn't do that. I know that I have no right to hear his whole life story, as I've only known him for a little over a week, but I feel like he already knows me better than most of the people in my life back in Chicago. Other than Tiffany and my therapist.

"You can tell me, you know. If it has to do with the monster. You can be honest with me."

His eyes shine with emotion, and his voice cracks when he opens his lips. "I cannot."

"If you can't tell me, who can you tell? We're both cursed, Erik. We're both stuck here."

"But you can be saved."

"You could, too. If you just trusted me–"

"I wish you would refrain from speaking of this," he says, sitting up abruptly. I follow, wrapping an arm over his shoulders and trying to parse out the look on his face, but it's hidden behind the shadow of his hair.

"It isn't right that you deal with it all alone. I can help."

"You are already." He faces me then, and that's when I see it. Tears fall silently down his cheeks. His calloused hand grips my thigh as he takes a deep breath and continues. "You are right. It is unfair to you, to resist your charms so inconsistently. It gives you the wrong impression."

"What's the right impression?"

"That I cannot be with you in the way I want to. Because He..." He closes his eyes, tilting his head down with a pained expression on his face. I reach up to smooth the lines creasing the corners of his eyes, wanting to see the understanding dawn on his face when I say my next words.

"Erik, I want you. I want to be with you. And I believe that you're strong enough to be with me."

"But you do not *know*," he pleads, grabbing my hands and cradling them between his. "What if I hurt you? What if *He* hurts you?"

I will not hurt Lillian.

We both jump at Phorkys's voice. Fuck, I forgot how *low* it is, how gravelly and all-consuming, and how it makes my whole body tremble with its power. Maybe it's because I was only half-conscious last time I heard Him, or maybe it's because we were underwater at the time, but now that I'm fully aware of everything that's happening and not in denial about the curse...

It's a lot. It's scary. I see my fear mirrored in Erik's eyes as we stare at each other, unblinking, as if maybe, if we stay as still as fucking possible, the monster will leave us alone.

A low, long-suffering sigh seems to fill the entire shelter, almost as if the earth itself is taking a breath. And then something absolutely crazy coo-coo bananas happens.

A tentacle brushes my cheek.

CHAPTER 24

ERIK

What are you doing? I want to scream it, but I am paralyzed. Lillian's eyes are blue-flecked orbs that dance with fear in the firelight as a powerful, prehensile limb that is entirely outside of my control caresses her face.

It is attached to my body. Without realizing it, I allowed Phorkys to transform my lower half into that of the monster, giant and writhing, curling its tentacles along the base of the shelter walls as far from the fire's heat as they can manage.

Except for one. One of them has its suckers set on my treasure.

You do not need to be afraid, Lillian. This is what you asked for, is it not? You wished to know what Erik was afraid of. Well here I am.

"You... you're on land."

Yes.

"And you... you can take over his body."

Yes. It is not difficult.

"I thought… When we had sex–" Lillian's eyes search mine, and I realize she is speaking to me now, and not the monster. Looking to me for guidance. Reassurance. Truth.

I open my mouth to answer her, but I cannot form words. Another sigh rings in our minds as Phorkys once again loses patience with my inaction.

I granted you privacy, yes. But I did not disappear. I cannot. I have been very clear about the terms of the curse.

Lillian swallows, and I watch the movement as it slithers down her neck. "So that's it, then? You're taking my body, whether I want it or not? Just like you took his?"

The seconds that follow are long. Painful. I do not breathe as Phorkys keeps his silence, torturing us both.

No. I am not.

The gasp she takes in is one of surprise and desperation. She, too, was holding her breath.

"Why not?"

Has Erik told you there was another maiden once, a maiden that he admired?

She nods, sympathy in her gaze as she searches my face. "Yes."

I do not want you to meet the same end.

Lillian closes her eyes, then takes a shaky inhale before nodding once.

The tentacle moves lower, brushing its tip over her collarbone, wrapping back upon itself to wind around her shoulder, then swirl around the curve of her breast. She trembles at its attention, and I hold back a curse as I watch.

I can feel it. Feel her soft, heated skin as the appendage skirts across it. I take in the supple weight of her breast as if I were cupping it in my own hand when the tentacle curls beneath the swell of it. And I can feel the slight resistance of her firm nipple as it plucks it with one of its many cups.

She gasps again, involuntarily this time.

Just as I use your body for my purposes, Erik, I will remind you: you, too, can use mine.

Another tentacle sweeps toward us, wrapping Lillian up by the waist and coiling about her, squeezing in a gentle embrace that has me reveling in the sensation of her soft skin all about me. It is *me*, I realize. *My* limb holding her, *my* cups plucking at the pebbled pink skin that peaks her luscious breasts, *my* insatiable tentacles itching with impatience to reach and feel every inch of her beautiful body.

Somewhere amidst the mass of powerful limbs, I feel my cock thicken with desire. I know without looking that it is, in fact, mine—my *human* organ—and that, if I wished it, I could bury it inside her as I did that night without impregnating her with the monster's brood.

Her eyes, which fluttered closed in pleasure as I kneaded her chest, open hastily at the Phorkys's words. There is heat there, so much fire that I can see is not just the campfire's flames reflected, but from within.

You desire this? I ask her, using mind speak without realizing it.

Blood rushes to her cheeks as she seems to come back into herself. She had succumbed to the pleasure, as I had, and now she is taking in the absurdity of it all. The terror of my half-shifted form. The repulsiveness of it all.

This was a mistake. Phorkys never should have interrupted us, not when she is not yet well enough to escape, not when we were just beginning to repair whatever friendship between us could be salvaged—

"Yes."

She whispers the single word, and my very heart ceases to beat. I cannot have heard her correctly.

Phorkys purrs.

Enjoy, humans.

CHAPTER 25

LILLIAN

My body is suspended in the stifling air of our lakeside shelter, my head inches from the slanted roof. Erik's—Phorkys's?—tentacles are wrapped around my waist and legs, lifting me with three while pawing at my breasts with two more, as the remaining three spill about the cabin as if searching for even more of me to explore. I swallow greedily as Erik searches my eyes with disbelief.

"Lillian. My treasure, you wish–"

"Yes," I practically gush (well, to be honest, I've been gushing ever since Erik's transformation), panting as I feel the thick tentacles pulse around me and knead into my flesh. "Fuck yes!"

I expect to see disappointment, disgust, or panic on his face. After all, Erik has been crucifying himself over his monstrous half the entire time we've been together on this little island. I can only assume that he finds my perversion disgusting. Wrong. Unforgivable, even.

Maybe this is the moment when he'll finally learn that of the two of us, *I'm* the real deviant, the actual monster:

craving things like tentacle sex so much that I'm having literal wet dreams about it on a near daily basis ever since drowning in the lake. Ever since I read that book. Ever since I learned it was possible, my thighs have been squeezing at the mere suggestion that the monster might take over his body and claim me for its own.

To be fair, my mind always kind of glosses over the "being filled with Phorkys's eggs" part of that equation. I haven't even thought about the possibility of kids (let alone *monster demigod* kids) since the doctor's diagnosis of my infertility. The idea that I could literally birth a brood of aquatic young is dubious at best, so why even consider it? Why let that stop me from living out a literal fantasy of hot tentacle sex?

Especially if I get to look at Erik's top half while it all happens.

Another rush of fluid warms my upper thighs as I take in my captor. His linebacker-wide shoulders. His eight-pack abs. His arms, Jesus *fucking* Christ his arms that are as thick around as my fucking calves—*fuck* me this man is exquisite. Half of the reason I've been going so mad over the past four days is because it's been agony to be rejected by him every night since our crazy hot hookup.

I've only known him for a week, but I already *miss* the guy, dammit.

He's sweet and considerate and gorgeous and...

And he's looking at me with so much heat, my entire core is set alight.

His eyes are glowing with lust. Not monster-glowing, not the fluorescent cyan that I saw in the underwater cave when I was first rescued and cursed. No, his eyes are like black opals in the light of the fire: the crystal gray smokey with desire and flickering with the embers of every possible thing he's about to do to me.

It's heady as fuck, and I'm here for every second of it.

"You know what you are asking of me?" He growls, and yep—another gush. *Fuck* I'm drenched for him. "What I plan to do to your pert–" he plucks a nipple, and I whimper– "round–" the tip of a free tentacle grazes down my ribs, and my voice turns into a whine– "*eager* body?"

"Tell me," I pant, lashes fluttering across my cheeks as I lean my head back in pure bliss and anticipation—

"*Eyes!*" He bellows, and fuck if my whole body doesn't snap open at the command, finding his fiery gaze in an instant.

A toothy smile I can only describe as feral uncurls across his face like a bow. "I am going to explore it with every limb until you release each precious piece from your chest of treasure. I'm going to take it all. Every jewel, every creamy drop of honey, and every sweet song that crosses your lips. I will make you sing for me, my bird. Only for me. Until *my* monster is satisfied."

My mouth gapes as I stare at him, this poor tortured soul who looks as though he's finally been set free from his captor. His human fingers ghost across my face, swiping away a few errant hairs and tucking them behind my ear before curling around my jaw and cupping my cheek tenderly.

Warmth swims in his gaze, gooey and affectionate for a moment, the tiniest respite from the hunger that accompanied his words. Like he's asking one last time for my permission to free the beast he's kept hidden from me since the moment we first spoke.

"Take me, Erik."

And he does.

. . .

THE LIMBS WRAPPED around my calves twist themselves further up my thighs, bending my knees up as my waist is drawn down and baring my center until I'm hovering spread-eagle in front of Erik's chest. Two more tentacles sweep forward to cushion my back and shoulders and secure my arms behind my back, and I'm amazed at the sheer size of this half-man, half-octopus form of his.

I don't even know if an octopus this size exists in nature, with arms easily twelve feet long or more, and thick as tree trunks where they split from his waist, twisting and expanding from his obliques and obscuring any human organs that might still be hiding out under the massive collection of tentacles. His body takes up the entire lean-to. While it wasn't ever that big of a shelter, it was still the size of a small bedroom. Seeing the grayish-purple arms folded and curled across every inch of ground and wall and gripping my body with their little suckers is...

Well, it's terrifying. Exhilarating.

Hot, I think to myself, as the image of his tentacles thrusting in and out of me, holding my wet, glistening pussy lips open as a sucker attaches to my clit and the limbs alternate, pushing and pulling me to orgasm–

A low, sexy chuckle rumbles through his chest, sending a vibrating shockwave through each of the tentacles wrapped around me. I shudder at the sensation, and I feel my empty insides clench with desire. I've got to be leaking like a faucet down there. I've never been more aroused in my life.

Your thoughts are so loud, my treasure, he speaks to me in my mind. *Loud and erotic and delightful.*

It's like something in him snapped when I admitted

that I wanted this. The steel threads of control he used to contain this form have frayed and split, and he is embracing his full self in this moment, monster and all. And if I thought he was sexy before? It's nothing compared to this.

This Erik isn't afraid of what he wants. Not anymore.

And I'm more than happy to let him take it.

Then shut me up, Viking, I tease back. *Make it so I can't think of anything but you.*

I'm still spread before him, held aloft by his giant tentacles, and he's yet to even finger me. Then again, I'm so keyed up just from this, I doubt it'll take me long at all to–

"Oh God!" I wail, as two things happen in concert to make me almost come on the spot.

First, two thick fingers thrust inside me and curl at just the right angle, tucking behind my pubic bone where that secret, sensitive spot hides. And then, the tiniest suction cup at the end of his last free tentacle closes around my clit.

It's like he just targeted my pleasure centers in a controlled demolition. Every muscle in my body spasms and clenches in pure ecstasy as he wiggles his fingers mercilessly inside me while his tentacle does this pulsey-sucky thing on my clit that has me seeing stars.

My vision goes black as I shudder from head to toe, flailing helplessly in his hold while I come undone.

I don't feel it happen, but I hear it. The sound of his fingers thrusting inside me goes from "stirring mac and cheese" to "belly flop at a waterpark."

I just squirted—*hard.*

My eyes burst open and I look down just in time to see a literal fountain of fluid lessen to a trickle, leaving a mess of clear liquid dripping from Erik's cheeks and beard. My face turns up to about a thousand degrees as I'm flooded with embarrassment. I'm about to apologize for the absolute mess I just made, but then I see his expression.

His eyes are lit up like a goddamn Christmas tree, and his tongue darts out to lick at the liquid covering his face like he's Augustus Gloop at Willy Wonka's fucking Chocolate Factory.

My orgasm is building too quickly for me to take in more, and my head falls back with pleasure as another wave starts to crest. It's his fingers—they're *relentless*. Pushing and curling and scraping against my g-spot with unending fervor, while the kiss-like pulses of his tentacle pull at my clit in a perfect rhythm.

When two more suction cups attach at my nipples, I know I'm done.

I cry out, eyes fluttering open in time to see another gush of fluid burst out of me like a fountain. Erik's eyes burn with satisfaction as he sees me fall apart a second time, tracking my pleasure in every part of my body: from the spurting geyser at my core, to my trembling breasts being massaged by his tentacles, up to my face, which is flushed and twisted with pleasure as I scream from the violence of my release.

A bed of tentacles cradles and pushes my ass up to his face, and his tongue laps at me, swirling around my folds. His beard and mustache tickle the sensitive skin of my thighs and bury in between my lips, scrubbing my most intimate parts as he wiggles his face back and forth and sucks my pussy greedily.

Laps turn to nibbles, nibbles to kisses. He trails his mouth lower. The tentacle takes back up the mantle of keeping my clit and pussy satisfied as his nose pokes against the stretch of skin between my holes, and I wriggle ineffectively.

"Erik!" I gasp. "That's–"

"Have you ever explored this hole, Lillian?" He asks, stroking a single finger up and down along the crease of my ass. A shiver runs through me.

I've been waiting for this since our little talk about butt sex back on that first night together.

The contact feels good when he does it, despite the fact that the few times I *have* engaged in anal I haven't really enjoyed it all that much. It takes a long time to work me up to it, and none of my partners in the past have been patient enough to take things at my pace. And they never use enough lube. But I also don't know how to spell all of this out for him while I'm still reeling from the most intense orgasm I've ever experienced.

He pulls back, and the limbs wrapping and teasing me let up a bit. I exhale, my body trembling still from after-shocks, as my nipples and clit are exposed to the relatively cool air of the shelter. Slowly, I reconnect with my body and breathe.

The fire has died back some. I must have lost track of time as Erik fucked me with his fingers. It felt instant, me coming when he touched me, but as I look around the shelter I wonder just how long Phorkys was speaking to us, how many minutes Erik waited before finally taking me at my word.

If it's easier... his voice whispers in my head, and I physically sigh with relief as I realize I don't have to find exact words if I just let him into my head. Still, I do my best to order my thoughts.

I've tried it. It's never felt that good. It takes a while to work me up... my explanation fades away, and I can tell that he's trying to read the unwinding threads of my spinning mind. I see his gaze dart to the fire, and in a flash three tentacles grasp at logs and toss them onto the dying blaze without adjusting their grip on me in the slightest.

Having eight separate, prehensile limbs in addition to two arms must be pretty fucking nice.

It has its advantages, Erik admits to me, shrugging. I grin. *You wondered how I was able to build my shelters... it helps to have more than two hands.*

One tentacle grabs a plate and uses it as a bellows to fan the flames, while another brushes some hair out of my face. The two at my pussy slowly resume their soft suckles and strokes. Yet another teases up the back of my legs, wedging itself in between my cheeks and finding my puckered hole.

A puff of breath resembling an "oh!" falls from my lips as the tiniest tip of the limb squishes itself against the tight ring, wiggling back and forth without pressing too far forward.

It feels odd at first, the easy, insistent pressure, then kinda nice. I find my eyes fluttering shut as I push back a little into the gentle probing and...

Oh.

It's like the tightness just falls away, opening up to allow the tentacle easily past the outer ring, where it pushes ever so slightly inside until it reaches resistance again. I clench, but Erik's hand strokes my thigh, and I meet his gaze.

"It is okay, my treasure. I will not hurt you."

The confidence with which he says those five words releases the last bit of tension lingering in my heart.

I hadn't realized how much his fear had been weighing on me. It's really hard to give yourself over to someone who keeps telling you how broken they are. I've been wanting to trust him, believed I could, but he wouldn't let me in.

It made me wary of him these last few days, and I was

still holding onto some of that fear… but looking at him now, meeting his eyes and seeing the confidence there as he embraces his monstrous form, as he allows *me* to embrace him…

The final brick in the wall between us crumbles away.

My life as I knew it is over. And even if I had a chance of returning, I know now that I wouldn't want to. Not when I could accept my circumstances and end up with a man like this.

No, not just a man *like* Erik.

Erik.

I want to give everything to this man, this beast. Who fought so hard to keep the humans of this land safe from an evil he didn't fully understand. Who stood sentry at the precipice of an army of demigods swarming the Great Lakes, and stopped them in their tracks. Who would have let himself wallow away in loneliness and never feel the love of a woman—as a man *or* a monster—if the terrifying god living inside him didn't set him free.

He deserves more than I could ever give him.

But he wants me. And I want him.

"I know you won't," I whisper.

"Will you let me take you like this?" He asks, as if I haven't already given him permission to take me every way he could possibly imagine.

"I'm yours, Erik. Take me."

CHAPTER 26

ERIK

I take in the sight of the spectacular woman spread before me. Her skin is flushed and dotted with perspiration, her thighs soaked from her release, and she lies back on a nest of limbs that ebb and flow beneath her.

Each moment I spend with her is a surprise. She welcomes every challenge; any setback to her freedom is merely something to be overcome. Even now, as I surround her with my monstrous form, she accepts me with open arms.

By nature, I resist this form on land, but there have been moments I have itched for the efficiency it affords me. But its convenience comes with a price. Phorkys is present just below the surface. I feel Him lending me this body as I always do; it is the source of my fear, the simmering itch of his presence that whispers in my mind, urging me to take whatever I desire.

But something has changed. Instead of the loud impatience to which I have grown accustomed, the monster seems content to merely hum in the background of my mind.

At first, He overwhelmed my lower half when Lillian requested intimacy. But by the time I realized what had happened, she had already seen. I thought, in that moment, that I lost her. That my weakness finally revealed to her how wretched I truly am.

I never could have guessed that instead of fear, she would greet the monster with...

No. I shall not dwell, nor shall I question the blessings of Odin. I will not doubt her sincerity, even if it does defy nature.

I have been granted a glorious gift: my treasure, spread before me, and an abundance of limbs with which to cherish her.

All of my arms surround her. Suckers pinch and attach to sensitive points across her body, latching onto the creases of her knees and the hollow of her throat. Arms twist about her ribcage, massaging her trunk and exploring the stretch of her soft skin. Tips brush against her nipples and clitoris, stiffening the pink buds into turgid peaks. The tentacle probing her backside pulses and twists against the inner ring of muscles, and I delight in the sensation of her.

The way I perceive the world in my shifted form is so much louder, so much brighter than that of my human form. My arms are only the beginning. The texture of her skin is mapped in a thousand nerve endings at my finger-tips, translating and relaying from limb to limb to communicate how best to serve her pleasure. The cups that pluck and tease her pink, pebbled nipples take in every pucker and quiver of her softness, resonating with each shudder.

Their reactions inform the slow binding twist of my arms at her waist, raising or lowering her as needed to coax the perfect gasp from her pouting lips.

Vision becomes feeling, sound becomes taste, as my

senses coalesce. Every limb becomes its own center for thought and sensation: seeing, tasting, smelling. As I explore her with my tentacles, it is as if I am seeing and tasting every place I touch.

Every sense, consumed by Lillian.

Her body rumbles with a moan, and I feel it radiate through my limbs. Oh, how I glory in her happiness!

Of course, I do not merely explore her for her pleasure. Every sensation in her body is magnified in mine. Each shudder and gasp sets my nerves alight with rapturous sparks, relaying across my skin like a lightning storm. It makes me greedy, hungry for more of her. I want to draw out every ounce, drink it from her pores, until she is completely sated.

Lillian unfolds under my attention like the treasure map of the Pirate Queen from the book she reads to me; I follow every twist and turn across her latitudes to find my prize at the end.

She is the journey, and she is the destination.

My treasure.

She gasps as the words ring true in her mind as they do in mine, a mantra I cannot resist repeating again and again as I push and pulse against her entrance. A moan like music falls from her lips, and I can no longer resist tasting her on my tongue.

I dive between my limbs, dropping my head between her slick folds once more and glorying in the salty tang of her. Every sense becomes taste as her juices saturate my tongue. She reminds me of the ocean. Of my life, hundreds of years since past, when I, too, crossed an ocean in search of gold and glory.

Erik!

Her beautiful voice rings in my mind as her body opens

to me, and my tentacle pushes deeper inside. It is time to fulfill her fantasies, the ones she hides within her mind. The shelter becomes dappled and unfocused at the edges of my vision as my tentacles begin to secrete a lubricating gel. It is frustrating, as it clouds my vision, but I know it will make the process more pleasurable for her.

My tentacles see and feel as one sensation. Slick with their secretion, they probe her back hole, relaying shivers of pleasure throughout my body as she squeezes me. My human organ responds enthusiastically as the pressure travels from the ends of my limbs to my center. It is almost as good as if I were thrusting my cock inside her, the sensation is so complete. She writhes above me, and her sweet honey thickens around my tongue.

She is close. Her pussy leaks into my mouth as I thrust inside of her ass.

Do you like the feel of me inside you? My tentacles twist within her, the suckers scraping against her inner walls, and her hips buck. *Tell me, please.*

Yes, she replies, and it is like a whimper even as she thinks it. I smile into her center, rubbing her swollen button with my nose. It is my favorite quirk of female anatomy, this bundle of nerves above her center. I breathe in the scent of her womanhood, heady and tangy, and it amplifies the sensations ricocheting through my limbs.

She keens. "Yes, God—Erik, *yes!*"

Through it all, I do not hear an iota of shame or fear. How is it that I have been so blessed to have been found by such a woman as Lillian? With a sharp tongue and clever mind, a curious spirit, hair like the fairest gold and a body that could launch a thousand ships? If I were not so sure of my own damnation, I would swear that I had at last passed from this mortal torture and been rewarded with Valhalla.

Until she clenches down upon my tentacle, and the overwhelming grip pulls me back to earth.

My own release threatens to spill forth as my torso tightens with ecstasy.

The rest of my limbs squirm in impatience, seeking the peak of the pleasure building within me. I feel every bit of contact with my limbs as if it is a hundred fingertips, sensitive and probing, seeking, yearning. I want to surround her with my body, only to drown inside her soft and welcoming heat.

It's so good, Erik! She screams to me wordlessly, her mouth slack and drooling around a wordless cry. *How is it so good?*

It is you, I think. *You are incredible, my treasure. I want you. I need you...*

Her eyes find mine, and the connection of our gaze threatens to overwhelm me. It is like our first night together, when she prevented me from losing myself, except now...

I know the fire burning in her eyes is not some outside force. It is not Keto, just as mine is not Phorkys. We are still Lillian and Erik. Our bodies can contain a heat that burns hotter than that of mere mortals. Together, we are more than human. We are–

"Lillian!" I scream, and then her face swims out of view. My tentacles reach of their own accord, wrapping her in my full embrace. I entwine her arms and legs and trunk with all of my limbs, drawing her closer until our centers grind together. Her lower lips, slippery with want, split around the length of my cock, and my entire body trembles with the anticipation of burying myself within her.

"Fuck!" I hear her voice, muffled amidst the mass of swirling tentacles, and I part the sea of limbs to find her face. Her cheeks, pink with excitement, dimple from the force of her giddy grin. "You know how to manhandle a girl, dontchya?"

"I do not see a girl." I pull her in closer, brushing away the errant strands of gold that fly about her face. I comb my fingers through her long, soft locks, then cradle the nape of her neck in my hand as I press my lips to hers. "Only a woman. And I will handle her in any way she permits."

She crashes her mouth back to mine, swiping her tongue against my lips until I open for her. When she penetrates me with her tongue, I return the favor: lining myself up against her entrance and sliding home.

It is *bliss*.

Sweet, perfect bliss.

She groans into my mouth, and I feel her arms wriggle against my hold. A series of small *pops* sound as I peel my suckered tentacles off of her upper half, and she uses her newfound freedom to wrap herself around my shoulders. She drapes over me, her small, human fingers digging into the meat of my back and denting my skin with her nails. My tentacles surround us, and I sink into her body in every way I know how.

My senses are on fire. Everything is more intense in this form—even my human parts are alive with touch and smell and taste and sight. I taste her wherever our bodies make contact, which is everywhere. Every point our bodies grip, squeeze, and rub together is like her essence exploding upon my tongue.

Even as I let her go, she grasps me right back, and I return the sensual embrace by twisting my freed arms—human and otherwise—around her back.

She sighs as she rubs herself up and down my length. I use my grip on her legs to assist her, suctioning hard around her thighs and binding her in spirals down to her ankle—making sure to keep the grip around her injury gentle. I pulse her body up and down, meeting her with a rhythm of my own as my hips move in concert with my limbs.

She weaves her fingers through my hair, and even that sets my senses aflame. The world dims around me to accommodate the overwhelm buffeting each of my other senses: as taste and feel become more intense, sight and sound fade away, until it is like we are once again underwater.

This is how I feel pleasure, the monster whispers. My eyes burst open to see if Lillian hears His voice, but her head is thrown back and her eyes fluttering closed, a soundless cry of pleasure floating on her pillowy lips. My own eyes shutter as I allow my sight to dim once more, assured that He whispers only to me.

It is incredible, I confess to Him. *I did not know it was possible to feel pleasure so complete.*

More awaits you, Erik. If you seek it...

The voice fades, as all the sound around me fades, and my sense of touch encompasses me completely. The wet velvet of Lillian's channel squeezes my cock as I bottom out inside her, and my entire monstrous body clenches from head to tips.

My arms and legs constrict, practically crushing the woman in my grip, but I cannot stop now. We are tied together in a knot of overwhelming pleasure, the waves of sensation cresting until–

Erik!

Lillian!

I explode. A jet of my release bursts within her, and the *feeling* of it is so overwhelming it is as if I can *see* the streams penetrate and fill her womb. My senses blend and twist until I no longer know what is real and what is a sex-induced hallucination.

Lillian gasps and I loosen my grip on her immediately, worry assaulting me. Odin help me if I ever hurt this woman...

But she is trembling. Not with fear, or pain.

All-consuming pleasure.

Shaking, her fingers spread and gnarled like claws, she consumes me as wholly as I have her. The sounds emanating from her break through the sense-queer fog and overwhelm encompassing my brain, and when her voice hits my ears, pure happiness fills my chest.

"Yes! *Yes!* Fuck, *Erik*, yes!"

She squeezes me again, and I allow myself once more to give over to pure touch, pure sensation, as her climax crests with mine.

More awaits you, Erik. If you seek it...

CHAPTER 27

LILLIAN

I'm pretty sure Erik and I both pass out after we share what feels like a marathon of orgasms. My God, if the Guinness World Record people had been around to record that, we'd both be in the book for "most intense and all-consuming sexual experience."

Then again, I'm pretty sure you have to be human to get a Guinness World Record. And I'm not wholly convinced that either of us *are* human anymore.

When I wake, Erik's arms are wrapped around me. His legs (human legs—the tentacles disappeared some time after the multitude of orgasms) weave in between mine, pressing his semi-hard cock into the small of my back. His hands paw at my breasts from behind, feeling me up even in his sleep as if he can't get enough of me.

Truth be told, I'm already aching for him again, despite still being able to feel the massive amount of cum he filled me with dripping from my thighs and soaking the fur beneath us.

Seriously. We're lying in a fucking puddle of the stuff, and it's looking like I'm going to need to clean our bedsheets all over again, despite the fact that I literally just did laundry in the lake yesterday. *Sigh.* I guess that's just the price we pay for pleasure.

In the back of my mind, there's a nugget of anxiety, though. Towards the end of our lovemaking, I could've sworn I heard a voice. Not Erik's, and not Phorkys's, but the one I've been trying to ignore. The one that I know I've heard before, but can't place.

A woman's voice. Dark and seductive.

More awaits you, Lillian. If you seek it...

The same one that called to me at the lake. But the more I reach for it, to try to figure out who or where it's coming from, it slips like water from my fingers.

It has to be Her. Keto. The monster that even Phorkys fears. The mother of his brood.

Erik's hands continue to knead and stroke, sinking from my breasts down to my stomach, where his large palm and strong fingers span the width of my abdomen. It's hot and possessive, but gentle, and I can't help but imagine if we'd met in another life, if circumstances were different... if I wasn't infertile, and he wasn't some thousand-year-old Viking, that maybe...

Ah, so you do desire children of your own.

Cold terror grips my heart. I stay perfectly still, as Erik's hands continue their sweet exploration of my body. There's no indication that he hears the voice like I do. His breathing remains steady, whereas mine has frozen solid in my lungs like ice.

Do not be afraid, sweet Lillian. I can help you.

There is a smile in Her voice that somehow makes it all the more terrifying. This invisible goddess, with the power to sink ships. What could She possibly want with me?

I am more interested in what you want, Lillian. The

depths of your desires. Did you enjoy your tryst with my lover?

Your lover? My hand brushes against Erik's arm—the warmth of his skin grounding me in the chill of the morning air—before pulling my fingers away. *But Erik...*

Not Erik, sweet one. Phorkys. His form is exquisite, is it not?

No. No, no no no *no*, that wasn't the deal. That's not what the monster said last night, when Erik transformed and swept me up in his many, many arms, that was–

The two of them together are quite magnificent. You are a lucky woman.

A deep, sensual laugh sounds in my head, before seeming to wrap around me on a breeze and echo out beyond the shelter and over the calm lake waters.

I shiver.

But then I remember the exact words. What Phorkys was really giving us, when He said He was granting us privacy.

Just as I use your body for my purposes, Erik, I will remind you: you, too, can use mine.

I try to swallow, but my mouth is bone-dry. The water skin is on the other side of the shelter, and the last thing I want to do is wake Erik. Not when he seemed so relieved last night, so open. Seeing him finally accept me, that I accept him...

I freeze, unsure what to even think. I barely know this man. We've lived together for a little over a week, just seven —eight? Nine?—days? I've lost track.

But at the same time, he knows more about me and my trauma than any other human on Earth. More than my coworkers. More than my family. The only person who even comes close is long gone. She abandoned me for Dean, and ran back to Chicago without me.

Are you sure about that?

What?

What—what do you mean?

Your friend is not in Chicago, sweet one. She is looking for you.

Looking for me?

Erik stirs behind me, and I feel the voice slipping away. Her presence lifts so suddenly, it's as if I emerge from being smothered by it; a sudden intake of breath shudders through my lungs and fills my diaphragm, and my head spins.

How long was I not breathing?

"Mmmm...y trehzhrr..." His endearment is slurred with sleep, but he wakes at the sudden jerk of my torso. As if he can feel me tensing, he rouses himself. "What is wrong?"

"Nothing!" I chirp. I don't trust myself to say anything else.

Does he know? Does he realize that last night, the monsters were just as much with us as we were with each other?

I turn in his hold, and he's staring at me with those beautiful icy gray eyes, so full of warmth and affection that the ice inside my chest melts instantly. He brings the heat back into the shelter, the morning chill erased completely as I snuggle into his wide, muscular chest.

"Mmmm..."

Mmmm, I think back, and nuzzle him. I reach my hand to his waist, ghosting over the head of his dick, which springs forward a little at the contact. He chuckles.

"Already, my treasure?"

I smile at him and nod, still not trusting my voice. I use

my arm to push him onto his back, and he humors me, a grin tickling the corner of his mouth as I shift myself over him and straddle his strong waist.

"I quite like this angle," he says, and his breath catches as I notch his head at my entrance. I slide back and forth, rubbing his shaft between my wet folds and over my clit. Maybe if I can orgasm again with only his human form, if I can bring us back to that height without any supernatural assistance, maybe then I'll prove that we don't need Them. Maybe then They'll go away.

"Perhaps you'd like it even more if I...?"

A blunt, squishy something pushes between my ass cheeks, and I jump—pushing my hips forward until my body is ramrod straight above the knee. "No! No, I just—I just want you, Erik. Just you, today."

The tentacle withdraws, and I know for sure he's back to normal when I feel his leg hair tickling the inside of my thighs. I don't look down to verify.

I'm afraid to.

"You face is so red," he murmurs, reaching a hand to stroke my face. I lean down into it, wrapping myself around him once more. He reaches his other hand to my breast and squeezes, and I spear myself onto his hard cock in one smooth go.

"Ah!"

"Yes, Lillian! Yes, you feel so good."

"You too, Erik," I pant, rubbing back and forth, sliding his cock in and out and rubbing the swollen head into my g-spot. "Fuck, you feel so good."

"Bend down, my treasure. Let me suck your perfect tits."

I do, posting my arms on either side of his head and letting my titties sway down over his face. He grabs one with his mouth, fastening around my nipple with his lips like he's bobbing for apples. It sends a shockwave rocketing through me—a zing of pleasure straight from tit to clit.

"Ah! Yes!"

He moans, grabbing the other breast and pinching at my nipple with his fingers while I increase my pace, grinding his cock into my core until I can feel the waves building.

It's good. It's very good.

It's just not as good as it was last night.

"Fuck, Lillian," he gasps, pulling off my breast with a soft pop and panting for air. "I need more of you, more–"

"I know." I bare down on his pelvis, pushing my clit into his skin as I speed up even more. "Grab me, grab my hips!"

Instantly, I feel his calloused hands wrap around me, fingers digging into my flesh as he puts those giant muscles to work. He stretches and contracts his arms, pushing and pulling me off and on his cock like a machine. I lean my torso back, changing the angle until he's pressing right into that spot, reaching down with my own hand and swiping furiously at my clit until I'm panting.

I feel the wetness soaking my pussy. I know I'm so aroused, *so* turned on, fucking the hottest man I've ever known—

But it isn't building anymore. Isn't cresting. It's just... torturously *fine.* Minutes turn to hours that we thrust and rock and ride, until my pussy is raw from the friction, but we can't seem to make it reach the tipping point.

We change positions: him on top in missionary, bent over me in doggy, holding one leg in the air while he kneels below me. I straddle his face. He fucks mine.

But he doesn't come. And I'm sore before I can get there. *Fuck.*

He sees me wince beneath him and slows down, finally pulling out of my raw, red channel, his eyes filled with concern.

"Are you okay, my treasure?"

Tears threaten to spill over, but I blink them away. My throat burns, but I force a nod. "Fine. I guess... we just overdid it last night, maybe?"

He nods slowly, considering my words, his light eyes cloudy and distant.

"Perhaps."

His cock bobs between us, looking achingly hard and swollen.

"Do you want–?" I sit up and lean my face towards it.

"No, no." He quickly pulls his hips away, twisting and kneeling to hide his erection, as if embarrassed that he, too, couldn't finish.

And just like that, I feel it. The wall, building back up, brick by brick, until he's shut off completely from me once again.

"I will gather firewood." He rises, avoiding meeting my eyes. "You rest."

"Erik, I–"

But he's gone before I can finish.

I'm so filled with hurt that I don't even remember what I was going to say.

THERE'S something else bothering me as I sit alone, stoking the fire to keep off the slight chill that nips the air. It's well into September now, and what summer heat lingered over Labor Day has given way to fall. Using a tin cup Erik found somewhere, I scoop the excess ashes from the pit and dump them out over the damp rocks in the high tide zone. I see yellow sprinkled through the leaves of the birch trees when I go to fill the water skin, and it reminds me that there's an expiration date on mine and Erik's tryst.

But whenever I think of leaving, an ache burns in my chest—so acute, it stops the air in my lungs. In the pain, I feel it. The thing I thought I'd gotten over.

Grief.

It's been three years. I assumed that time had been the thing to numb the pain, but as I work through the tears that overwhelm me, alone in the shelter, waiting for Erik to return, I realize it wasn't distance that healed me.

I know it as surely as I know my own name.

It was Keto.

Keto stole my grief.

I don't know how. But I do remember when: that night three years ago when I sat on the beach waiting for Tiffany to get back from her hike, when suddenly it was like the cloud over me lifted, and I found the resolve to move forward.

Somehow, Keto answered my cries that day. When, with streams of salty water pouring down my face, I screamed and wished and prayed that something would end the pain.

And that was the last day I shed a tear for my lost pregnancy.

Well, until today.

I know it was Her, because as I sit alone in front of the fire I feel Her presence, like a weight on the back of my neck, looming over me. She doesn't speak. Doesn't whisper those agonizing lies into my ear like She did this morning.

She waits for me to break the silence.

So I wallow. Every minute that passes, more and more of my own fucked-up backstory fills in.

From the first year that Tiffany and I stayed at the cabin, we felt called to return. It became tradition, a ritual. Whenever I had a particularly stressful week at work or the two of us needed a break, we'd talk about the cabin. We could hardly wait to get back.

It's like it called to us to return.

No, not it. Her. The Monster of Lake Superior.

The *real* monster. Phorkys is terrifying, sure, but He's had Erik to keep him in check. Who's been reigning in Keto?

What was it that Phorkys said that first night, in the underwater cave? When he first tried to convince me that I was Erik's mate, that He needed us in order for them to unleash Their brood onto the world?

Her influence is subtle, yet mighty. And her physical form is a magnificent force. We have both grown weaker with time, but she is still fearsome in her abilities.

I think about me and Erik together last night, and then this morning. How neither of us were able to come once he'd given in to his monster form.

Is this some kind of curse? She offered me an escape from my grief, a hint of unbelievable pleasure, only to steal it back? Forever?

When I prayed for the grief to just go away, for something to just take it away from me, She answered that prayer. But in return, She took a piece of me. When Tiffany and I said that this was the last time we were coming back here, our last girls' trip, Keto heard. She made it so I couldn't escape. She made it so I wouldn't want to.

But now She's exacting her price.

Your friend is not in Chicago, sweet one. She is looking for you.

I jolt as Keto's words from before come back in a rush. *Tiffany.*

It's not just me that can't leave. Tiffany can't, either. She didn't go back to Chicago with Dean. How could she? We're cursed; our souls are bound to the lake until Keto gets what She wants.

Her brood.

My breath grows shorter and shorter, until I can hardly fill or empty my lungs without gasping. My airways constrict until I'm clawing at my throat, as the irrefutable *truth* of my conclusions suffocates me.

Her presence is clear. This is what She wants. This is what She'll take.

And She won't let me or Tiffany escape until She has it.

I have to warn her!

Erik finally returns, arms filled with a stack of firewood that obscures his face. Not that he would look at me even if he could. I fight to quiet my breath, but I know it's obvious I've been crying. I don't know where Erik's mental state is at right now, but in this moment, I can't let myself care.

My best friend is in trouble. I need to find her, need to get her out of here, before Keto takes what She wants from me by force.

Erik stacks the wood onto the pile in the corner, and when at last he faces me, I break.

"I need to go back, Erik. Back to the mainland. Tonight."

CHAPTER 28

ERIK

Tonight.

She wants to leave me, and she wants to do it right away.

I should not be surprised. After all, last night I showed her just how terrifying I can truly be, when I embrace the monster inside me. But no—that does not seem entirely truthful, does it? She enjoyed last night, immensely.

It was this morning, when I was unable to please her, that must have pushed her away.

"Lillian–"

"Please, Erik." It is then I realize that her eyes are red and puffy from crying, and her whole body seems to be shaking. From what, I do not know. Surely our sex this morning was not so terrible? But her tone is hard when she continues. "I have to go. Now. Will you help me?"

She is asking for my help?

It is odd that *that* is the part of this situation that makes me realize something is off, and yet it is. Lillian never asks for help. She is stubborn and self-reliant to a fault. Even when she was unable to walk, I needed to force her to rest while I took care of her.

"What is wrong, my treasure?"

Her shaking intensifies. When she hears my pet name for her, her shoulders tense, and water once again beads at the corners of her eyes.

Despite being covered in splinters, I cannot stand to keep my body from hers. Her emotional discomfort is physically painful for me. I cross the shelter and wrap my arms around her, squeezing tight until I feel her breath push her chest against mine. My shoulder is wet when I finally let her pull away, and her face is shiny with fresh tears.

"Please," is all she says.

There is fear in her eyes. And that is when I know.

You can hear it.

She nods, as if she is afraid to confirm it in any way that Keto or Phorkys may overhear. They are in both of our minds now.

She is absolutely right. I must get Lillian to safety. Now, while she still may stand a chance.

"Let me take you to my main shelter. We can gather supplies there."

She nods, and I scoop her in my arms. A small snort escapes her, and I cannot help but grin at the return of my stubborn treasure.

"I can walk now, you know."

You need your strength, and you know it.

Her lips purse in response as I carry her to the shore.

The autumn sun is high in a cerulean sky, highlighting the burst of color that dots the leaves surrounding us. I have always believed this time of year to be so cruel: the flamboyant burst of colors, unseasonably bright, only to beckon the loneliest and harshest of seasons.

I step into the freshwater surf, and goose pimples pock my flesh as a light breeze rustles past. Lillian shivers in my arms, and I tilt my head at her.

This is the fastest way to my cabin. While I can traverse over the harsh terrain to my main dwelling, it is physically demanding to do so. This spontaneous forest is crescent-shaped; the shelter in which we have been staying is closest to the northern shore, while the other is in the thicker central arc of the island, more protected from vacationing humans. The forest is denser there, which is why it is my primary place of residence during the warm months. I worry less about being disturbed there.

But the rough, rocky, and heavily forested terrain surrounding it has a drawback: it is perilous to journey in and out.

Just dragging the wagon of supplies from the middle of the island to the tip when Lillian first arrived took an entire day, and we do not have the luxury of time. Swimming across the lagoon is the most efficient way to travel there, and it will be less strenuous on her recovering ankle.

And she will need to reserve every ounce of strength she can to make the swim back to the mainland.

I lower her into the water once it is too deep to keep my feet on the pebbly floor, keeping hold of her wrist as she tests out kicking her legs. Her face does not squint with discomfort, which is good. She nods at me, and I swim out in front of her to lead the way.

When I reach the central shore of the crescent, I look over my shoulder to gauge Lillian's progress. She is about a hundred meters back from me, her blonde hair a small golden jewel upon a dark, wavy sea. When her knees at last reach the sandy basin of the water's edge, she crawls ashore. She is breathing heavily, and favoring her injury as she rises to her feet.

My chest aches, and my throat is hoarse before I even attempt to speak.

"Lillian..."

"I'm fine," she chokes between breaths, and my heart tightens further. "I *will* be fine."

The fiery look in her eyes bars no argument. I relent, bowing my head as I turn away. "Remain here. I will fetch what we require."

As I run through the forest, twigs and rocks and pinecones scratching at the calloused soles of my feet, I use every ounce of willpower I possess to empty my mind.

I cannot think of the danger she is in.

I cannot allow myself to entertain the idea of aiding her escape.

If I think of it, then They will know our plans. Especially here, so close to the underwater cave in the lagoon where she was first cursed. I am certain that must be where Keto hides, when She is not lording over her subjects like the tyrant that She is. That is why Phorkys is so strong there: not simply because it is His base of power, but because that is where His mate sleeps.

You seek to deduce from that which you do not understand, Erik.

The growl seeps in from the base of my brain, and if I were a weaker man its chill would be enough to freeze me to the forest floor. But I surge onward, knowing that Lillian depends on me, even if I cannot think it.

You try to hide your thoughts from ME?

The further inland I run, the weaker His voice, but it is still there. A threatening chuckle lingers on the corner of my consciousness like the voice of a dream in the space between wakefulness and sleep. He is both there and not there, a figment and a reality, and for the entirety of my run I cannot shake Him loose.

All I can do is run. Crash through the door to my cabin. Gather a sealskin sack and stuff it full of what few clothes I possess that Lillian can use on the mainland: short pants, a sun-bleached shirt, senseless floppy shoes that affix to one's feet with a thong of rubber. A water skin. An odd, bird-shaped ring that can inflate with air to aid in flotation, which may grant her respite in the long journey to shore.

All the while, the monster laughs.

I slam the door shut, my arms laden with supplies, feet flying as fast as I dare over the uneven deer path back towards the shore. I cannot be too careful—if I were to fall, if I were to injure myself, what hope would Lillian have?

I cannot let her share my fate. I cannot—I will *not–*

The forest blurs at the edge of my vision, before a furious film emerges across my entire field of sight. My breath hitches as I rub at my eyes with my shoulder, slowing my pace just a hair to wipe my vision clear, only for my arm to come away wet.

Why am I crying?

I am saving her. I will deliver her to safety. It is not too late, I swear it, I will save her—

But you do not wish for her to leave, do you?

My chest is heaving. The exertion of this hike is too much, too fast, even for one as fit as I am. I spent all morning gathering wood, only to swim half the length of the island and sprint up a demanding forest path. I am tired, clearly. I have expended much energy.

Something is blocking my throat when I suck in a breath. It hitches, and a stitch buries itself in my chest.

When I hear myself inhale, it is broken and ragged, in a way that sounds eerily similar to a sobbing babe.

But I do not sob.

I do not weep.

That is not—has never been—how I process my emotions.

At last, my feet reach the forest's edge, where the mighty pines and birches give way to small shrubs and tall grasses. Fine sand overtakes the hard red clay of the interior soil, and I look up to see Lillian, clutching her knees to her chest and burying her face in her legs as she rocks back and forth.

"I have returned," I say, willing my voice to be as strong as she needs me to be. My beautiful, *beautiful* Lillian, with her waist-length locks and soft curves. Her steely resolve and curious mind.

My treasure. *Mine.*

Mine.

A shiver skitters down my spine. *No.*

If the only way I can claim her is by proxy of the monster, then I have no choice.

I have to let her go.

CHAPTER 29

LILLIAN

She knows.

She knows I'm trying to escape.

But instead of stopping me, insulting me, or baiting me, the voice in my head is doing something infinitely more terrifying.

She's *laughing*.

And I can't get away from it. She echoes in my head like it's an opera house, and I'm center orchestra, forced to listen as Her sensual chuckle saturates into every thought until I think I'm going to go insane.

And also? Remember how I couldn't come this morning, no matter how hard I grinded Erik's face and dick?

Yeah, well, Keto seems to find some sick, twisted joy in making me suffer. Because there's an ache in my core that won't go away. And I'm not talking about the "I just swam a mile and now my abs are on fire" ache. I'm talking about the horny kind.

So I'm exhausted, thirsty, terrified, devastated, and horny. If you're keeping track at home.

Erik returning to the beach only ramps up the tension curling in my belly. And Keto's laugh only gets louder.

I need to get off this island.

You can try, Lillian. It is so entertaining to watch.

I swallow around the lump in my throat, and it burns with thirst. Erik, seeming to read my mind, hands me a water skin from the mountain of stuff piled in his arms.

I sip greedily, taking a minute to absorb the tragic irony of seeing a Viking swashbuckler like Erik attempt to blow up a pink flamingo floaty while I burn with literal Titanic lust. All in a, if I'm being honest with myself, doomed attempt to flee the gods.

My ankle throbs in time with my core. I'm never going to be able to swim to the mainland like this.

The greatest sex of my life. And this is the price.

"It's useless, Erik," I croak. Even after emptying the whole skin, my mouth is dry with feelings I can't understand or control. "We're never getting off this island."

"I will not let you suffer as I suffer!" He belts, tearing the little plastic gasket away from his mouth before furiously pursing his lips around it once again.

It's ridiculous. And it's also the bravest thing anyone has ever done for me.

Oh, you think so?

Her words stop my heart mid-beat as an image flashes across my brain. It's gone as quickly as it comes, but it's so vivid I can't help but remember it.

Tiffany. A younger Tiffany: pre-Dean Tiffany. Standing on a boulder at high tide, tears streaming down her face, shouting at the waves.

How does it feel, to know that so many humans are willing to give up everything for you?

Another flash, and this time it's Tiffany as I know her

now. A slight bow to her stomach, bloated with the young life growing inside it. Strapped to a rocky cave wall, imprisoned by strong, slimy-looking ropes of seaweed, as Dean watches helplessly from his own underwater prison. Bubbles rise helplessly from their mouths and noses as they shout for someone to rescue them.

Tiffany!

My best friend. She took my best friend.

Why didn't I listen!? When she wanted to leave early, when she didn't want to swim in the lake? When she wanted to abandon the lake cabin and instead take a vapid, touristy trip to the Mall of America where we could Build a Bear and call it a day? Why couldn't I just do what she wanted to do?

But no. I had to be selfish. I had to run away, and now we'll never be free again.

You can be free.

This time, it's Phorkys's voice, and I know Erik can hear it too, because the innertube falls from his lips and bounces noiselessly into the wet sand below his feet.

We meet eyes, and the only word I can use to describe his face is pure terror.

Because he knows. We're playing a game we can't win.

She has my best friend, Erik. I plead with him with my eyes. *She's pregnant. I can't let Them...*

He nods slowly, shoulders sinking with defeat as his eyes rake over my face, then my body, before latching back onto my gaze.

Perhaps it is time for a reunion...

If I weren't seeing it for myself, I never would have believed it possible. But in that moment, the bright blue September afternoon sky turns a dusky purple-red, as angry clouds roll in from the horizon. From the center of the lake, I see a mound of water rise, giant and frothy, and come roaring at us like a stampede of wild horses. As it approaches, it rises, cresting higher and higher until it engulfs the entire sky in the wall of water.

In the second before Erik and I are swallowed, I see fish swimming in the massive wave.

Huh, I think. *That's funny.*

And then everything goes black.

CHAPTER 30

ERIK

I am no stranger to waking in the heart of the lake. Especially in the winter months, I spend every waking and sleeping hour burrowed in its depths, switching between forms and allowing Phorkys to hunt and prowl to His heart's content. He craves the open water in the spring and summer, but I always reign Him in until the tourists have long fled the harsh winter conditions.

And yes, there is always the errant adventurer out for a winter surf. But those are few and far between. And the humans rarely bat an eye when one of them does not return.

Although I rarely inhabit my fully human form whenever I am underwater, I feel my legs kick against the familiar resistance. Instinctively, I reach to check my gills, which are of course intact, before whipping my head around to take in my surroundings.

Something is wrong.

Why am I not in Phorkys's body?

Why is the water so warm?

And then my eyes adjust to the darkness, and I remember.

Lillian!

Light swirls of hair float in a lazy nest about her hanging head, glowing an eerie blue in what little refracted light makes it down this far to the lake's floor. This is not my usual cave. This is different, larger: with vertical tunnels swooping in and around us and letting in grayish beams that cast the space in chiaroscuro fields. My treasure is tied to a rocky outcropping with woven weeds. Her dress has been torn from her body: I can see the white stripes where the seams split across her shoulders and side. The fabric is bunched about her feet, translucent and inadequate, and a deep, all-consuming sadness overwhelms me.

I could not protect her.

Do not sorrow, Erik. You never could.

I cannot summon the energy to rage at Him. The creature who started this all.

This was your plan all along. You tricked me. I thought...

...

Now you are silent? Do not tell me you feel guilty. I do not believe it.

Even I am powerless to Her desires, Erik.

The conversation stops as I see Lillian stir: her sweet, soft hand twitches, then her body shifts. I count the seconds with bated breath until her head finally rises and her deep blue eyes meet mine.

My treasure.

Erik, she thinks, and her eyes swim with affection I do not deserve. *Where's Tiffany?*

My body stills, and I struggle to remember who she means at first. But then her eyes focus on a spot beyond my shoulder, and I turn.

Another human female, with mousy brown hair and an unnaturally rounded belly filling out her thin frame, hangs from weedy ropes similar to the ones restraining Lillian. A man, thin and sinewy with close-shaved hair that appears almost spikey, is tied up and unconscious beside her. I look over my shoulder back to my sweet treasure, and know from their wavery appearance that if we were not surrounded by water, tears would be flowing down her round cheeks.

These are your friends?

Yes. She nods, and I curse myself once again for not being able to protect her from this pain. But I do not have time to comfort her, because at that moment the entire cave goes dark.

No, not the cave. The tunnels. Something is covering the tunnels.

Prostrate yourself, Erik! It is her!

Phorkys's command rings to fill my brain completely, and my body complies without me telling it to. My face is forced into the sandy bed of the lake as I bow to the floor, covering my nose and mouth until I can taste its loamy grit on my tongue. My arms stretch out before me, and my body folds itself on my knees.

The stretch burns.

"Phorkys. You have returned to me. Let me see you."

I am never ready for the feeling of being held captive in my own skin. But when my physical being surrenders completely to the whims of the monster living in my veins, Phorkys is in complete control. I can see, but cannot react. I can feel, but cannot move. Even my mind is trapped within; the Titan is at the wheel, and I am but the boards of the ship upon the tide.

My body, large and gelatinous and many-limbed, rises

to meet Her. I take in all sides of the cave through eyes the size of tree stumps on either side of my massive head, feeling the top of it stretch up to the rocky ceiling of the now cramped cave.

But it is not me who fills the space.

It is *Her.*

The most beautiful woman in all of creation, as large as an ocean-crossing vessel, with the torso and face of a human queen and the lower half of a gargantuan octopus, larger than myself by a factor of ten. Her ten arms flare beneath her waist, their exterior skin coated in a flexible armor of glittering scales, protecting the rows and rows of squishy suckers within. The ends, instead of tapering to tips, flare out in translucent, webbed fins, giving her lower half the appearance of a party of dancing mermaids being swallowed by a scaley skirt.

But I only see her lower half in my periphery as my gaze is slowly drawn up her awesome body. The scales taper at her cinched waist, giving way to smooth, green skin that covers a powerful trunk and full, round breasts that shake with her subtle laughter. Laughter that lights in her hypnotic, silver eyes, that widen when she curls her wide, sensual lips into a sharp-toothed smile.

She towers over me, her massive grinning face surrounded by a quaff of eels and water snakes, who hiss at me in anticipation of what horror she is about to unleash upon me. And atop the terrifying locks sits a sparkling crown.

As if there were any doubt of the majesty of the creature before me.

I have never been more aware in my thousand years on Earth that I am prey, and my pathetic fate rests in the hands of one being, and one alone.

Keto.

CHAPTER 31

LILLIAN

We're all going to die.

It's the only thought running on a track inside my head as I gape at the real-life Ursula monster towering before us. It's almost like the cave got bigger once she was in it, like she's bending time and space to her whims.

I know it's a her, because her boobs are... well, they're fucking gigantic and perfect and like porn star titties, except for the fact that they're green. Seriously. She's like one of those Barbie cakes, where they stuff the doll into a tiered cake that's shaped like a skirt? Only instead of a skirt, it's a bunch of tentacle-fin things. And instead of plastic hair, she's got a mane of snakes and eels. And instead of–

Okay, you know what? Scratch that. She's nothing like a fucking Barbie cake. She's the most terrifying, sexy thing I've ever seen and I'm glad I'm underwater right now because I'm literally pissing myself with fear.

Erik, I plead in my mind, despite the fact that my Viking boyfriend has been replaced by a giant Octopus. Although, "giant" is relative. He looks like a chihuahua when he's next to Keto. *What are we going to do?*

He doesn't respond. I don't know if he can. The giant, bulbous eyes on the side of the Octopus's head are marbled with that haunting neon cyan that lets me know that Phorkys is at the helm. And He, like me, seems shocked to silence by the presence of His baby momma filling the underwater cave before us.

Baby momma...

Oh fuck.

The brood they want me to have. To... *incubate,* or whatever. The eggs they want to shove into my baby-maker. They're not just the eggs of some slightly-larger-than-average octopus monster.

They're *Hers.*

Fuck. Fuck fuck fuck.

I'm a big girl, sure, but there's a *big* difference between a size 22 and a size Empire State Building.

I'm going to die, I'm going to die, I'm going to die...

"Silence, human!"

Fuck. I piss myself again. The water around my legs goes warm for a second before blending into the mass of lake around it.

"Your thoughts are louder than you realize. Be silent like your male companion. Or, if you prefer, I'll hold you in stasis like your precious Tiffany."

I realize, for once, that she's actually opening her mouth as if she's speaking instead of just telepathing into our minds. It sounds like the voice in my head from earlier, that low sensual silk scarf of a voice that's as arousing as it is terrifying.

Shit, am I bi? I might be bi.

"Silence!"

Her voice literally bends the laws of physics, echoing around the cave and shaking me to my very core. The same core that is now dripping.

And no, I didn't piss myself again. I'm just super horny.

Fuck, I am bi, aren't I??

Why couldn't I learn this by scrolling TikTok like a normal thirty year-old white woman instead of through facing my own imminent mortality?

She's hot, dammit. And going to kill me.

Suddenly, a tentacle that's bigger around than a small sedan whips out and wraps around my body, suckers the size of my face gluing themselves to every inch of my skin before squeezing the air from my lungs.

Water from my gills?

What... even... ih...

"If you cannot quiet your mind, I will quiet it for you, human."

The unbearable pressure relents, and a stream of water across my neck makes the light come back into my vision.

She had been choking me. I almost passed out.

Okay, then. Time to calm down.

"Much better."

"What do you–" I try to speak, but unlike Keto, my voice comes out as a stream of coughing bubbles. I switch back to telepathy. *–intend to do with Tiffany and Dean?*

"Ah, these? Why, I am simply collecting the debt this one owes me."

Debt?

"Yes. Her first born child. In exchange for granting you respite from your depression."

I blink. Desperately attempting to keep my thoughts from spiraling again.

I want to stay conscious.

What are you talking about?

Her deep laugh rumbles through the water, the cave walls, and even my body—making it ache with that unrequited lust once again.

I really, *really* don't like it when She plays with my body like that.

"We both know that isn't true, Lillian. Otherwise, you wouldn't have enjoyed your night with my consort nearly so much."

Her luscious indigo lips curl into a knowing smile, and *fuck* if it doesn't kill me a little.

I can't speak. It's all I can do not to think too loudly, with so many feelings clamoring to form sentences in my mind. I'm caught in a web: feeling too much to process, but needing to process to know what I'm feeling. Right now, it's all just some horny/scared/confused milkshake that's giving me brain freeze.

I think I short-circuit.

"Ahhh, good girl, Lillian. Your silence is appreciated." Her eyes, fiery silver eyes that pull me in like a magnet, turn to the monster between us. **"My precious Phorkys. You have done well to bring them to me."**

CHAPTER 32
ERIK

There is one benefit to being in a prison of my own mind. Somehow, Keto cannot hear my thoughts. Unfortunately, neither can Lillian.

It seems the only creature with whom I am allowed communication in this tortuous state is Phorkys, who is currently quivering with anticipation before his lover. He is just as aroused by Her as Lillian appears to be—her flushed cheeks and heady scent a dead giveaway to her desire. I cannot blame her, when even the monster is unable to keep his hectocotylus from flushing with sperm.

He is ready to breed. Eager for it.

Which only increases my fear for Lillian.

"Because I am generous, Lillian, I will give you a chance to save your friend."

When the Titan speaks, her voice saturates every molecule around and within us. I see my treasure tremble, her breath quickening with every word Keto directs to her. Her pupils are so dilated I can barely discern the ring of navy blue from their depths.

I know what is coming. Because it is the same bargain

that Phorkys attempted to offer me. Freedom in exchange for lending our bodies to their mating ritual.

You cannot let Her do this, I plead to him. I have to shout to be heard from my cage within His body. He will just ignore me otherwise. *Please, Phorkys! Do not condemn her to the same fate to which you condemned me!*

Silence, human. I have no power here. We must beget our brood. It is either your mate, or her friend.

His eyes focus on the limp forms of the fragile humans still strapped to the cavern walls. Compared to Lillian, a sturdy lass with fire in her eyes, these two seem so...delicate.

She seems to be thinking the same thing, as Lillian's gaze flits to her friend and her mate. My treasure seems to wilt at the sight of them, but then her face steels with resolve. I am in awe as she lifts her head to the Titan before us, determination filling her gaze.

She is breathtaking. In that moment, even Keto's beauty cannot compare to hers.

My treasure.

For a moment, I swear her eyes flick to me, as if she can see the man trapped beneath the monster.

How can I say that?

She has *always* seen the man beneath the monster. Always accepted me. Always found me, even in the darkest of moments.

I may have failed her, but she is strong enough to save herself.

"Take my brood and bear my children, and I will let your friend go."

Lillian's chest fills with breath as she stares down the Titan.

If you guarantee that Tiffany, Dean, and their baby will be free to live their life back on the surface, that you will never hurt them again...

I will have your children.

"Wonderful." Keto's attention refocuses on Phorkys and me, and His body stills. **"Phorkys. Retrieve the eggs."**

CHAPTER 33

LILLIAN

Phorkys propels himself out of the cave, taking Erik with him. I couldn't hear his voice at all, but I sensed him in there.

I feel so helpless. All of my friends are being held captive at the whims of these monsters. Sure, I can agree to have Keto's babies, but how do I know She won't renege on the deal once She has what She wants?

Unbidden, those old words from the shopkeeper at the general store come rolling back to mind. *Lake Superior doesn't give up Her dead.*

But is that the lake? Or has it been Keto, this whole time? Sinking ships under cover of storms and fog, devouring up the victims before they become corpses? Before they leave evidence?

"*You do not trust me.*"

Her elegant face is stoic as She studies me, one emerald eyebrow raised. I meet Her gaze. At this point, I have nothing else to lose.

Either way, She holds all the cards.

You tricked me. You tricked my friends.

She tilts her head, narrowing her eyes. ***"How did I trick you?"***

You told me you could "fix" me. You used your magic to make me beholden to you. I'm just a human. How am I supposed to make any choice when you take all my choices away?

A long moment passes where neither of us speak. I'm getting better at silencing my thoughts. Sure, I'm still uncomfortably aroused, but I'm not afraid anymore—at least, not for myself. For Tiffany and Dean? Their young family? Sure.

This morning, the overwhelming grief for my own lost child came crashing back like a tsunami. Once Keto took away Erik's and my ability to satisfy our own desire, every emotion inside me started boiling. Lust, grief, fear—I've been in a state of constant overwhelm all day. And now?

I'm just numb.

Now that the fear and shock have ebbed, it's hard to feel too passionate about anything when my hopelessness threatens to drag me under.

Something seems to shift in Keto's expression. Her eyes soften around the edges. She finally opens her mouth to speak.

"When you came to my lake those many moons ago, broken and alone with grief, I never intended to take advantage of you, Lillian."

Slowly, with each word, the hopelessness fades. The heavy weight in my stomach eases, and my chest unclenches. The water flows more easily over my gills, my lungs expanding with a full breath for the first time since this morning, and my head clears a little.

She's playing with me again. Siphoning off my pain. I don't know if I'm more wary or grateful.

She continues, ***"You came here with your friend. I***

could feel your loss from miles away. It called to me. One kindred soul to another."

I blink.

Kindred... soul?

"I had children once. They were tricked and slaughtered by the spawn of the Olympians. Greek heroes, seeking glory, mercilessly hunted and murdered them one by one. All along the Aegean Sea, humans rejoiced in their demise. And Phorkys and I wept.

"When another brood swelled in my loins, we fled. Across oceans and rivers, rapids and puddles small enough to suffocate us, we journeyed west until we couldn't any longer. I deposited my brood. He fertilized it. And then that wooden ship crashed into my nest.

*"Thousands of my young—*destroyed.

"I flew into a rage. And when Phorkys returned to my side, wearing the body of a murderer, I–"

She sucks in a breath, Her chest rising with fury as Her cheeks tint an angry yellow.

"I could not look at him. So I ran away."

The shipwreck. Erik's crew and family.

Phorkys didn't tell us they crashed into their eggs.

I lost one embryo. Keto lost thousands.

The last drips of pain clinging to my heart squeeze in sympathy. Her eyes lock with mine, and whatever She sees there gives Her the strength to continue.

"Your pain was fresh. It called to me. I was quickening once again, and the grief and hope were overwhelming. I sought my mate, but he was still bound to the human. I could not mate with him.

"Then I found you.

"I did not realize humans could feel pain. They always seemed so brutal, so obsessed with glory and war. How

could they kill so many and feel the depth of pain that I felt?

"But you. You understood. I could have listened to you weep for hours. You knew what it was to lose a child. You felt it as deeply as me. Meeting another with my scars was... cathartic, somehow.

"Your pain drew me to the shore. It wasn't long before I met your friend, Tiffany. Her grief was different. She wept for the loss of her friend. Worried your friendship would never be what it was. Already missed you from your years attached to that unworthy male.

"She loves you, you know."

What?

I look over at her unconscious body, limp in the seaweed bindings. I remember the sight of her on the beach not even two weeks ago, tan and happy, sipping mocktails and reading on her Kindle in the gravity chair beside mine.

She's my best friend. Of course she loves me.

The Titan gives me a curious look. *"You deny her deeper affections. That is interesting. Why?"*

I... I shake my head. What affections? Tiffany loves *Dean.* That's why they're engaged. That's why they're starting a family.

"She asked if I could take away your grief. Grant you happiness once more. I told her that every magic has a price.

"When I asked for her firstborn, she said that that was an easy price to pay. She confessed she felt guilty, knowing in her soul that she wouldn't ever pay the price. She never imagined the two of you would have children together."

The two of *us?*

Wait. You're saying she had a crush on me?

Holy shit.

Keto tilts her head again. ***"I do not know that word. But she wished to spend her life with you, yes. As partners. As lovers."***

But... Dean...

"She loves Dean. It is true. But she dreams of someday having more. Deep in her heart, she desires a family of lovers. Her male mate does not know of this. Although he has fantasized about bedding both of you before."

Well, fuck. I thought Tiffany and I knew everything about each other. But I never would have imagined she was polyamorous. Or that Dean wanted a threesome with me.

I expect to feel some kind of betrayal at that. But I don't. I'm not disgusted by it, not even a little. In fact, the idea of the four of us—Erik, Tiffany, me, even Dean—somehow escaping this and establishing a little family somewhere far away from the Great Lakes...

It sounds really nice.

I'm having all sorts of realizations about myself today.

Can I speak to her?

Keto shakes her head. ***"No, Lillian. I cannot risk you fleeing before the debt is paid. I will give Tiffany her child, but my magic still demands its price.***

"Phorkys cannot fertilize my eggs as long as he is chained to share that human's body. With his seed, they will not develop unless their maturation occurs in a human womb. Even my power has its limits."

I don't understand how that works. Maybe something about shifter sperm having different DNA? But Keto doesn't seem concerned with the specifics.

"Your essence will complete them, Lillian. And I will consider my debt paid."

My grief is no longer overwhelming, but it also isn't entirely gone anymore. Where there was an endless torrent, and then an empty hole, it's now just a subtle ache in my heart. It's a part of me, and I know it always will be—as surprising and scary as it was at the time, I wanted that baby. It will always hurt to think of what could have been.

But the pain of it isn't all-consuming anymore. It's the type of pain that helps me understand.

Yes, Keto is a terrifying monster. No, I don't completely trust Her. But I do understand how seeing Her children murdered would make Her hate humans. How losing an entire brood of eggs would send Her into a rage.

Granted, I never wanted to kill an entire village of Vikings because I had a miscarriage. But you know, I see the logic behind the leap.

Kinda.

The water around me warms a little, and I look up to see Keto scowling at me. I realize Her anger is capable of heating up the lake. *Yikes.*

"We all grieve differently, Lillian."

Okay. Right. Don't make the sexy lake monster angry. Got it.

My eyes dart to Tiffany and Dean. I need to keep my cool. Not just for me and Erik, but for them. Their future depends on me.

In more ways than one.

I swallow.

"I will take them with me."

What? When?? Panic flits through me as a few eels detach themselves from Her hair and begin untying my friends. *Where are you taking them?*

"As happy as I am to have convinced you to incubate my children, I do not wish to watch my lover fill you with his seed."

I gulp. Uhh...

"I will hide your friends and leave you and Phorkys to the insemination. You can have them back when you have birthed my young."

Birthed... what??

Keto, wait–!

But in a typhoon of swirling bubbles and scaly tails, She's gone. Tiffany and Dean are gone with her.

Fuck. Fuck. *Fuck!!*

I didn't think this through. Getting impregnated with a bunch of eggs, sure. Octopus sex insemination. Right, yeah, that's fine... maybe even a little hot.

But birthing the monster babies? Actually pushing out a hoard of monsters through my hoo-ha?

How many eggs did She say She lost with the first brood? Thousands?

Thousands...?? In my...

Phorkys returns to the cave, an Ikea bag-sized bundle of gooey, opalescent eggs the size of marbles clutched in his ten tentacle arms, and I picture them growing. Maturing. Hatching

The logistics of what I just agreed to do hit me all at once.

I pass out.

CHAPTER 34

ERIK

"*Phorkys. Retrieve the eggs.*"

The last thing I want is to leave Lillian alone in the hands of the underwater goddess, but my captor pulls me away. Deeper and deeper we swim into the heart of the frigid lake, further than I have ever explored in my human form. As we put kilometers of distance between ourself and Keto, I slowly regain my ability to communicate.

Where are you taking me?

To get the eggs.

I shudder. Of course, I knew that this was their ultimate intention with Lillian and me. But I had not realized the eggs were stored somewhere. Hidden. Somehow, had assumed they were somewhere in this body of mine, that Phorkys would implant them if I ever lost control.

But, of course, that does not make sense. Despite His shifting powers, Phorkys was decidedly male. If He could carry eggs in His own body, He would not require a female to incubate them.

Eventually, we reach a small passageway, with an

entrance that is far too small for my human body to squeeze through. But the squid-like form of the monster morphs effortlessly through the tiny opening, and as we emerge, I realize where it carried us.

My ship.

Or the wreckage of my ship. The oiled wood still glows faintly through the thick layer of algae and lake scum it has accumulated. My very soul weeps at the sight.

Our once great vessel, crushed by the all-powerful monster that now has Lillian in her clutches.

There. Beneath the hull.

A clutch of perfectly round, gelatinous eggs is nestled beneath a cover of seaweed underneath the inverted hull of the ship. It is then I realize exactly what the two Titans are asking of Lillian and me. Not just to participate in some erotic breeding ritual, but to doom the humans of this land to another generation of cursed monsters.

Will they wreak havoc like you did to my people?

I feel the monster stir, an uncomfortable twisting in our belly.

It is your people who murdered our young.

The memory of the crash, the ship in the storm—the wave cresting and pummeling our vessel into an outcropping of lake rocks.

And then another image: the hull smashing into a bundle of shining eggs, destroying them into swirling ribbons of dying magic.

You have been without your family for hundreds of years, Erik. Keto and I have been without ours for thousands. You have found your mate. You will have a family. Allow me to have mine.

And that is when I feel it.

An unfathomable loneliness consumes me as the

monster gives me the briefest glimpse into His own emotions. I have felt His drive before, His desire, His lust. But I realize now that there was some mercy in His heart in that He never shared with me His sadness.

My very soul aches, the despair weighing heavier than all the wreckage of my ancient ship. Were I in control of my limbs at this moment, I would surely buckle under it.

I thought before that I had been privy to all the monster felt, his lust and greed and hunger, but I was wrong. He held back. He protected me. The loss of His children, first in the Aegean Sea and then again when my people crashed into His nest, is a pain I will never know for myself.

I lost my family once, it is true.

But the loss of a thousand children?

It is enough to ruin a man.

Do I not also deserve a taste of what you call hope?

I ponder that. In truth, I do not know.

Together, we stare at the clutch of eggs. Marble sized and shimmering with an otherworldly glow, stuck together with a gelatinous glue that shines like opals, I am struck by the sheer amount.

Lillian will bear these eggs.

There is an accusation there, but there is also fear. My treasure is beautiful and strong, but she is human.

She is not merely human anymore. Just as you are more than human. Keto has chosen a worthy surrogate.

I nod, feeling something akin to understanding for this monster. For the first time, I feel empathy for Him.

Did Lillian see this in Keto? She is a magnificent mate indeed, to offer so much of herself to repair the damage of my people. A responsibility not her own.

We scoop the clutch of eggs into our many arms,

spreading our webbing to surround them as we slowly swim back to Keto's lair.

THE FORCE with which I buck inside of Phorkys's body when I see my sweet Lillian faint at our approach almost causes us to drop the eggs.

Lillian!

She is alive. Just shocked.

Where is Keto?

Securing her friends.

Anger burns within me, and I yearn to gain back control of my body, if for no other reason than to flail with my rage. I feel unbearably helpless, carried on the whims of my captor.

Calm yourself, Erik.

She promised She would let them go!

All in due time.

He settles the brood into a nest of weeds before finally allowing me control once more. I half-shift, reclaiming my human head and chest and arms while keeping my tentacled lower half to allow me more control of my movements in the water. I propel towards her, grabbing her soft body and cradling it to my chest.

At last, her breathing quickens, and she rouses in my hold.

Erik?

Please, I beg her, though I know it is useless. *My treasure. Do not do this.*

I have to, Erik. I've decided.

We cannot know how many humans will die by these actions–

She twists in my hold, placing her hands firmly against

my chest. Over my shoulder, her eyes flicker to the nest of eggs, and I watch the swallow bob within her throat. When her gaze returns to mine, it is filled with determination.

Erik, humans die every day. And we kill more humans than Keto or Phorkys ever have. We slaughter them in wars, we exile them to live in slums, we deny them life-saving medical care. We elect miserable jackasses to office! Who's to say that humans aren't the real *monsters? Shit, my ex was a monster for leaving me.*

As she rants, pictures of the devastation of modern humanity plague my mind. She is showing me the carnage. Videos she has seen on mass-communication devices. Announcements from deranged leaders. Every one more horrifying than the last.

My resolve wavers. *Lillian, is this the world that awaits us?*

She closes her eyes, and her chest rises with a deep inhale. I clutch her tighter, and she gives her head a small shake.

What I mean to say is, Phorkys and Keto don't need our help to hurt the humans, Erik. Even if that was their true purpose, they have plenty of competition out in the real world! We can't know for sure that resisting them will save anyone. But by doing this, I can save three good humans—humans I love. Humans who never deserved this punishment.

You *do not deserve this punishment.*

Neither do you.

She nuzzles into me, and I hold her even tighter, surrounding her with as much of my human half as I can. She deserves everything good in this world, and yet she is willing to sacrifice her womb to these monsters to give to others.

I want you, *Erik. I want to be with you, and Tiffany and Dean, in the real world. As war-filled and broken and fucked up as it is. And if I have to have a bunch of monster babies to make that happen, then... so be it.*

She kisses my sternum, her lips a balm to all the hurt in my soul. Phorkys stirs within me, and I feel a flash of guilt for still wanting to deny Him His happy ending.

Seeing you two, the love you have for each other... I am almost sorry that you and your mate were not able to escape, he murmurs to me. ***I know that was your plan.***

Would you have let her walk away? With all that we have endured today, it is difficult to believe.

When He begins to answer, His intention is not immediately clear.

When my Keto left me, I did not understand. I was angry. I blamed her. I blamed you. My grief was great, and I was without a partner. My family was dead. My mate abandoned me, blamed me for trying to protect myself. It left me skeptical of our bond, of any bond between two mates.

But seeing the love you and Lillian share, as fleeting and insignificant as it is, has opened my eyes. Though she is destined for you, you do not see her as yours unless she wishes it. I saw Keto's departure as a betrayal. But when Lillian attempted to leave you, you would have helped her. Even though it would have left you broken and alone.

I did not understand before. But now that Keto has returned, now that I see the pain she endured at my return, unable to mate with her and help her heal from her loss...

You give me pause, human.

Your mating with Lillian. It was soft. Caring. You did not seek to reproduce. You did not seek mere pleasure. There were times when it felt as if it was not about your

pleasure at all, but simply a means to be close to her. To make her *feel pleasure.*

It was not about bearing young. Nor was it wholly to seek release. It was an expression of love.

I shift a bit in Lillian's arms, uncomfortable at keeping this conversation from her. But Phorkys's voice is only for me in this moment, and my response is only for Him.

It was also pleasurable.

I wish for that with my mate.

Are you even capable of that kind of affection?

A thoughtful growl sounds in my mind as the monster considers my question. I almost feel guilty for asking. But given his other confessions tonight, I believe, for once, that he will not attempt to deceive me. That he will be honest.

I love her, human. With all that I am, I love her.

Can we help who we love? I look down once more into my treasure's sweet, round face, her eyelashes tracing dark arches on her cheekbones, her hair flowing about us and glinting in the dim light of the cave.

I know it is a minimal chance, but if it would save her the pain of birthing a thousand monsters...

Just because you love, it does not mean you must have children.

Is it so bad, to help two beings who love each other have a family?

Lillian opens her eyes, and our gazes meet. She heard Him. She knows I have been trying to protect her, to convince Him to let her go free.

It is if Their children are monsters.

When the response comes, Lillian and the monster speak in unison, and the fact that they are united in their feelings surprises me more than all of today's events combined.

Monsters are born everyday.

Paired with Lillian's indifferent expression, and followed by the love in her eyes as she holds me tight, I have no response.

All I want is to protect the one I love. My treasure. My mate. *I do not know what to think anymore, Lillian.*

Her eyes grow hooded, and the water around us changes. I know in that moment that the time for philosophy is past.

Then don't think, Erik. Feel.

CHAPTER 35

ERIK

The softness that was swirling in Lillian's eyes is replaced with a blazing fire. I lick my impossibly dry lips as I feel a gush of wetness slick between her folds, as she wraps her legs around my torso. A sharp tug yanks inside me, drawing me closer to her.

I lower my head to center myself, only to find myself staring at her breasts. They heave as she breathes in deep, sending a current rising along her collarbone as the water rushes through her gills.

What will it feel like? To be filled with your eggs?

Her thoughts project wonder as she leans in closer, her nipples brushing against my chest.

I hold back my hips as the tugging sensation returns low in my stomach. I remember bedding her in this form, the intensity of it unlike anything I have ever felt before.

I want to buck into her, wrap my tentacles around her body, feel the soft skin of her breasts press into me.

And then, suddenly, I am once again not entirely myself. Phorkys rises within me, sharing my body, meeting her gaze, and it answers her.

I will deliver you both pleasure unlike you've ever experienced.

His low voice ripples through our spines, and both Lillian's and my body flush at the vibrations.

Erik will fill you with his seed, and together we will open you to receive Our young. Your inner gate will open to our administrations, and your womb will grow with Keto's eggs. You will be transformed, magnificent, god-like, as Our brood grows within you.

The tentacles climb and suckle up her legs, leaving red marks in their wake as they leapfrog up her body.

Lust overwhelms me, and a flush rises in her cheeks. This is a fetish of Phorkys, I realize, to see his mate expand with eggs, but one that He has never experienced with Keto.

His lust transfers to me, filling our shared body with heat. We reach to fondle her between her legs, up the cleft of her ass.

I remember the feel of her asshole, circling me and my tentacles tight, as she writhed in pleasure.

Our eyes meet.

She clearly remembers it too.

Her pulse flickers at her neck and her gills flutter faster as her heart rate increases. I too, find myself breathing harder in her presence, my cock growing even harder, pressing insistently against her folds.

You will expand to fit them all, and they will incubate. For one cycle of the moon, you will continue to grow. Erik and I will feed you, nourish you, and pleasure you at your command.

Until, at last, you will deliver our young.

As eggs? She asks. *Or…?*

I feel the transformation overtake me, as the monster fully consumes my body.

Lillian jumps and floats back, her eyes widening, her mouth opening in a perfect *O* as she takes in the form of the fully transformed monster once again.

They will be born as I float before you. Some will resemble me. Others, Keto. And many others yet in forms you cannot imagine. They will not be as large, but they will have hatched by then.

You will birth a full clutch of our young, and then you will be free to live as you choose.

Her pulse jumps again, and she searches Phorkys's giant, bulbous eyes.

Me and Erik?

Yes.

The monster retreats, and I feel my body return to my own, fully human once more.

I gauge her reaction.

She has never shown any sign of full transformation with her curse. Only the gills at her neck and the slightest webbing between her fingers and toes indicate any deviation from her humanity. Will she truly be able to endure such a pregnancy?

She is so beautiful, her skin glowing a creamy peach in the dim luminescence of the cave, with only her eyes giving any indication to the curse lying beneath her skin. They glow a bright purple now, instead of the reassuring navy they usually hold. I can scent her lust on the water.

She swims up to me, caressing her fingers up and down my torso. My hips jerk again, as memories of her supple body beneath mine, beneath the monster's, flash once more behind my eyes. His words still ring inside my ears: *the human will fill you with his seed...*

I want to feel my human cock inside her, want to fill her with *my* young, watch her expand with *my* child. I fear for her, what this transaction might do to her.

And yet...

No woman has occupied my fantasies for hundreds of years. Living with Phorkys, it has distorted what I desire. Seeing my tentacles penetrate Lillian's puckered red hole, feeling my arms coil and twist inside her as I wrench climax after crying climax from her pliant body...

No completely human woman could understand my perversions after this curse. Not one.

I need a monster now. A monster like me.

The hope she lights inside me, that in one month's time I will be free of this curse and rewarded with my perfect mate, burns as hot as the lust she ignites in my veins. I do not just want her. I *need* her. She is my only chance at someday living a normal human life. Or, as normal a life as I can have, as separated by time and isolation as I have been.

She speaks inside my mind, directly to Phorkys. And in her words, I feel the final, sealing oath.

I accept. I will incubate your eggs, and I will bear your young. Tiffany and Dean and Erik and I will walk free after a month's time, and in those weeks...

Her eyes shift back to the deepest blue I have ever seen. Even in the heart of the lake, they hold more life and mystery than any I will ever know. Our gazes meet, and the love we share in that connecting thread is palpable.

You will give me the most amazing fucking orgasms I've ever had.

She stares directly into my eyes as she completes her vow. Two intense desires swirl within me, so strong and all-consuming that I cannot separate which is the monster's and which is my own.

Time to give the woman what she wants, Erik.

CHAPTER 36

LILLIAN

I can admit that I'm not entirely sure what I'm agreeing to. But when you wake up in an underwater lair surrounded by Titans and the unconscious bodies of your best friends, you don't just sit back and do nothing.

I have the power to save my friends. And from how Phorkys is making it sound, despite it being more than a little terrifying, it might not actually be all that bad.

Hell, beats filing corporate lawsuit paperwork for a month.

No wonder no one had looked for me. Tiffany had been kidnapped just like I was. There was no one to sound the alarm, no one who knew me well enough to try to figure out what happened when I didn't return to Chicago. I would get fired from my job whether or not I let Phorkys and Keto fill me with their babies. Not to mention the fact that if I *had* managed to escape, I'd still have fucking gills to cover up for the rest of my life.

In the back of my mind, a question wriggles. Keto had mentioned she had the power to heal me. That someday, I might be able to have a family after all.

Was that all lip service? Or some thinly veiled attempt to get me to agree to letting her lover breed me?

Deep down, did I think that agreeing to this bargain would heal whatever's wrong with me?

Erik, fully human and fully erect, stares at me, curiosity in his eyes at my hesitation. I want him so much. But I don't just want him—we've been through *hell* together. We're straight-up facing the flames, walking into this thing with eyes wide open, and he's supporting me.

I can't imagine a better man. I don't want to.

I love him. And if I return to civilization after this, he's coming with me. Either that, or we just live off the grid for the rest of our lives, roasting squirrels and fish and fucking like animals. Maybe Tiffany and Dean will want to live with us, and maybe whatever kids they have will be like ours, too.

Maybe family means more than just a man and a woman. Maybe this whole ordeal has me seeing love and family through completely different eyes.

Erik reaches for me, and for the first time in my life, I know how it feels to be loved. This man looks at me with fire in his eyes. He calls me beautiful, precious, his treasure. And even as I agree to let Phorkys and Keto use my body for their purposes, in the end, it's him that I want filling me with these children. His gorgeous, sculpted chest hovering over mine. His face breathing into me, his tongue swirling in my mouth. His cock spearing me open and changing my life forever.

I worry that it can't last. That it's too good to be true. Even amidst all this ridiculous, apocalyptic bartering of hoards of monsters and eternal curses, a part of me still believes that no man will ever truly want *me* if he has other options.

I want to ask you something before we get down to it.

A tiny little line forms between his eyebrows, and a shadow passes behind his eyes.

Please. Ask me.

When the Titans set us free, when it's just you in this body again... I stroke a finger up and down the valleys of his chest. He shudders, and his gills flutter with an intake of breath. *Will you still want me? Or has this all just been because of the curse?*

His eyes flutter closed, and tiny bubbles shoot out from his mouth as he heaves a sigh. I tilt my head, worried that maybe I've read him wrong all along.

This is it, I tell myself. This is where I learn the truth. That this was all just a bunch of horny Titans using his body to find a surrogate, and once Erik is free from it all he's running away for good.

Tears spring to my eyes, dispersing immediately into the lake around us.

But he was going to let me go. He was going to help me escape this, back on the island, and then he never would have been free.

Why would he do that if this was all a trick?

Lillian, he says, and I force myself to look at him. To truly listen to him.

No matter what he says this time, I'll believe him.

You are the most enticing human I have ever seen. His eyes open, and they bore into mine with an intensity that takes my breath away. His hands, which have been floating idly at his sides since he was turned back into a human, suddenly wrap around me. He pulls me close, and his whole body is rigid against me, from the tightly wound muscles of his arms to the washboard ripples of his abs, all the way down to the impossibly hard ridge of his cock.

He leans his forehead against mine, and I feel him tighten around me in a bone-crushing embrace.

I have not been with a human woman as a human man in many, many years. My body has had some... enhancements with the curse. Whereas you, in your human form, are perfection personified... I am afraid that, when we escape this and are free once more, I will not be enough for you. I want—so badly—to please you, Lillian. You are the light of my world. I cannot imagine a life outside this lake without you. I love you, my treasure. For now and forevermore, you are my true mate and my heart's desire. I will always want you.

I tilt my head up, blown away by his words. But I told myself I would believe him.

And staring into those clear gray eyes, I know he's telling the truth.

I kiss him, and his grip around me tightens. He swallows me with his lips, pressing against my mouth with his tongue until I open for him. He delves deep, before darting back out and sweetly running his tongue along my lips, gently dragging my bottom lip between his teeth.

Oh my god.

He smiles against my mouth, and I realize that that little thought transferred to him as well. I giggle a little, and bubbles pour from my mouth between us. We pull back from each other, realizing at once how different this will be for both of us, from anything we've ever experienced before.

It's not just the fact that we had tentacle sex. With this curse, we're connected on a deeper level than what's possible between humans. We speak into each other's minds, we see into each other's souls. We have a history that no one else, save maybe Tiffany and Dean, will ever understand, and that's going to make reintegrating into society a challenge.

My heart pounds as I look up and down his perfect body, remembering all we've done together.

He is a literal Adonis. Sculpted to perfection. He says he might change after Phorkys sets him free, but I think he was mostly talking about his giant wang—which, to be fair, is bigger than I strictly need on a regular basis anyway.

Besides, with the type of sex we've had? We'll probably be investing in a colorful collection of toys once we're back on the mainland anyway.

I think about how *my* body will change with all of this. The brood of eggs. Erik might know what it's like to shift into a giant squid, but I'm going to become an *actual* monster before this is over.

He tilts my chin up with his finger. He searches my face with such love, I think I might burst. Then he grabs onto my hips and pushes me up, floating me above him and kissing his way down my body until his face is level with my chest.

I want to explore and taste every inch of you.

Okay.

He kisses me again, sweetly this time, tracing the curve of my breasts with his lips. Slowly, he moves across my body, drifting up to my neck and my collarbone, reaching down lower around me to cup my ass with his giant hands. I moan, and the vibration of my chest resonates through both of our bodies, bubbles floating lazily above our heads. He raises my body again and latches onto a nipple, sucking it into his mouth before releasing it with a pop and swirling away the tenderness with his gentle tongue.

I feel the giant ridge of his cock twitch against my leg, and in that moment, I want him inside me more than I've ever wanted anything in my life.

Erik! I want you. Just *you. This one time, before…*

I leave the rest unspoken, but he seems to understand.

Before I'm prepped for breeding. Before we become monsters again.

Before my body becomes a tool for the Titans, I want to be with him as we are. As we met. As we fell in love.

One more time.

His eyes meet mine. The swirling cyan shadow that lets me know Phorkys is lingering below the surface winks out, and in its absence I'm met with the beautiful, crystalline silver eyes of my Viking warrior.

My heart leaps to my throat. He nods, and together we float down to the soft, sandy bed of the cave.

Gently, he lays me out across a bed of drifting lake grasses, lowering his mouth to my breasts. I feel his tongue lap at one nipple as he teases the other with his fingers, rubbing small circles with his thumb. The slight current of the water around us makes me feel weightless as I arch into his touch, my hips rising easily so I can rub my lower lips against his cock. His whole body tenses, and his lips close around my nipple. An electric sensation zips from my breast down to my core, and I feel a warmth spreading between my legs.

It doesn't matter that he doesn't have tentacles. Erik is a man that knows how to use his human fingers and mouth and cock just fine.

This man… I need him. Now.

Please, Erik.

He lifts his eyes to mine and nods, releasing my nipple and tweaking the other, sending another zing of pleasure between my legs. I buck my hips forward, the movement oddly slow in the heavy water, and he lines himself up with my entrance.

It's heady to watch him rub his cockhead up and down my glistening seam. He's going to stretch me out in the most delicious way. Fill me utterly and completely with his human cock.

And next time, I'll be filled even more.

That thought sends a barrage of lewd images flicking through my brain, and I'm shuddering even before he enters me. Just the thought of him spilling his seed inside me, filling me full, his semen bursting through my cervix and flooding my womb with his cum is an idea that I've never pictured before, but now that I've imagined it it's all I can think about.

And that, combined with the sensation of his cock spreading me wide as he slowly thrusts himself inside me all the way to the hilt, is pushing me hurtling towards oblivion already.

Is this the curse? Or have I had a breeding kink this whole time?

Erik smiles at me, a laugh rumbling through his chest.

Man, this being so horny I can't control which thoughts transfer and which ones stay inside is a real pain in the ass.

I would be happy living with you for the rest of my life, my treasure. But if Keto keeps her promises... maybe, someday, I could fill you with my children, too.

And with that thought echoing in my brain, he pulls out almost completely and thrusts inside again, pulling my hips down until I'm seated on the base of his cock.

As I feel him split me open, stars erupt behind my eyes. It's as if the heat and desire that Keto spun within my belly was a balloon about to pop, and he just pierced it with his cock. An explosion of pleasure erupts within me. Wetness gushes out between us as he pierces me again. I'm already convulsing around him, wave after wave of pleasure engulfing me.

He reaches between us to rub my clit with his thumb, and my legs fly straight out, jerking wildly with my orgasm until he shifts us, hoisting my hips with his strong arms and forcing me to meet him thrust for thrust.

He braces my ankles on his shoulders, wrapping one arm under my back, still tracing tantalizing circles around the tiny bundle of nerves with his other hand. All the while, his cock pushes inside me again and again.

My eyes roll back in my head. Impossibly, the pleasure builds even more. Despite feeling like I've come a dozen times already, a secret, deeper peak lingers in the outer reaches of my awareness, my body convincing me that there's a bigger climax waiting for me at the end.

His rhythm grows more erratic, his fingers on my waist digging in tighter as I become delirious with pleasure. Are his eyes flicking between cyan and gray again? Are mine? Is this real?

Eyes!

Every fiber of my being protests as I search within myself for that unbreakable connection: Erik and me, our bond, our love. I find him, his human eyes locked onto me as he loses himself inside me, his body tensing at last as he finds release.

The walls of my pussy swell and spasm around him, and I finally fall apart.

I scream, the sound actually reverberating around the chamber as a deep, unfamiliar voice erupts from me. Erik thrusts again: once, twice, three more times, before he grunts in harmony with me, and I swear I can feel his cum shooting inside me. Thick jets of it, deeper and deeper, with every involuntary shudder.

He collapses on top of me, bumping gently into the sand and grass as we come down from our orgasms. Minutes pass, and I'm still trembling with aftershocks, curling my fingers in his thick, long hair.

Kiss me.

He obliges, pressing his lips to mine, and I feel my pussy tighten around his softening length again. With his tongue and lips entwining with mine and his cum filling my every crevice, a sweet heat spreads throughout my whole body. My inner walls flutter gently around his cock, which gives a few spent twitches, and we slowly come down together. Our lips and arms and legs locked together in a perfect, warm embrace.

A moment later, he rolls to my side and snuggles against me, running his fingers in light, lazy scratches up and down my body, sending little tingles racing across my skin.

That was amazing.

We both think it at the same time. I giggle, and he chuckles beside me.

Rest now, brood mother. When you awake, you will feel pleasure you've never known possible.

I shuddered at the monster's voice, my imagination running wild at his words. How could pleasure be any better than that?

As Erik's cum dribbles down my legs, slowly dispersing through the water around us, I wonder once again just what I've signed myself up for.

Erik pulls me closer into his arms, and I nuzzle into his firm, warm chest, and together we drift off to sleep.

CHAPTER 37

ERIK

It is time.

Phorkys speaks, and his deep voice rouses us from our floating slumber. My body shivers—but I hold off the transformation so I can squeeze Lillian close as a human one last time.

This will require a change from both of us. Holding her like this, feeling her soft hair graze my cheek as I rest my face against her temple: it grounds me.

You are mine, my treasure. I love you.

She squeezes me in return. *I love you too, Erik.*

I hold her for a second more before the transformation begins. I push away from her as I feel the familiar tingling take hold, enveloping my legs and spreading up to my waist as my lower half splits and stretches into ten writhing limbs. Although this time, two of them are different.

At their ends, there is a flared bell-like tip. From within its open chamber, a sticky white goo beads at the inner core.

Phorkys stirs within me, and for the first time I feel it when He rises to my face, my eyes burning a neon glow that shines in Lillian's face. I can see the cyan highlights in her assessing gaze.

Mate.

His voice is a growl, a purr. Immediately, her pupils dilate. Our tentacles swirl around her body, and she reaches for one, twisting it delicately between her fingers as she takes in my hybrid form.

Erik? Are you still in there?

Yes, my love.

I pull her closer with my monstrous arms, and Phorkys growls again.

The impregnation will require another transformation from you.

Me? I ask, surprised at the intention behind his words. Lillian blinks and tilts her head at me.

Lillian has proven that she can accept quite a sizable probe.

My treasure blushes a bright red, and I taste the tang of her juices inundate the water around my tentacles. She is aroused, and her vision is distant, as if she is picturing lewd acts inside her mind while Phorkys whispers to us.

You have to fill her with our eggs. It will require a larger member than you possess.

Instantly, a blazing fire fills my belly. I bow forward, and Lillian clutches at my human arms, eyes widening in fear.

What is going on?

The two odd tentacles are twisting together unnaturally, pivoting themselves to the front of my body and dissolving unnaturally into the gel-like skin beneath. They meld together, until they resemble a human cock.

But this is no *human* cock.

It juts from below my waist, proud and hard and *giant.*

Just its existence causes me discomfort, my head light and woozy from the blood rushing to fill its girth. Its base is wide like the eight tentacles around it, but its taper is slight. Its tip, which bobs achingly close to my chest, is rounded, peeking through a sleeve of reddish-purple skin.

This member is somehow neither the monster or me, but a mix of us both. Beneath its base, surrounded by the swirling tentacles that spread from my waist, I feel my sac hanging heavy and full with seed.

Lillian rushes over to me, and her arms wrap around my body, the shape of which I am too dizzy to discern. Am I still man? Monster? How do I appear to her, and how much of my body is within my control at all?

Slowly, I tilt my head to meet my mate's eyes, and find her deep blue gaze waiting for me. Her eyebrows rise in surprise as my member twitches between us. Recognition fills her features, and her lips thin into a resolute line.

I can see that the new appendage is terrifying. As thick around as my human legs, and half as long, I shudder in horror at the thought of this giant... *thing* entering my mate.

My Lillian. My treasure.

You will use this to deposit the eggs within her.

It is impossible, I argue, but her eyes are already hooding with lust, and I can see the acceptance of her fate fueling the fire of her lust.

Her body is already changing in preparation. Keto has blessed her for this task. She will feel no pain...in this phase.

I cover my face with my hands. My head is light, my vision blurry in the way it only gets when my monstrous senses wrest my human reasoning from me. I try to breathe through the pulsing in my lower body, try to steal back control, but Phorkys's grip on my body is unrelenting.

I do not want to acknowledge the desire burning like an ember deep in my belly. The cursed lust that longs to see my mate take this giant cock as easily as she let me spear her hours ago.

I feel soft fingers grasp around my wrists, and slowly, Lillian pulls my hands away from my face. The monster's tentacles wrap around us, creating a bubble in which only she and I exist.

Erik. She grasps the sides of my face and forces me to meet her eyes.

I swallow at the lust I see there.

I agreed to this. You agreed to this. It's time. Fill me with Their eggs.

She lowers one hand down below my waist and strokes my terrifying length, brushing its shaft with her palm and fingers.

Lust and desire like I have never felt before overwhelm me, and more blood rushes like a river from my head to my cock. Impossibly, it hardens more, taught as the leather skin of a drum, and milky white fluid leaks from its bulbous head.

Insert the eggs, Lillian.

Black spots erupt into my vision as my head spins with lust, and the creature's senses overwhelm me. I scent my mate as she swims about my body, the waves of the movement building a picture in my mind of the cave around me.

I am seeing with sound. Feeling through taste. And then my love is kneeling before me once again.

My tentacles stroke her body as she drags me down to the soft lake bed, entangling with her legs as her breasts brush against my throbbing member. I blink, and her face swims before me, shadows swirling in her eyes as her whole body flushes pink with desire.

I can taste the arousal between her legs as her thighs part around my waist. And something else... something salty. Something foreign that I cannot place...

I groan as my cock grows even harder, because my vision fails me at last. It must be, for the images that play before my eyes are disconnected from my body.

One by one, tentacles rise and fall about our bodies, cupping and scooping the opalescent marble-like eggs of Keto's brood with their suckers and feeding them between Lillian's lips. Her mouth pouts sensually, and her pink tongue stretches to lick the delicate balls into her mouth. She lets me feed her, more and more, until her cheeks bulge with them.

The ember in my belly flares as she resumes stroking my cock with both hands, running her soft fingers up and down its length and surrounding it in her grip. I almost jerk out of her hold when I feel her pillowy lips kiss its throbbing tip.

My eyes roll back into my head, and I can see no more. I only feel her press something smooth against the opening of my cock, and, unbelievably—impossibly—push it inside of me.

Suddenly, it is like the rising desire within me expands against the constraints of my body, as if I were a bottle of ale that someone has shaken. Pleasure pushes against my skin from inside, spiraling and pulsing more and more densely with every smooth press of her mouth to my cock.

Again and again, she rubs her hands up and down my shaft, the sleeve of skin pumping with her movements. She swirls her lips and tongue around my head before pressing another ball against its tip and pushing it inside, increasing the pressure. For an eternity, she pumps and licks and pushes, until I feel like I am about to burst.

My senses swirl and mix, my body not my own, anchored only by the unnatural fullness that is stretching my body to its capacity, filling to its utmost—

And that's the last egg.

My eyes burst open in time to see her push the final ball —no, *egg*—inside the tip of my transfigured cock with her devilish tongue, before licking a line from the flare of the head down to its base. Milky fluid leaks from the strained opening, gathering in a stream around the foreskin and slickening the glide between it and the throbbing organ within.

My dizzy human brain is not prepared for the information my eyes are giving it. My hips jerk forward, and I almost spill my seed and all the eggs right then and there, until the squid-like tendrils of my lower half wrap tightly around the base of my cock, choking its connection to my sack and stifling the eruption. An aching, lusty numbness spreads within me, until the buzzing pleasure is just shy of unbearable.

I breathe deeply, feeling the water rush up my chest in a cooling current to my gills. Lillian smiles at me, and we both hear the voice of the monster announce:

Lillian, spread your legs.

CHAPTER 38

LILLIAN

This is it. The point of no return.

I don't know if it's Keto's influence or pheremones or what, but since I woke up with Erik's cum still coating my insides, my libido has been off the charts.

Let's be real, everyday with Erik has been an exercise in restraint just to keep my hands off him, but the tsunami of desire that's been pummeling me for the past 24 hours is finally reaching a breaking point.

I'm grateful that Erik and I got one last time to make love as ourselves before our bodies started to transform to accommodate this weird mating ritual. There's an odd, yawning-like sensation happening in my core: like a mix between a stretch and a relaxing, and a little bit like I need to pee.

And with each passing minute, the sensation in my core gets headier and headier. My brain is fuzzy with lust, and that only grew as my body instinctually gathered Keto's clutch of eggs and kissed them into Erik's giant sex-organ.

Seriously. Pretty sure that was the hottest blowjob ever.

Phorkys' commands are a stream-of-consciousness murmuring in the back of my mind as He directs me through each step of the mating process. Gathering the eggs, stimulating Erik's semen production, filling him with the eggs so he can saturate them with his essence before he deposits them inside me.

I'm in something like a trance as He explains to me the changes that are taking place in Erik's body, the way his cock is something between a human penis, a *hectocotylus*, or "breeding arm," and an ovipositor, or a mating organ specifically modified to deposit eggs into a mate's body. The lesson weaves in and out with directions of what to do with my body, and the way His voice purrs within my brain is hypnotizing.

It doesn't matter what He says: how ridiculous or how alien it is. My body understands the meaning and obeys, but my mind simply hears it as sweet-nothings and dominant commands.

My eyes hood, staring at the half-shifted man before me. Memories of our passionate night in the shelter with him half-transformed like this play on a loop underneath the monster's sexy murmurs, and it only spins my desire into overdrive.

I smile at Erik, my unexpected mate, and widen my kneeling stance before him until my thighs no longer touch. The tentacles that emerge from beneath Erik's hard torso wrap around me, two grabbing my legs, two encircling my arms, and two more exploring my body with their sinful suction cups. I feel myself being lifted off the sandy ground until I'm suspended, spread eagle and completely vulnerable.

My pussy is practically a waterslide after using my mouth to fill Erik's cock with the monster's eggs. Even so, he's so *big*. Bigger than any cock or dildo or tentacle I've ever taken.

I am beyond questioning it. I can feel the transformation taking place, and it's leaving my reason and logic behind. In its place, there is only lust and a growing emptiness in my core.

I'm ready to be filled.

The four free tentacles tease my body, circling my nipples and leaving suctioning kisses all along my curves. Their administrations leave no part of my body unexplored save one, stroking me into a tizzy as they lavish attention on every place but the one where I need it most.

Please! I beg, not knowing if it's a cry to Erik or the monster within.

I could question it: how I've become fatefully entangled in a breeding ritual with the Titans. But then I would be distracted from the incredible pleasure tingling through my body. I am outside my mind right now, inhabiting solely in my skin and nerves and core.

Ripples of lust and pleasure course through my body, as if my very skin is a conductor for some octopodal current passing through me. The tentacles coil around me. Suckers attach to my skin and tug, leaving rows and rows of simultaneous hickies covering my entire body. Then three tentacles reach down and suction to my pussy lips.

I buck in my restraints, but my arms and legs are completely restrained in those powerful limbs. The final one slithers down my sternum and flicks at my clit, agonizingly slowly as the three tentacles below it pull at my entrance, stretching my labia tentatively like a rubber band.

Erik's head meets my body, and I feel his tongue lick a line from my navel to the swell of my mound. He buries his face into the patch of small curls there and laps at my folds between the tentacles tugging them apart, making absolutely sinful noises as he sucks at the juices dripping out of me.

It's like being ravished by ten lovers at once, between the tentacles holding open my legs, pinning my arms, flicking my clit and spreading me open for my lover. I gasp as Erik withdraws his face and replaces his tongue with four fingers.

He spears me with his hand, and my body accepts him easily, *eagerly*. He twists his fingers inside me, brushing up against the tentacle arms from inside my inner walls. Between the inner pressure of his movements, and the suction cups pulsing against him with my sensitive folds sandwiched in between, my pleasure is stretched further and further until I'm tight as a bowstring.

I'm close, I'm close!

The tentacle which has been languidly circling and stroking my clit increases its pace, rapidly passing back and forth over the sensitive bud. With each pass, its suction cup pulls at it, coaxing it stiffer with each pass. My breath comes in pants, bubbles forming at the eddies swirling around my gills, the passing current over my collarbone only adding to the heady sensation building inside me.

Eric withdraws his arm, and I whimper at the loss. But when I look down, I see the reason for it.

The tentacles holding me in place are lining me up with his giant, mutated cock. Spreading my pussy wide while wrecking my clit and securing my limbs from fighting it.

Eriks fingers find my ribcage, and he pulls me as flush to his chest as he can without impaling me. His head hovers around my navel, licking and kissing while his fingers grasp at my breasts, squeezing the fleshy globes like he's claiming them. A zing of pain sizzles down my spine at the strength of his grip: those strong, warrior hands not sparing me from their power.

And part of me loves the monster inside him. The way he can't hold back or control himself anymore. He doesn't look to me for permission, he doesn't meet my gaze with an apology in his eyes.

No. This time, when he tilts his head back and sees me staring back at him, the glowing silver-cyan swirls a challenge. The head of his throbbing cock meets my entrance, nudging into the wide-spread lips until I can feel him covering my whole pussy with it.

The strokes around my clit work to a fever pitch, and I'm coming. The neon fire in his eyes sparks as mine flutter closed, and I'm shaking, bucking, wrenching against his hold.

You are ready for my eggs, mate.

I force my eyes open, and see that lusty cyan gleam in my Viking's eyes: the hungry fire of the Titan's primal need to breed me shining through my lover's human face. At once, he is both monster and man: his torso, arms, and face that of the beautiful human I'd come to love, his lower half a chaotic swirl of tentacles, tendrils, and one massive, terrifying, egg-laden cock.

It notches into my entrance, my pussy slick and primed from my release. We both look down at the physical impossibility before us.

And then he starts to move.

I thought the tentacles had stretched me to my breaking point, but I'm proven wrong as the hard, relentless head forces me to open even wider. The suckers pull and suck me open, and I open my throat around a wordless scream as a tingling heat rushes to my pussy. Every inkling of pain is soon consumed by a river of heat as my body thrums with adrenaline.

I'm still coming, still shuddering around the tip of him, and each spasm opens me a little more as the smooth muscle walls unclench.

Millimeter by millimeter, he pushes further, wrenching me apart at the hips, the Titan's magic working overtime to retroactively repair my human body as it splits around him.

I writhe in Erik's hold, riding my hips forward and back against the writhing and probing of the monster cock. It isn't until the tip of a tentacle traces the cleft of my ass that I realize his head is fully seated in my channel. There are no tentacles sucking my lips apart.

Instead, two suction to my breasts. The third still tortures my clit, keeping me on the edge of some forbidden pleasure I've yet to even fathom, while the fourth teases and pulses against my other hole.

No. There's no way my body could stand it. With my pussy stretched so far beyond its capacity...

The tentacle withdraws, and I look down to see it swirling around the lip of foreskin circling the ovipositor. It gathers a dripping mass of precum, scooping a generous glob on its end before retreating behind me once more.

Thick and slimy enough to keep its viscosity even underwater, I feel its warm slickness slide between my cheeks, lubricating my back hole as the tentacle circles the tight pucker.

And then my entire body is pulled down over his entire length.

In a smooth glide that should be impossible, I feel his giant cock fill me past my limit in one long stroke. My stomach visibly bloats with his girth, and I swear I can feel every egg inside him as the straining organ pushes into my inner walls. My whole body bears down on him, and as he strikes my innermost point, the tentacle between my ass cheeks pushes inside.

Heat rises and expands from my center, rumbling higher and higher up my belly like an approaching peal of thunder. He withdraws until he almost leaves my channel completely, before spearing into me again, faster this time, and I cry out, water filling my mouth, my lungs, heating and expanding until I feel like I'm not fully real.

An entirely alien voice builds inside my chest, moaning and whimpering as my holes are mercilessly stretched and pounded.

I didn't know how many tentacles are filling me anymore, but as my mouth opens on another cry I feel one slide past my lips and swirl around my tongue. I suck greedily, every cell in my body striving toward one singular purpose:

Open wide.

Stars erupt behind my eyes as the pleasure builds to its peak, and I fall apart in Erik's hold, shaking uncontrollably as the tentacles withdraw from me almost completely, until only one thing is filling me up.

Now!

One, two, three thrusts up inside my pussy, until he is seated to the hilt and my belly bulges with the force. I feel it when the final gate opens and his tip kisses the entrance to my womb.

It doesn't hurt. My body is beyond pain, above pain now. Each stretch is just another extension of the Titans' curse, of Keto's magic, of Lust itself, as my body floods with heat and pleasure.

Erik cries out, his voice saturating my mind and ears. I feel his cock undulate from within, knots of eggs rising from its base up to the tip, building and swelling and bulging until at last, they spill inside me, exploding with a force that has me and Erik spasming around one another.

My orgasm is about to split me in two. My body grows, expanding and stretching, spiraling higher and higher.

The alien voice cries from my throat again. I can't fathom what gibberish I utter as my entire awareness is consumed by the bruising stretch of Keto's brood. *They were wrong,* I think, as my brain threatens to split from my body completely. *I can't handle this much pleasure.*

My mind breaks. Screaming, shouting, pulsing—all of it melds together in an orgasm that literally shatters time and space. I am split upon the colossus of monster and man, I am a vessel and a sacrifice, and I am consumed by ecstasy.

When I come down, Erik is still inside me, a final, bulging knot of eggs keeping our bodies locked together. His whole body trembles, including the tentacles holding me captive. With my last remaining strength, I crunch my abs to pull myself upright.

He lets me, and the tentacles fall away so I can collapse over his shoulders, my swollen belly cradled in our embrace. He shudders, and his monstrous limbs shrink back, exposing his heavy balls and still swollen base of his cock aching for that final release.

An aftershock zips through my body, and it's enough to send him over the edge. The knot within him pushes up my channel, as deep as it can go, followed by a stream of cum that stretches me to my very limit.

My womb is full. Our bodies heat. The afterglow of our climaxes grow hot, and I feel magic swirling inside me. Emotions, too big to be human, flood my consciousness as another orgasm overtakes me, making me blackout as two Titans call out to each other in complete bliss:

Phorkys!

Keto!

I float, adrift in a sea of black, impregnated with the Titans' brood.

EPILOGUE

TIFFANY

Cold. It's very, very cold.

I open my eyes, and immediately realize something is wrong. It's dark, for one. And for another, I'm not lying down. I don't know about you, but I'm pretty sure every time I wake up, I find myself in a horizontal position.

Not hanging, completely vertical, strung up by my wrists and ankles against a rocky wall and surrounded by dark, wet–

Wet.

I'm underwater.

I can't breathe underwater!

I gasp for air, reaching to clutch at my throat but held back by the slimy weeds knotted around my wrists. *Where am I, where–*

"Relax, human. Your thoughts are so loud. You're as bad as the blonde one."

My heart beats double-time in my chest. How am I not

dead by now? Who is that? And why does her voice sound so familiar?

Ti..ff..nee...

Dean?

Dean! I shout with my mind as I see my fiancé dangling across from me, hanging by his hands and feet like I am. He seems much groggier than I feel, his eyes barely flicking open as his chin lolls against his chest.

Oh, Dean. My rich, spoiled boyfriend. He's hopeless in a crisis.

So I guess that means it's up to me to face our mystery captor.

Until we suffocate, I guess.

Who are you?

"You humans and your pesky memories. Always so slow to return when you wake from comatose..."

Coma...?

And then it hits me. Girls' trip, at the lake with Lillian. Dean sneakily following behind us the whole drive so he could "surprise" me with midnight trysts.

He'd known how nervous I was for this trip, but he hadn't known *why.*

"You are a very lucky human, Tiffany."

Oh yeah? I turn to face the goddess lurking in the shadows.

Or Titan. Primordial sea creature. Whatever She is.

She pushes herself out into the hazy light that just barely filters into the cave, enough to highlight the seafoam glow of Her skin, and the hypnotising silver of Her eyes, and the dozens of yellow eyes of Her mane of snakes.

What makes me so lucky?

"You're about to be set free."

What? I look at Dean, wondering if maybe he stood up

for me after all. Made some unholy sacrifice for me and our child.

Never, in all my years, would I have ever imagined I'd get to hear a goddess snort.

"Oh, Tiffany. As if."

As if?

"As if he would ever possess the fortitude to resist me."

I sigh. Keto is right. I may love Dean with all my heart, but a Golden Retriever has more bite than that man ever will.

Poor guy is gooeyer than a cinnamon roll. No wonder he's out cold.

"Don't despair, child. You have someone looking out for you."

My blood freezes in my veins as the rest of my memories come pouring back.

My fight with Lillian. Her swimming away, not returning. My absolute panic when I realized something must have gone terribly wrong, and sending Dean out for help, only to–

You're going to set us free? But I thought you were keeping us prisoner. So you could claim our child to pay off my debt.

From the deal we made, years ago.

"Please, God, just lift her grief away. Give my friend her happiness back, I will trade anything…"

Anything?

Keto, like a glowing, sexy Ursula rising from the waves. Making me an impossible deal. Convinced that, without Lillian, I'd never have a family of my own anyway.

And then I met Dean.

"I no longer require your child. I am going to have many of my own."

My eyes flicker to Her stomach, which is taught and flat. No sign of pregnancy.

She snorts again.

"Even if my body shared the odd quirks of yours, young human, the days of delivering my own young are behind me."

What do you mean?

"I've found a surrogate to have my children. She was more than willing. Eager, even, one might say, given her attraction to her partner. And once I gave her an offer she couldn't refuse, convincing her was child's play."

Why are you telling me this?

"Because it is good news, Tiffany! Once they have been born, I will remove your gills and you can return to shore!"

Gills? Ah. So that's why I'm not suffocating. *You're really letting us go? Why? What does finding a surrogate have to do with paying my debt?*

A smile curls at the corners of Her lips, and She rockets toward me, grabbing my chin and dragging a long-tipped finger down the curve of my cheek. I suppress a shudder as Her touch sends sparks skittering across my skin.

The beautiful, powerful Keto brushes Her lips against my ear, and whispers the devastating news.

"Lillian is my surrogate. Your precious friend agreed to have my babies if I would set you free. Now they are growing inside her, and we...

"Well. We shall have to find a way to occupy ourselves, won't we?"

∼

At the mercy of monsters, can our foursome of heroes escape their destiny intact?

The story continues in *Bride of the Kraken*!

If you want to read Tiffany and Keto's secret history, claim your copy of *Deal with the Kraken*!

AUTHOR NOTE

Thank you so much for reading *The Kraken's Castaway!*

I have so many more monstrous stories planned for you. Please take a moment to leave a review so I know which scenes were your favorite!

Your honest review will help future readers decide if they want to take a chance on a new-to-them author. In a world full of beautiful, diverse stories, it can be hard to find the book that hits all the right buttons. So if this one tickled your fancy, recommending it on Storygraph, Goodreads, or social media can help you find more stories it!

And if you want more awesome book recommendations, consider joining my book club on Discord! We have monthly book chats, bingo, prizes, accountability and more —completely free!

All that and more can be found on my website, www.cassandramedcalf.com.

Hope to see you soon,
Cassandra

Acknowledgments

This book has been a long time coming. I've known since I started self-publishing that I wanted to write monster romance. The more I consume stories, the more I want to explore deep worlds, relationships, and the absolutely peaks of pleasure. But I never would have had the confidence to put it out into the world without a whole community of people.

First, my partner, Andy. Herner, you are the absolute light of my life. My biggest cheerleader, my support system, and my best friend. I love you and the puppies more than I will ever be able to put into words (and considering I'm a romance author, that's saying something!). Thank you for putting up with my early mornings and late nights as I claw my way into a *hopefully* successful author career.

I am so fortunate to have a supportive family, even if I'm never letting them read this book. Thank you all for understanding. I love you SO much.

And now we get to the authors who have helped and inspired me through this journey. Ariel Dawn, you are such a talented badass, and you have been rooting for me since I wrote the original novella of this story back in 2022. Thank you for being my friend and inspiring me to keep going!

Kathryn Moon, Katee Robert, Lillian Lark, Bebe Harper, L.E. Eldridge, Emily Antoinette... man, the list goes on. You all are incredible, and you've made this subgenre such a cool place to explore. Thank you for being awesome!

Christina Mattingly and Vera Valentine, thanks for letting me give voice to your stories in audio, and supporting me in my own writing endeavors. I frickin' ADORE your books.

I'm also lucky to be part of an amazingly supportive writer's group called The Bi+ Book Gang, led by the incredible Bailey Merlin. Y'all kept me writing through some of my toughest times this year, and the book wouldn't have gotten done without you. Thank you so much!

And finally, my readers! A few of you go above and beyond to support me on Patreon, and I cannot tell you how grateful I am. This year has been a tight one for me, and there have been months where Patreon has kept the puppies fed. So thank you. Thank you, thank you, thank you SO much for supporting me and reading along as I write my monster smut:

Danielle S

Gennifer N

Bryce N

Jess T

Kitt3n Bree

Terri V

And my beta readers,

Ari the Wandering Bard

B.M. Light

Kaiidth

Hilary

Author Ash

THANK YOU!

About the Author

Cassandra Medcalf is a writer, narrator, audio engineer, food enthusiast, wine taster, do-it-yourselfer, and an amateur film critic (despite barely having seen any movies). She lives in Duluth, MN with her adorable husband and their even more adorable dogs. You can follow her and her family's hare-brained schemes and lofty pursuits on her website, cassandramedcalf.com (or, if you're just here for the smut, on Instagram @CassandraMedcalfVO).

ALSO BY CASSANDRA MEDCALF

STAND-ALONES

Fowl Play, A Small Town Sports Romance

FIXER UPPER SERIES - LGBT SMALL TOWN ROMANCE

Betting on the House

Betting on the Bird

Hot Rod Hookups

Here Comes the Bride

FOR THE LOVE OF TITANS SERIES - LGBT PARANORMAL ROMANCE

The Kraken's Castaway

Bride of the Kraken

* 9 7 8 1 9 6 0 4 4 5 1 0 0 *